THE FOG DIVER

JOEL ROSS

HARPER

An Imprint of HarperCollinsPublishers

The Fog Diver

Copyright © 2015 by Joel Ross

Library of Congress Cataloging-in-Publication Data

Ross, Joel N., date

The Fog diver / Joel Ross.

pages   cm

Summary: "In this futuristic high-stakes adventure, humanity clings to cities on the highest mountain peaks above the deadly Fog, and airships transport the pirates of the skies. Daring 13-year-old tetherboy Chess and his salvage crew must face the dark plans of Lord Kodoc and work to save their beloved Mrs. E"— Provided by publisher.

ISBN 978-0-06-235294-1

[1. Adventure and adventurers—Fiction.   2. Survival—Fiction.   3. Recycling (Waste, etc.)—Fiction.   4. Environmental degradation—Fiction.   5. Orphans—Fiction.   6. Science fiction.]   I. Title.

PZ7.1.R677Fog   2015   2014034154

[Fic]—dc23   CIP

                                                                         AC

Typography by Joel Tippie

18 19 20   BRR   10 9 8 7 6

First paperback edition, 2016

THE
FOG
DIVER

THE
FOG
DIVER

MY NAME IS CHESS, and I was born inside a cage.

Imagine a wooden platform jutting from a mountain cliff. Now picture a chain falling from that platform and vanishing into the Fog, a deadly white mist that covers the entire Earth.

That's where I was born: locked in a cage, at the end of a chain, inside the Fog.

And I would've died there, too, if Mrs. E hadn't saved me.

When she saw my face for the first time, wisps of Fog swirled inside my right eye, shimmering white shapes that marked me as a freak. That's why I've spent thirteen years keeping my head down, staying quiet and afraid—but now Mrs. E needs help, now *she* needs saving.

It's time to stop hiding. Everything is going to change.

1

AFTER A LONG MORNING searching the woods, I spotted a school bus through the Fog. The broken windows looked like rotten teeth as I edged closer, hoping to salvage hubcaps or engine parts.

Then a growl rumbled through the swirling mist. A low, warning sound, maybe a mountain lion or a jaguar. Probably just telling me to stay away.

I wasn't about to argue.

My heart clenched and I reached for the hand brake on the harness buckled around my chest. A long cord—my "tether"—rose three hundred yards upward from the harness. If I squeezed the brake, my crew would reel in the tether, heaving me to the safety of our raft, which floated in the clear blue sky high above the Fog.

But when I touched the hand brake, the growling stopped.

Hm. I didn't know if that was a good sign or a bad one. I peered toward the rusty school bus, but even I couldn't see ten feet through the dense foggy whiteness. And the Fog muffled sounds, so for all I knew the big cat was padding closer, paws crunching through the leaves.

People died in the swirling mist, but animals thrived. They ran wild in the forests and the rubble. Packs of ferocious boars and troops of rowdy monkeys didn't even notice the whiteness. Only *humans* were blind and deaf in the Fog, stumbling around like accidents waiting to happen.

Or tasty treats.

Sweat trickled down my forehead and pooled on my goggles. I wanted to squeeze the hand brake and flee, but I needed to stay in the Fog. I needed to stay strong and brave. My crew was counting on me. So I took one slow step backward, then another and another. Two minutes later, I slumped in relief. I really needed to find a better place to search for valuables than a school bus where a jaguar made her den.

My crew and I lived in the slums of a mountain-peak empire called the Rooftop, one of the few places not covered by Fog. We flew our rickety air-raft over the endless white vapor every day. As the "tetherboy," I dove into the Fog and searched the ancient wreckage for stuff we could sell back in the slum for food and clothes and rent.

But these days, we needed more. These days, we flew deep into uncharted Fog, hoping to find something big— something *huge*—to save Mrs. E's life. We were running out of time.

I spent the rest of the afternoon prowling through Fog-covered hills, keeping my tether free of tree branches, rummaging in heaps of concrete and searching the husks of pod-cars. I wasted an hour digging through rotting planks, hoping to find pipes or plastic, but all I unearthed was thousands of beetles. Then the hand brake on my tether jerked: three fast yanks.

It was a message from Hazel, the captain of our ram-shackle raft, signaling me from above the Fog. *Come back,* she was saying. It was getting late, and nobody survived a night in the Fog—even I was afraid to stay after sunset.

I started to sign back *okay,* then stopped when I heard something in the distance, a muffled *eee-huuurk.*

I smiled at the sound and squeezed the hand brake. *Not yet.*

Come back.

Not yet, I told Hazel again.

Not the most fascinating conversation, but cut me a

little slack. We couldn't say much with a hand-brake cable connected to a bell on the raft deck.

After a minute, she signaled, *Okay*.

"Cool." I peered at the sky. "Dinner's on me."

I didn't expect to find salvage this late in the day, but I hoped to find food. Meals were scarce in the slum, and that *eee-huuurk* had sounded like a goose. Like delicious roast goose for dinner.

Adjusting my goggles, I headed downhill through the underbrush. Wisps of whiteness surrounded me. The Fog felt like cool breath against my skin, with the faint pressure of air before a big storm. Leaves crunched under my boots, and my tether unspooled with a *whirr-click-whirrr*.

Eyes wide and ears pricked, I stalked through the Fog. I crossed a meadow full of dandelions and smelled water. I listened for the burbling of a stream as I edged past some brambles . . . and an animal lunged at me through the mist.

My pulse rocketed. I yelped and leaped straight upward—eight feet into the air—and spun like a bat chasing a moth, feeling the world slow down around me.

On the raft or in the slum, I moved like an ordinary kid, but inside the Fog, I was *fast*. Rattlesnake fast. I jumped like a kangaroo, tumbled like a monkey, and climbed like a squirrel. That was me, a rattlaroo squirbat.

My body felt weightless as I flung myself through the

mist, tracking the dark shape of my attacker with my gaze. Then I fell to the ground in a crouch and saw it clearly. It wasn't a mountain lion or bear or baboon—I'd been assaulted by an angry goose.

"Okay, feather-face," I said. "Come and get me."

The goose glared with beady eyes—it didn't even notice the billowing Fog—and made a hissing sound like a broken valve: *hhhhhhh, hhhhhhh*. Uncoiling its neck, it beat the air and snapped at my face.

But this time, I was ready, and I trapped its long feathery neck under my arm.

The goose struggled and thumped my chest with its wings. *Mee-hurrrrk-ee!*

"Ha!" I clamped its wings tight. "Gotcha."

It hissed and wriggled, and its webbed feet pedaled in the air.

"Sorry," I said as I started to wring its neck. "But we're hungry, and you're dinner."

Then I heard a faint *eep*.

Eep eep eep eep!

I looked down and saw four fuzzy little goslings waddling toward me through the haze. The one in front tilted its downy yellow head upward and stared at me with big eyes, like it was begging for mercy.

"You're out of luck," I told him, gripping the mother goose's neck harder. "We've got to eat."

Eeep, he informed me.

"Easy for you to say," I muttered. "Shoo!"

Eeep, he repeated.

"Go away!" I stomped, trying to scare the goslings off. "I can't do this with you watching!"

Honk, the mother goose cried.

Eeep eep eep! the little ones said, bumbling closer like puffballs on webbed feet.

The crew needed food—we *always* needed food—and we never ate anything as tasty as roast goose. But something about four defenseless babies who needed a mother stopped me cold.

"Fine!" I sighed, loosening my grip. "But if we starve, it's your fault."

I set the mother goose down near her babies, and she said *hooooork!* and whacked me so hard with one of her wings that I fell on my butt. Then she led her goslings away, honking and hissing.

"You're welcome!" I called after her.

I sat there feeling like an idiot. We were hungry all the time, and I'd let a perfectly tasty goose get away. I didn't even want to *think* about what Swedish—our raft pilot—would say. And I couldn't stand the thought of watching Bea—our mechanic, and the youngest member of the crew—go to sleep hungry again.

After a while, I pushed to my feet and started plucking dandelion greens from the meadow. They were bitter, but they'd fill our stomachs. I was shoving one last handful into a sack when a breeze blew a perfumed scent toward me. *Flowers? Maybe roses.*

A grin tugged at my lips. I'd learned that roses meant fancy gardens and houses, which were good places to scavenge.

I followed the scent uphill, and a shape loomed through the Fog: dark bars in the whiteness. I edged closer and saw an iron gate, a row of black posts with sharp points. Good, thick, valuable iron, only slightly rusty.

I smiled. "Now we're talking."

I reached for the hacksaw in my leg-sheath, and the hand brake on my tether jerked three times: Hazel was saying *Come back.*

Not yet.

Come back, she signaled. *Come back, COME BACK!*

I frowned. That was pretty bossy, even for Hazel.

Then I noticed the Fog darkening around me. I'd lost track of time. Dusk was falling and long shadows were creeping across the field.

"Yikes," I muttered. Hazel was right, of course. Sometimes she was more "boss" than "bossy."

I signaled back: *Ready.*

A moment later, my tether straightened in the air above me. With a tug at my harness, it lifted me off my feet and reeled me upward.

I rose into the air as white clouds billowed around me. Higher and higher until finally, in an instant, the Fog fell away and my full weight returned. The harness dug into my chest, my arms and legs turned to lead, and even my boots felt heavy, like they were suddenly filled with mud.

The endless Fog spread below me, touched by the rays of the setting sun. It looked more like a cool mist than the plague that had almost destroyed humanity. And that still hid the treasures we needed to survive.

2

OUR SALVAGE RAFT WAS a hodgepodge of mismatched parts and tattered patches. It floated above the Fog, dangling from three balloons lashed together with fraying ropes. A wicker basket swayed in the tangled rigging beneath the balloons, the "crow's nest" where Hazel usually stood.

Below that, the raft itself was a weather-beaten deck of canvas, wooden floorboards, and copper pipes. The winch for my tether rattled beside my diving plank and, farther back, Swedish spun the ship's wheel and clattered at the steam organ that controlled the rudders and propellers.

Under the deck, Bea tinkered with the clockwork engine that powered the fans and pistons and vents. And hanging below the whole thing, the empty cargo net

11

swayed in the stiff breeze. It wouldn't be em̲ṫy.
That iron gate would cover food for a week or two̲̲ ̲e̲a̲
after the bosses took most of the money.

But we still needed a much bigger score to help
Mrs. E.

The tether winched me toward the underside of the
raft, bringing me close enough to grab the boarding
ladder.

"Chess!" Bea called to me, with a smile on her freckled
face. "You're okay!"

"Of course!" I struck a pose on the ladder. "For I am
Freakula, Lord of the Fog."

She giggled. "You're a chucklebutt! How come you
stayed down so long?"

"I found something," I told her. "Float a buoy!"

She flashed a salute and disappeared into the gearwork. It was too late to grab that iron gate today, so she'd
mark the site with a buoy and we'd return tomorrow, after
drifting all night. We couldn't hover in one place over-
night, not without a pilot at the wheel, and even Swedish
needed to sleep.

I climbed on deck, shoved my goggles to the top of my
head, and started unbuckling my harness.

"Next time come up when I tell you to!" Hazel called
from the crow's nest. "Look at the sun."

From above, the Fog usually looked like an endless
ocean with motionless white waves. But now, the orange

light of sunset brushed the high crests.

"Sorry," I said. "I got busy."

"Doing what?" she asked. "You look messed up."

"Chess always looks messed up," Swedish said from the wheel.

"I got into a fight," I admitted.

Hazel frowned. "Are you okay?"

"Was it wolves?" Swedish asked. "Baboons?"

"Worse," I told him.

"Not driftsharks," Hazel said, giving me a worried look.

"Of course not," I said. "You don't *fight* driftsharks, you just . . . die."

"Hyenas?" Swedish guessed.

"Um . . ." I didn't want to tell them I'd lost a perfectly tasty goose. "I found an iron gate that's in good shape. And I'm pretty sure I smelled roses nearby."

"Finally!" Hazel brightened, forgetting that I looked a mess. "I knew that flying this far would pay off. We'll grab everything in sight, and make enough to help Mrs. E!"

"If the troopers don't arrest us first," Swedish grumbled.

"Nobody's going to arrest us," Hazel told him.

"They will if Lord Kodoc hears about Chess."

I swallowed. Lord Kodoc was more than the tyrant who ruled the Rooftop and commanded the roof-troopers—he was the reason we lived small and quiet in a remote corner of the slum. *Everyone* with half a brain was scared of Lord Kodoc, but it was different for us. He was the bogeyman Mrs. E had scared us with since we were little. The monster in all our nightmares. She said that if Kodoc found us, he'd tear us apart.

"Yeah," Hazel said, "but he won't. He doesn't even know Chess exists."

"Not yet," Swedish muttered darkly. "You've heard the rumors."

I ducked my head. Swedish was right. We needed to escape the slum to find a cure for Mrs. E's fogsickness—but also to get far away from Lord Kodoc. He thought I'd died thirteen years ago, after he'd lowered my mother into the Fog. Recently, though, we'd heard terrifying rumors about a kid with a Fog-eye. If Kodoc found out I'd survived, he'd hunt me down. He'd lock me to a tether and dangle me in the white until the Fog killed me.

Hazel shot Swedish a dirty look, then turned back to me. "So what'd you get in a fight with?"

Apparently she *hadn't* forgotten about me looking messed up.

"Here." I tossed my sack to Swedish. "Dinner."

He peered inside. "You got in a fight with dandelion greens?"

I sighed. "Fine! It was a goose. I got in a fight with a goose."

From behind me I heard Bea's familiar giggle, and she teased me while Swedish started dinner. He soaked the

14

greens in rainwater, tossed the last of our seagull jerky into the broth, and simmered the whole thing over an exhaust vent.

I plopped down under the balloons while the soup cooked, feeling drowsy and content. I'd follow the scent of roses tomorrow, and with any luck I'd find a drawer of silverware or even—in my wildest dreams—a cabinet full of unbroken wineglasses. Rich people on the upper slopes of the Rooftop paid huge for stuff like that.

Hazel sat beside me, gazing at the sunset, her braids falling around her shoulders, as Bea fiddled with a handful of wires. She made figurines out of cables and wire, what she called "twistys," miniature people, airships, and animals.

She handed me a twisty of a cute little bird. "Here!"

"What's this?" I asked, even though I already knew the answer. "A chickadee?"

"A silly goose," she said. "Like you!"

Swedish poured the soup into bowls and handed them around. "A *rabid* goose. Nothing else could beat Chess."

"It probably had fangs," Hazel said. "And glowing red eyes."

Bea wiped her mouth with her sleeve and asked, "What really happened?"

"She had baby geese with her," I admitted. "They kept looking at me with their big eyes. I just . . . couldn't."

"You fog-face," Swedish grumbled. "We could be eating

roast goose right now."

"Of course Chess couldn't kill her!" Bea told him. "She's a mother! She had babies."

Swede grunted. "They're probably all adopted."

"*We're* all adopted!" Hazel reminded him.

"Sure," he said. "But we're not delicious."

3

NIGHT FELL, AND a million stars freckled the dark sky. We climbed into our hammocks to sleep as the engine ticked and the rigging fluttered. When a cool breeze rose, my hammock began swaying.

"In the old days," I said, pulling my blanket to my chin, "before the Fog came, people used to see shapes in the stars."

"You already told us that," Swedish said. "They called them constipations."

"Constellations," Hazel said with a soft laugh.

"That's what I said!"

Gazing at the stars, I almost told them the old tale of "Skywalker Trek," about a space war between the Klingons and the Jedi, set in a future when people lived on distant planets, and fought Tribbles, Ewoks, and Borgs. I decided to stick with constellations, though, because sometimes my stories got a little garbled.

"They saw archers and bulls and foxes," I said. "They gave the stars names, like 'Elvis Parsley' and 'Greta Garbo' and 'Michael Jackson.'"

"There's no way anyone was ever named 'Garbo!'" Bea said in the darkness. "That's too silly, even for the old days."

"That's what it says in my dad's scrapbook." When my father died, he'd left me a notebook filled with historical facts he'd pieced together. "Greta Garbo."

"'Greta' is nice," Hazel said after a minute.

"'Garbo' sounds like the noise you said bullfrogs make," Swedish told me. "*Garbo, garbo.*"

"It sounds bossy," I said. "Like a command. Swab the deck! Garbo the sails!"

I turned toward Hazel's hammock. "That could be your name. Hazel Garbo."

Bea giggled. "I'm Bea Parsley!"

"Swedish Jackson," Swede said. "I kind of like that."

The raft rocked in the breeze, and we fell silent. Snug in our hammocks, safe and together, far from our troubles. The rich green scent of trees and meadows rose through the Fog, so much sweeter and cleaner than the stink of the slum where we lived.

My eyes closed and my mind began to drift—

18

"I can't sleep!" Bea called out. "Tell me the story again."

"No!" Hazel and Swedish said at the same time.

"Pretty please?" Bea pleaded. "With pigeon on top?"

"Be quiet," Swedish grumbled.

"Count the stars, sweetie," Hazel told her. "Until you fall asleep."

"Pretty please, with churro on top?" Bea asked. "Pretty please with *cucumber*?"

"Would you tell her already, Chess?" Swedish smacked the bootball he used as a pillow. "I'm getting hungry just listening to her beg."

I yawned. "You've heard it a hundred times."

"I don't care," Bea said. "It's *our* story. Nobody else even knows it, because Mrs. E only told *us*."

"Some people on the Rooftop know," Hazel said. "A few of them, at least."

"You know what I mean! None of the other slumkids. Pretty please, with frog legs on top? Pretty please with—"

"Just tell her," Swedish grumbled.

"Sure." I rolled over in my hammock, gathering my thoughts. "Um . . ."

"'Before the Fog rose . . . ,'" Bea prompted, in a sing-song voice.

"Before the Fog rose," I said, "there was something called the Smog. The Smog covered the whole Earth, like the Fog does now, except it made *everything* sick. Not just people—but also grass and trees, and every animal in the sky and sea and land. The Smog choked the entire Earth, slowly killing every single living thing."

"So the gearslingers . . . ," Bea prompted again.

"They called them engineers back then," Hazel told her for the hundredth time. "Nanotech engineers. They made tiny machines to clean the Smog. So tiny that a million of them could fit into your smallest freckle. But—"

"It worked!" Bea interrupted. "You can always count on gearslingers."

"Engineers," I said. "And yeah, it worked. Sort of. At first. The tiny machines—"

"Nanites," Swedish grumbled. "She knows they're called nanites—she's heard the story a thousand times."

"Do you want to tell it?" I asked.

"I want to sleep. Hurry up and finish."

"Fine," I said, trying not to smile. Swedish loved to complain, but I could tell that he was listening to the story, too. "The nanites fixed the Smog and healed the Earth. They cleaned the water and the air, they scrubbed the poison and pollution from every crack and crevice. Only there was one problem. . . ."

"They didn't stop cleaning after they finished," Hazel said, taking over the story. "They were designed to attack any new sources of pollution, and they calculated that because we humans *made* the Smog, they needed to stop us. The nanites turned themselves into the Fog."

20

"You mean they *created* the Fog," Bea said like she always did.

"No, they *became* the Fog. Some of the engineers had been afraid the nanites might go haywire, so they built a 'command password,' a secret code inside each nanite that automatically killed it after three months."

"That way," I said, "if the nanites went loco, the engineers could just shut down the nano factories, and boom. A few months later, no more nanites."

"What they didn't expect . . . ," Bea prompted.

"They didn't expect the nanites to build their *own* factories. Nanites started making more nanites. More than humans ever built, zillions of machines so small that they floated like droplets of fog."

"And we had no way to stop them," Bea breathed.

"The nanites programmed themselves not to bother animals," I said after a moment's silence. "They don't block the sunshine—plants grow like crazy in the whiteness—but they keep *us* out. They only target *human* brains. If we enter the Fog, we become blind and deaf. And if we stay too long, we die of fogsickness."

"But not *you*," Bea said.

"Not yet," I said.

Bea shook her head. "You're different."

"I'm a freak."

"Yeah," Swedish said. "You get beat up by birds."

21

I went on, ignoring him. "Nobody knows exactly when the Fog started rising. A hundred years ago? Two hundred? We only know that the nanites rose slowly, inch by inch, foot by foot, until they covered the entire Earth in a thick white mist, and nothing remained but a few scattered mountaintops. The Rooftop and Port Oro."

I fell silent. We lived on the Rooftop—except slumkids weren't allowed on the mountain itself—but we'd never even seen Port Oro. The Rooftop troopers didn't let anyone get that far from home.

We'd heard stories, though, and we knew that on Port Oro we'd find a cure for Mrs. E . . . and would finally be safe from Lord Kodoc. Ever since the mutineers of Port Oro broke away from the Rooftop years ago, airship skirmishes between the two settlements were common, so the Port was the only place where Kodoc couldn't follow us.

"Do you think there are people on other mountaintops?" Bea asked.

"I *know* there are," Hazel said from her hammock. "Somewhere across the Fog, if you fly for months or years. There must be."

"If they're too far to reach, it doesn't matter," Swedish said. "It's like they don't even exist."

"I wonder," Hazel said with a wistful tone in her voice, "if they also think they're the last people on Earth."

I watched the stars through the rigging and imagined distant mountaintops across the Fog. Foreign places where everything was different, where nobody feared Lord Kodoc.

Although he'd been born into a minor branch of the Five Families, Kodoc became a captain of the roof-troopers at a young age. In those days, the scientists known as the "Subassembly" worked for the Five Families, but Kodoc suspected that they were hoarding information. So he attacked them. He seized their labs and research, he took hostages and lives. And as the tattered remains of the Subassembly fled to Port Oro, Captain Kodoc used his newfound knowledge to become *Lord* Kodoc, head of the Five Families and ruler of the Rooftop.

"Tell the rest of the story, Chess!" Bea demanded. "The part where there's gear inside the Fog that controls the nanites."

"You just told it," I said. "The myths talk about ancient machines that can lower the Fog."

"Do you honestly think they had these machines and didn't use them?" Swedish asked. "They just sat around and watched the Fog rise? That's loco. That's beyond loco."

"Not if they didn't know about them at first." I swayed in my hammock. "What if the nanites built them? Either way, Mrs. E says Lord Kodoc is obsessed with finding them. He thinks if he controls the Fog, he controls the world."

"He's right about that," Hazel said. "If anyone messed

with him, he'd bury them in Fog. Entire families, whole neighborhoods. All of Port Oro."

"That's why he'll kidnap Chess if he finds him." Bea rolled toward me in her hammock. "And force you to search for the machines."

I swallowed. "Well, yeah. . . ."

"Because nobody dives as well as you."

"I'm the only freak around."

"You're not a freak," Hazel told me. "You're a garbo."

"He's a total garbo," Swedish said. "Now go to sleep, Bea, before I toss you overboard."

"Tell me the story of Robbing Hood first!" she insisted.

She loved the story of the hoodie-wearing thief who lived in Sherlock Forest and stole from the rich. She loved the Hood and his crew: a robot called Made Marian and a monkey named Fryer Tuck. We used to play Robbing Hood when we were little, with Hazel as the Hood, Bea as Made Marian, and me as Fryer Tuck. We'd make Swedish be the evil Sheriff of Nodding Ham, of course.

"Bea, let Chess sleep," Hazel told her firmly. "He needs to stay sharp for tomorrow. This is our big break."

"Oh, okay," Bea said in a small voice. "Sorry."

"Night, everyone," I said.

"Night, Chess," Bea said. "Night, Swede. G'night, Hazy."

"Good night, honeybee," Hazel said, a smile in her voice.

I smiled, too, then snuggled under my blanket as the

scent of pine trees washed over the raft. The gyroscope spun, the gears clicked, and I swayed in my hammock and gazed at the sky. So many constellations: archer, crab, Oprah. Was there a constellation for us? For salvage crews and slumkids?

Was there a star for *me*? A tetherboy and a Fog-eyed freak?

4

THE NEXT MORNING, I walked the plank. The cool air gave me goose bumps, and my boots tingled from the ticking of the engine under the deck. My heart beat even faster than usual before a dive. This time I was searching uncharted Fog, following the scent of roses.

"Settle down, Chess!" Hazel called from the crow's nest. "We're almost there!"

"I am settled," I yelled back.

"You are not!" she laughed. "Go check your tether."

I mock saluted her. "Yes, *sir*!"

"That's me!" Hazel gestured with her battered spyglass as her skirt whipped in the wind. "Admiral of the fleet!"

Some fleet. Our rigging looked like tangled ropes, and goofy-looking whales were painted on the bulging balloons. Still, things worked better when Hazel was in charge, so I stepped off the plank and checked my tether while she scanned for the buoy Bea had floated the night before.

"I don't see it," Hazel muttered a minute later. "It should be right here."

At the back of the raft, Swedish spun the ship's wheel a few inches. "I have a bad feeling about this."

"You have a bad feeling about *everything*," I told him. "If you ever had a good feeling, you'd get a bad feeling about it."

"Keep laughing," he grumbled. "That's what *they* want."

"They who?"

"*Them*," Swedish said ominously.

Swedish was convinced that *they* were watching us—not Kodoc, some other *they*. He'd been paranoid about it for years, though he'd never managed to explain who *they* were or why *they* were so fascinated by a bunch of slumkids.

"You always say *they*'re watching," I told him. "But you never say who *they* are."

His eyes narrowed cunningly. "If I knew who they were, they wouldn't be *them*."

Arguing with Swedish always made me dizzy. "So—because you know absolutely nothing about them, you're absolutely sure they exist."

Swedish nodded. "Now you're getting it."

"That doesn't make any sense!"

"That's what they *want* you to think," Swedish said.

"A few wisps to the left, Swede!" Hazel called.

"Can you see the buoy?" I asked her.

"Not yet," she said. "But it's close."

I didn't ask how she knew. Hazel charted the Fog better than anyone. Just like Swedish was the best pilot, and Bea kept our raft in the air better than anyone could.

"Close is good," I said.

I tugged my goggles over my eyes. Bubbles of excitement rose in my chest and I started rolling my shoulders.

"Take a hard left, Swedish," Hazel said. "And stop fidgeting, Chess!"

"I'm not fidgeting," I informed her. "I'm limbering."

"Then stop limbering! You're making me nervous."

"Why?" I asked innocently. "Because if there isn't great salvage even this far from home, we'll never escape the slum?"

"And you'll never afford those pink boots you want," Swedish called to Hazel, tapping on the steam organ.

She glared at him. "I don't want pink boots."

"Yeah, Swede," I said, crossing to the plank, "she wants *yellow* boots and pink *ribbons*."

We teased Hazel about ribbons and dresses because she was such a weird combination of "girly" and "commanding." She wore long, flowing skirts, dreamed of fancy dances, loved pretty sunsets . . . and could bark out orders faster than the toughest junkyard boss. She was about fifteen, a few years older than me and a dozen times smarter. And pretty, with light brown eyes, dark brown skin, and dozens of silky braids.

I looked like every other tetherkid who ran with a salvage crew. I was compact, wiry, and undersized. My boots were stained and my goggles were scraped, and the leather bracers I wore on my wrists to catch the tether were scarred. The only difference was that I always kept my head down and my hair over my freak-eye.

Swedish looked more like a thug or a bootball player than a raft pilot. He was so burly, shaggy, and bearish that he barely fit in the thoppers—sleek, narrow airships— that he flew in drag races to earn extra money. And Bea was our kid sister, with short red hair, big green eyes, and smears of grease on her face. She didn't dream of roast meat and conspiracies like Swedish, but of gears and pistons and building crazy new thoppers that looked like demented dragonflies and flew like hunting eagles.

"On Port Oro," Swedish said, trying to mimic Hazel's voice, "everyone wears yellow boots."

"And there are no junkyard bosses," I added.

"Pigeons lay scrambled eggs," Swedish said.

"It rains soup," I added, "and snows rice!"

"And apples grow on trees!"

I gave him a look. "Um, actually, they kind of do. . . ."

"Oh," Swedish muttered. "Right."

"If you two are done," Hazel said, eyeing us, "can we get back to looking for the buoy?"

I laughed and bounced slightly on the plank. Maybe today we'd finally catch a break. Those roses were a great sign. I started scanning the Fog for the buoy again, and—

A deafening *POP!* shattered the calm morning. It came from beneath the deck, from the engine where Bea was working, adjusting a faulty propeller.

My blood froze. "Bea?" I called. "Are you okay?"

No answer.

"Chess, *go!*" Hazel shouted. "Swedish, cut the engines!"

I dove from the plank, caught a cable with one hand and swung under the deck as a bubble of fear expanded in my chest. What if something had happened to Bea?

5

I SCRAMBLED PAST THE side rudder and the vents, and spotted Bea beside an exhaust pipe.

"Bea!" I said, slumping in relief. "What happened?"

She didn't answer, her usually pale face so dark with soot that she looked like she was wearing a mask. She tapped a bolt with her wrench and told the engine, "Not funny."

She talked to the machinery, the rotors, cables, and gears. That wasn't so weird, except she was sure that they talked *back*. Of course I couldn't argue with the results. No other gearslinger could've kept this scruffy raft in the air.

When I tapped her shoulder, she jerked in surprise.

31

"Chess!" she shouted, even though I was only a foot away. "What are you doing down here?"

"We heard a huge pop and—"

"What?" she shouted. "I can't hear you! There was this huge pop!"

I eyed her. "Are you okay?!"

She eyed me back. "Are you okay?"

"Hoo boy," I muttered. "I'm fine!" I shouted. "Are. You. Okay?"

She gave me a thumbs-up. "No problem! The hydraulic valve's just mad because I didn't adjust him yesterday!"

"Right," I said.

"Valves are moody," she explained.

I shot her a dubious look, and she grinned back. She knew we all thought she was whackadoo, but she didn't care.

I tapped her leather cap twice, saying good-bye, then climbed back onto the deck.

"She's fine," I told Hazel. "Just bickering with the spark plugs."

Hazel rubbed her face. "Do *other* captains have these problems?"

"Other captains have airships," Swedish told her. "You have a floating rattrap."

"That's what I have *for now*," she said.

Swedish and I shared a bemused look at Hazel and her big dreams.

"But I can't find the buoy," she continued. "Chess, help me look."

I shoved my goggles to the top of my head, started to brush my hair away from my freak-eye, then hesitated. Like I was afraid that someone might burst out of the clouds and spot the white wisps drifting across my right eye.

This was the fear that never left me. The clouds of nanites in my eye helped me see farther, hear more, and move faster in the Fog than anyone else, but they also marked me as a freak. As Kodoc's freak. He wasn't just my enemy, he was also my *creator*. Millions of tiny machines swarmed through my brain because of him. Cobblers made shoes and weavers made cloth and Kodoc made me. Like I was nothing more than a tool he'd crafted to help him find those ancient fog-machines—so he could kill his enemies in the silent rise of white.

I'd felt his power every day of my life, before I'd even heard his name. Not just because of the big things, like not having a mother. Kodoc was also the reason I'd worn an eye patch as a little kid. My dad was the one who'd given it to me. He knew I had to hide my eye, but he'd hated how ashamed I felt. So after he died, I vowed that I'd never wear a patch again. And I hadn't: I'd just kept my hair long, my head down, and my mouth shut.

Of course the crew didn't care about my freak-eye, because they were my family. The only family I had left.

So I brushed my hair away and scanned the sky again for the buoy.

"No luck," I called. "I don't see it anywhere."

Hazel swung down from the crow's nest. "It's gone."

I stared at her in disbelief. Buoys didn't just disappear. "What do you mean, it's gone?"

"It should be right there," she said, pointing to an empty stretch of Fog. "But it's not. Full stop, Swedish."

Swedish clattered on the organ keyboard, and the raft jerked to a standstill.

I shaded my eyes. "How can it be gone?"

"Only two ways," Swedish muttered.

Either the buoy malfunctioned or someone messed with it. And if someone messed with it, they might start messing with *us*. A worried silence fell . . . then a hatch slammed open and Bea popped through, her leather cap askew.

"Look at that!" she cried happily. "She still stops on a thumbnail! This raft is purple as a real airship." For some reason, Bea considered "purple" the highest praise.

Hazel quirked a grin. "I don't know what we'd do without you, Bea."

"We'd sink," Swedish muttered. "We probably still will."

"She *likes* stopping," Bea said, her soot-smudged face flushing as she looked past us. "Um, guys, where's the buoy?"

"Gone," Swedish told her.

"Oh." Bea fiddled with her tool belt. "Where'd he go?"

"Now that," Hazel told her, "is a good question."

"I've got a *feeling* about this," Swedish declared.

"Yeah?" I said. "What *kind* of feeling? Surely not a paranoid, doomed sort of feeling?"

"No," he said. "A realistic one. Someone stole our buoy."

"Who'd steal a buoy?"

"Who knows?" Swedish said as he nervously squeezed the bootball he kept beside the wheel. "We're too far from home this time. Probably in mutineer airspace."

My stomach clenched. Everyone knew that the mutineers sometimes shot trespassers on sight. "Don't even say that!"

Hazel tucked a braid behind her ear. "We're not in mutineer territory. We're in no-man's-land."

"Oh, that's much better," Swedish muttered.

"Maybe the buoy just deflated?" I asked.

"It's possible," Hazel said. "Bea, check it out."

"Sure thing, Cap'n!" Bea knelt at the bin where we kept the buoys. "Remember that buoy who went out yesterday?" she asked the spare buoys. She "listened" for a moment, then nodded. "That's right, Bumbleboy."

Hazel and I exchanged a glance. Now Bea was naming them?

"How was he feeling? Hmm? Purple as the day he was

stitched." Bea frowned, then raised her head to Hazel. "The buoy's fine. I don't know where he is now, but he definitely didn't deflate."

"So somebody took it," Swedish said. "We're not alone out here."

6

THE DAY SUDDENLY FELT cooler. The raft swayed in the breeze, the rigging creaked under the balloons, and foggium whooshed through the copper pipes.

"You mean mutineers?" Bea finally asked.

"They're not so bad," Hazel said.

Swedish snorted. "Yeah, they just shoot down any airship that gets too close to Port Oro."

"They're defending themselves," Hazel said. "You know why they're called 'mutineers'?"

"Because they rose up against the Rooftop?" Bea asked. "A long time ago?"

Hazel nodded. "They were ordinary people, like us. Not nobles or merchants. They got fed up with paying the Five Families for the chance to breathe clean air. They gathered on Port Oro, fought off the Rooftop, and started ruling themselves."

"Roof-troopers." Swedish snorted. "They're the worst."

"They're not as bad as Lord Kodoc," Bea said, fiddling with her cap.

"Kodoc's not worse than the roof-troopers," Hazel told her as a breeze rose around us. "He *is* the roof-troopers. They're his private army. Nothing's worse than him."

"Except driftsharks," I said. "But they stay in the Fog."

Swedish tapped the steam organ keyboard to keep the raft in place, but nobody spoke. They knew how much driftsharks scared me, swimming through the air with lashing tails and gaping jaws.

Driftsharks were about the size and shape of real sharks I'd seen in pictures, except they didn't have solid bodies. They were dense swirls in the Fog, with bulky heads, misshapen fins, and wispy tails. They were made of billions of tiny nanites, but they seemed like a single animal, driven to destroy any human in the Fog.

A year earlier, I'd seen a driftshark kill another tetherboy right in front of me. I still heard his screams in my nightmares.

"Um," Bea said after a second, "now *I'm* getting an itchy feeling."

"Let's find a different site," Swedish said. "Something closer to the junkyard."

The "junkyard" was what everyone called the slum where we lived, because it was a sprawl of floating platforms jam-packed with shacks and trash, held aloft by rusty fans and creaky balloons. It was shaped like a huge, uneven ring and encircled the base of the craggy Rooftop mountains that towered above the Fog.

The Five Families lived high on the rich green peaks of the Rooftop, descendants of the people who'd grabbed the best land when the Fog started rising. The farther down the mountain you lived, the less powerful you were, until you came to the junkyard, where the air stank of garbage. Rats swarmed the streets in the night, at least until someone trapped them for dinner. It was dangerous and dirty, and the only home we'd ever known.

We lived in a run-down shack crammed in among thousands of other run-down shacks. And we didn't even *own* our shack, or the raft. We weren't allowed to. Instead, we rented them from the junkyard bosses, who called us "bottom-feeders" and took all of our best salvage. They answered to Lord Kodoc, and we were lucky if they left us enough salvage to buy a sack of rice every week. Some neighborhoods weren't so bad—like the ones where servants lived, crossing the bridges every day to work on the Rooftop—but most were shaky, violent, and mean.

So, after swallowing my nervousness over the missing buoy, I pleaded my case. "We *need* this. There's an iron gate waiting, and probably more. We didn't come this far to turn back now."

"Forget it," Swedish said. "There's enough salvage near home to buy food, if we look hard."

"We need more than food," I said.

"Tell that to my stomach."

"If we stick close to home, we'll never raise the money to reach Port Oro."

Swedish snorted. "You really think they can heal Mrs. E?"

"They can!" I said. "I know they can."

"And there's food in Port Oro, Swedish," Hazel said. "Enough food that you won't be hungry."

"We do okay in the slum," he said stubbornly.

"Enough food," she said, "that *Bea* won't go hungry."

Swedish looked at Bea and his expression softened. Ever since she'd joined the family, we'd tried to protect her from the worst of the slum. Maybe we were used to it, but she deserved better.

"There are real houses, instead of living in shacks," Hazel continued more gently. "Real jobs, instead of dropping Chess into the Fog. And no Lord Kodoc. Port Oro is—"

"It's *paradise*," Swedish scoffed, tossing his bootball from hand to hand. "They'll heal Mrs. E and we'll live on a cloud. You keep saying that, but you don't know what it's like there. Nobody does. All we know is that the mutineers will blow us from the sky if we get too close."

40

I started to answer, then hesitated. He was right. Port Oro reminded me of a magical island in one of Hazel's storybooks, a golden land of fruit trees and freshwater springs . . . guarded by a ferocious sea serpent. Maybe the island was great, but the serpent would eat you before you even saw the beach. And it didn't help that the roof-troopers arrested anyone who tried to move to the Port. They didn't care if you lived or died, but they'd be damned if they'd let you join the enemy.

Still, we needed to try. For Bea. For Mrs. E. For all of us.

"I'm diving." I grabbed my harness. "What's the worst that could happen?"

"You could slice yourself on broken glass and bleed gallons," Swedish said. "Again."

"That was a scratch!"

"Hazel gave you twenty stitches," Bea reminded me. "And I heard alligators are coming back."

"You don't even know what alligators are," I said.

"Like snapping turtles," she said. "Only bigger."

"And what are snapping turtles?"

"Turtles," she said. "That snap."

"It's not animals I'm worried about," Swedish said. "Someone's out here. They're probably watching us right now."

I didn't bother answering. I just turned to Hazel and waited.

She tapped her spyglass against her leg, her forehead furrowing. I knew she was thinking that we needed a big find, to save Mrs. E—and ourselves. But she also worried that we couldn't afford to take stupid chances, and that every day I spent in the Fog, I came closer to losing my strength and my mind.

"That missing buoy means trouble." Hazel rubbed her nose. "Are you sure this is a good site?"

"Well, nobody's scavenged here in forever," I told her.

"Nobody else is dumb enough to dive in the middle of nowhere," Swedish grumbled.

"Plus, I smelled roses," I said.

"What does that mean?" Bea asked.

"They used to plant flowers around fancy houses, so it means this is a good site." I looked to Hazel. "There are roses on the Rooftop, right? On the upper slopes, near the fancy houses?"

"Red and white and pink," she said with a wistful smile.

"How would you know?" Swedish growled at her. "You've never been to the Rooftop. Born and raised in the junkyard. If it weren't for Mrs. E, we'd all be working in a refinery for a bowl of gruel and a beating."

"I know," Hazel told him, "because I *read*."

Swedish cracked his knuckles. "You can't believe those stories. *They* control the books."

"*They* don't control my dad's scrapbook," I told him.

"That's just odds and ends from before the Fog."

"It's history," I said a little defensively, because the scrapbook was my only connection to my father. "How else would we know about the weird animals that used to exist? Spelling bees? Hello Kitties?"

"How *did* kitties say hello?" Bea asked.

"The same way bees spelled, I guess," I said.

"Someone took the buoy," Swedish said. "And even if the roses—"

"I'm diving," I interrupted. "This site is special."

Hazel took a breath. "Promise you'll run like a cockroach at the first sign of trouble?"

"With all six legs," I told her.

"And hope you don't get squashed," Swedish muttered.

"You know me," I told him, crossing toward the diving plank. "I'm unsquashable."

Swedish jostled me as he headed for the wheel. "Just watch out for geese, okay?"

I strapped my harness around my chest and attached my tether to the winch on the deck. Bea checked my buckles; then I stepped onto the diving plank, my heart beating fast and hard.

"Goggles down," Hazel called from the winch.

I lowered my goggles. "Goggles down!"

"Tether free?"

I checked my tether. "Tether free!"

"Dive at will, Chess, and—" Hazel paused. "Come back safe."

"Every time," I told her.

Behind me, Bea asked, "What do roses smell like?"

"Like a full belly and a warm bed," I said, and dove into the Fog below.

7

My TETHER HISSED THROUGH the air, uncoiling from the raft.

The winch squeaked as I fell—then I hit the Fog, and the world disappeared into a silent blur of white. Wind whipped my face and ruffled my pants, and I whooped in excitement, forgetting my worries as I somersaulted through the mist.

I loved diving. Sure, the Fog scared me half to death—but it was also the only place I felt fully alive.

I'd been a salvage diver for three years, and most divers didn't even survive one. There were too many dangers in the Fog: wild dogs, driftsharks, and—worst of all—the jagged branches of trees and the spiky edges of crumbling buildings. I knew Hazel had nightmares about hoisting my tether above the Fog and finding an empty harness.

The Fog was treacherous and brutal, but it was beautiful, too. Shimmering shapes tumbled in the mist, and my body felt different. Buoyant, weightless. I jumped impossibly high, I twirled and flipped and sprang.

I never talked about how much I loved diving. I knew the Fog was terrible, I knew that millions—billions—of people had died when it rose. I hated the Fog for that, and I hated that the Fog was inside me. Most of all, I despised Kodoc for making me like this: afraid of strangers, afraid of exposure, afraid of myself. Scarred for life by a freak-eye that affected me—or *infected* me—in ways I didn't understand.

But I loved how the Fog carried me like a leaf in the wind, how it freed me. And I loved that diving would help me care for Mrs. E.

The junkyard bosses had taken my father's shack after he died, so I'd been sleeping under a pile of molding roof shingles when a gray-haired lady with sharp eyes and a hawk nose started bringing me food. I'd spent my days stealing and my nights trying to spear rats with a stick. I'd almost turned into a rat myself, filthy and skinny, and driven by exactly two things: fear and hunger.

Sometimes I'd hang around marketplaces, keeping

my right eye closed and whining for food, but the beggar gangs usually chased me off. One day, though, I'd found a bag of potato peels. I'd scampered into a gloomy alley, and shoved handfuls into my mouth.

"I've been looking for you!" a woman's voice rang out.

She stepped toward me from the end of the alley, and I stopped chewing, my gaze darting everywhere, looking for escape.

"Don't be frightened," she said soothingly. "I knew your father."

I wasn't loco enough to believe that. I figured I'd stolen from her, and she wanted to get close enough to kick me.

"I have food." She reached into her bag. "Grilled pigeon feet."

Even from ten feet away, the meat smelled delicious. My mouth watered and my stomach gurgled, but I looked at her kindly face and followed my instincts: I ran.

Two days later, she found me again. She put a pickled egg on the ground and walked away. The day after that, she left me a bunch of toasted grasshoppers, and a pair of shoes.

Over the next few weeks, she kept feeding me . . . and I kept mistrusting her. What could she possibly want? What horrible thing was she planning for me?

She treated me like a skittish wild animal, slowly guiding me across the slum toward her shack. She'd already adopted Swedish and Hazel, which reassured me. She hadn't cooked *them* in a pot and chewed on their bones. I figured that was a good sign.

Finally one day, after giving me a bowl of corn mush, she told me, "When you're finished, bring the bowl inside, please."

Against my better judgment, I went inside and put the bowl on the cabinet. And from behind me, she said, "Chess?"

I spun toward her, tensed to flee.

"Welcome home."

Her name was Ekaterina, but we called her Mrs. E, and she raised us like some combination of mother, teacher, and boss. She made me practice my tetherskills until my fingers bled. She made Swedish fly thoppers in under-slum drag races. When Bea came, she made her fix engines in the dark, until she knew every valve with her eyes closed. She was the hardest on Hazel, though; she made Hazel make the rest of us do our jobs. And at the end of the long, exhausting days, she taught us to read and told us stories of the time before the Fog.

She was the kindest thing in our lives. I once woke up in the middle of the night and caught her sewing scraps of cloth by candlelight, making a poufy dress for Hazel's doll. She did the same years later for Bea—except instead of a dress, she made overalls and a tiny wrench. And when

Mrs. E teased him, Swedish used to laugh, this big booming laugh.

Then the fogsickness began to sap her strength. And nobody could cure the sickness except the Subassembly. They were our only hope. We just had to find them.

Only a few "fogheads"—Subassembly members—had stayed on the Rooftop after Kodoc's attack. They lived in hiding, though, and studied the Fog in secret. If they were discovered, they were sentenced to hard labor in the stinking refineries that produced foggium.

Somehow, Hazel had tracked down one of their hideouts in the junkyard. And after Mrs. E started getting feeble and confused, she'd dragged me to a Subassembly meeting in a dank chamber that dangled under the floating slum platforms.

We'd covered ourselves in cloaks, but the fogheads still stared at me like they knew all my secrets.

"We can't cure your friend," a hard-faced woman told Hazel. "We don't have the right gear."

"Who does?" Hazel had asked.

"Our brothers and sisters on Port Oro," a younger foghead had told her, eying my cloaked face. "They're your only chance."

"But you'll never reach Port Oro by yourselves," the woman said. "Now, tell us how you found us. We never meet in the same place twice."

"You always meet in whichever hideout is closest to the Fog," Hazel told her. "I looked for the highest peaks of Fog under the slum."

The woman inhaled sharply. "You read the Fog as well as one of us! Who are you?"

She reached toward me and brushed my hood back a few inches before I knocked her hand away. The younger foghead gasped at my roughness, but I didn't care. At least he hadn't seen my eye . . . or so I'd thought.

"We're nobody," Hazel had said, and led me away.

As I swooped through the Fog, I somersaulted at the end of my tether until I felt the ground nearing. I slowed suddenly and dangled in midair as a line of metal spears came into focus five feet below. Any one of them would've skewered me like a kabob.

"Ha!" I said, though the thick mist swallowed my voice. "Direct hit, Hazel."

She'd dropped me right over the iron gate I'd spotted the previous evening, even *without* a buoy.

Except . . . where was the buoy? If Bea wasn't wrong—and she never was, about mechanical things—then some airship had stolen it. Hopefully not the roof-troopers, who'd sink us on suspicion of trying to escape the Rooftop. Of course, the muties were just as deadly, even if all they cared about was protecting Port Oro.

I unspooled my tether until I landed on the ground, then wiped my goggles and got to work. First I cleared the shrubs twining through the rusting gateposts, enjoying the rich scent of greenery, so unlike the stink of the slum. Then I pulled my hacksaw and started cutting the gate from the earth. Still spooked by the missing buoy, I stopped to peer into the Fog every few minutes, but after an hour the gate finally toppled.

I attached a cargo tether, then squeezed the hand brake on my harness, telling the raft to raise the cargo.

Nothing happened for a few seconds; then I felt four jerks on the hand brake. It was Hazel, asking me to confirm. When I repeated the message, the gate lifted into the air and winched toward the raft, tilting and swaying.

In a minute, it was ten feet above me, out of sight.

I squeezed the hand brake, telling them I was safe and wanted to scout for more salvage. The iron would pay for food, but we needed a big score. So big that even after the bosses took most of the money, we'd still have enough to hire "coyotes"—smugglers who secretly transported people from the Rooftop to Port Oro. That was our plan. Dive like maniacs in uncharted Fog until we raised enough money to pay for coyotes, then dodge roof-trooper warships and angry mutineers to sneak onto Port Oro and cure Mrs. E.

"Easy as falling off a pie," as they used to say. Which didn't make any sense to me, but they also used to say

"May the horse be with you," so as far as I could tell, they talked gibberish pretty much all the time.

When Hazel signaled that it was okay, I followed the crumbling asphalt uphill, and a sudden humming sounded through the muffled quiet. A flowering bush loomed into view, covered in bees. Even insects thrived in the Fog—it was only the humans who died.

Sometimes fogsickness struck a few days after contact with the Fog, or sometimes it took a few weeks or months. Sometimes nothing happened for over a decade. Like with Mrs. E: she was dying now because she'd braved the Fog to save my life, thirteen years ago.

Most people got fogsick if they spent even a few hours in the white. Only tetherkids built up resistance as little kids, so we could dive all day and stay healthy for years— though we didn't usually live that long. Of course I'd been diving over three years and still hadn't gotten sick, but I was born in the Fog itself, with nanites in my brain.

When I stepped closer to the bush, dozens of peach-colored roses came into view. I stood there for a moment, clearing my mind. I loved diving, and I loved *this*: exploring the Fog-hidden Earth. Nobody in the slum ever saw roses or deer tracks or moss-covered rocks in burbling streams. Heck, none of them even saw *trees*.

Humming to myself, I snipped a big blossom for Bea.

I tucked the flower in my pocket, sat down on a pile of stones, and ate a snack of dried locusts. I didn't like eating bugs, but a swarm had flown over the slum a few weeks back, and food was scarce. One thing every slumkid knew was hunger, the kind of hunger that made you dizzy and desperate.

When I started off again, a slithery motion caught my eye. I lifted my head and saw a swirl of Fog thickening in the air as the nanites formed dense white cords above me. My breath caught and my mind blanked with terror: a driftshark.

8

I STARED INTO THE whiteness, eyes wide and heart pounding. Horror tightened my throat and terrifying images rose in my mind—memories of a tetherboy, limp in his harness.

Last year, we'd teamed with another crew to salvage a load of broken glass I'd found in a half-buried truck. I worked alongside a tetherkid named Bilal, a scrawny boy with a goofy smile. We didn't say much at first, because silence felt natural in the Fog. At the end of the second day, though, he grabbed my arm.

"What's wrong with you?" he demanded.

I gulped, worried that he'd seen my eye. "You mean other than my personality?"

"No, I mean . . . you're not afraid."

"Are you kidding? I'm scared of everything. I'm even scared of *butterflies*." I shuddered. "With their creepy wings."

Bilal smiled but somehow still looked serious. "You're not scared in the Fog, Chess. I know you're not."

"Yeah," I muttered, ducking my head. "I don't know."

"And you're . . ." He eyed me suspiciously. "You're too good at this. You *like* it."

"Right," I scoffed. "I'm a huge fan of broken glass."

He didn't mention it again, and by the end of the week we'd become friends. Spending days in the Fog forged a special bond. Nobody else knew the muffled quiet of that whiteblind world.

Then early one day, after we'd loaded the cargo crate, Bilal stretched his arms overhead. "Almost done."

"Two more loads," I said.

"Maybe we can keep diving together," he said almost shyly. "I mean, when we're done with this. If you want."

"That sounds cool," I said. "If our crews are okay with it—"

A driftshark lashed forward from the mist, thick cords of nanites forming a sleek fishlike body with wispy fins and foggy jaws that opened way too wide. Trillions of tiny mindless machines acting in unison—but it looked like a fraying, hazy shark diving through the Fog.

As I shouted a warning, the knot of whiteness closed around Bilal's head, the nanites invading his brain. There wasn't a crunch of bones or splatter of blood. Just one thin scream, and Bilal sagged in his tether. By the time his crew winched him back to his raft, he was dead without a mark on him, except for his flat, white pupils.

I'd watched helplessly from only a few feet away as the driftshark had twirled into the distance, leaving me limp with grief and guilt. The same Fog that had killed my friend swirled inside my own eye.

The memory faded as the haze of nanites above me dwindled into nothing. Just another puff of Fog. Not a shark at all. I exhaled in relief. I should've known better. Driftsharks usually appeared only in ruined cities and towns, and I was in the middle of nowhere.

After catching my breath, I headed uphill . . . and almost fell in a ditch.

Instead, I sprang upward, spinning in midair. I landed in a crouch on the other side of a wide rectangular hole that looked like what Mrs. E called a "swimming pool." She said that people used to swim for fun, but c'mon: even in the old days nobody would waste good drinking water like that. A huge puddle in the yard, just to splash around in? The whole idea was ridiculous.

When I searched the hole, I found pillbugs and black ants and beetle shells. And then, finally, a scattering of broken blue-and-white tiles.

"Nice," I said.

I stuffed the tiles into my bag, jumped from the pool,

and caught sight of a dark doorway half covered with thick green ivy.

I frowned. I hated untethering in the Fog, because if things went wrong I'd never get back to the raft. Not unless I learned to fly. But searching inside a building was tough with a tether, and this site looked worth the risk.

So I squeezed my hand brake, telling Hazel I was untethering and going inside the house.

The hand brake jerked twice, giving me the answer: *No.*

"Thinks she's an admiral," I muttered, and sent the same message again. *I'm going inside.*

Nothing happened for a while, and I pictured them as they argued on the raft above. Then, finally: *Okay.*

"Ha," I said, and sent another message: *I'm detaching my tether.*

The reply came immediately. *No.*

I grumbled and sent the message again.

No. No. No. NO!

Okay, I told her, and muttered aloud, "Hazel Garbo."

I pushed aside the curtain of ivy. My tether scraped against the doorway for a second; then the Fog muffled the sound as I stepped inside.

The darkness smelled of rust and mud and hungry wolves. I mean, I wasn't sure what hungry wolves smelled like, but the shadowy gloom looked like the perfect den for *something* with fangs and claws. I stood very still, trying not to look tasty, until I was able to make out a small room, with rotting leaves carpeting the floor.

Completely empty. No fangs or claws. Just how I liked my shadowy dens.

Another misty doorframe led me into a room with the remains of an altar, what Mrs. E called a "teevee," a screen that told everyone what to wear and eat, and showed them pictures of royalty like the Burger King and Dairy Queen. The teevee itself lay on the floor, a shattered shell of plastic, with wires and circuit boards inside. Not worth much, except as building material.

Down a hallway, the Fog glowed brighter, like the house was missing a wall or part of the roof, letting sunlight in. I clambered over the rubble toward a staircase that rose into the white—and something fast and gray blurred through the mist.

I jumped backward, my heart pounding. I didn't carry a weapon, because if you fought anything in the Fog, you lost. Instead, you ran: you tugged on your tether and rose into the sky. Unless of course you were trapped inside a building with a hungry wolf pack.

Holding my breath, I scanned the misty whiteness. A scrabbling sounded behind me and I sprang upward until I was jerked back down—my tether snagged in the other room.

The tether jerked tight, but I kept moving, like a ball at the end of a chain, and smashed straight into a crumbling brick chimney.

Pain burst in my side, and the bricks collapsed around me. I moaned, half covered in rubble. I should've untethered, no matter what Hazel told me. Now I was trapped, dazed and defenseless, while the wolves prowled closer—

A gray squirrel dashed across the stairs.

Oh. Not wolves. I'd almost killed myself running from a *squirrel*. Maybe I wouldn't mention that to the others, especially after yesterday's epic goose failure.

With a groan, I began pushing the bricks aside. Then a glint of metal caught my eye, a dented box that must've been hidden in the fireplace. Still half covered in rubble, I grabbed the box and opened the lid.

"Nice!" I said when I saw a stack of what Mrs. E called "cash," faded green rectangles with weird faces printed on them.

And numbers, too. Most of *this* cash said "100," though some said "1000." But that didn't really matter. What mattered was that cash made excellent toilet paper—the best in the Rooftop. The 1000s weren't any softer than the 100s, though.

I shoved the "cash" into my pocket, and saw the second box. Smaller, and almost cube shaped, with a tattered felt cover. Inside, I found a ring nestled on a puff of discolored satin.

A gold ring with a sparkly stone. A diamond.

My breath caught in my throat. "No way."

Impossible. We'd spent weeks diving for a jackpot in

uncharted Fog, and it was a *squirrel* that finally led me to the biggest haul ever? Completely impossible. I mean, I'd never seen a diamond, but this looked exactly like one of the pictures in Hazel's books.

And the Rooftop paid huge for diamonds. Heck, only members of the Five Families were even allowed to own them. They were illegal for slum-dwellers and lower slope crafters and even for the merchants on the middle slopes. In fact, I'd heard that if you got caught keeping a diamond for yourself, Lord Kodoc would personally cut off your hand.

But that didn't mean you couldn't sell them.

I closed my eyes for a second, then peered again at the ring. Still there.

"You're not dreaming," I told myself. "You're not fog-sick. That is one big honking diamond."

I was grinning like a garbo as I tucked the ring into my belt pouch. I wanted to shout and sing, but I dug myself out of the bricks instead. I almost scrambled outside to return to the raft, because we didn't need any more salvage, not with a diamond like this in my pouch. But I'd been a tetherboy for too long, and I couldn't leave good salvage behind. So I filled the bag with bricks from the chimney, smiling the whole time.

I couldn't wait to see everyone's faces when I showed them the diamond. Bea would jump up and down, Swedish would spin his bootball on his finger, and Hazel would make a triumphant speech. And to think we'd been *worried* about today's dive! No driftsharks, no accidents—no problems at all.

All our work, rewarded. All our troubles, solved.

Port Oro, here we come.

9

AS THE CARGO TETHER rose, I gazed into the Fog, daydreaming about life on Port Oro. Imagining a place without hunger, without Kodoc, without junkyard bosses or roving gangs. Imagining a cure for fogsickness.

Chewing my lip in excitement, I squeezed the hand brake. A moment later, my harness yanked me upward. My boots left the ground and the whiteness blurred around my face as I rose toward the clear world above.

I laughed as I passed through the highest fringes of the Fog, eager to show everyone what I'd found. When the blue sky burst into sight and my full weight returned, it felt like I was carrying a fifty-pound backpack, but for once I didn't mind.

Twirling toward the underside of the raft, I saw pistons

chugging and vapor hissing from valves. Before I reached the boarding ladder, Bea's face popped over the side.

Her leather cap was askew and her green eyes were wide. She gestured wildly toward a peak of Fog.

"What?" I called.

She raised a finger to her lips, shushing me, then disappeared from view.

I almost yelled, *Don't shush me—I found a diamond!*

The winch stopped suddenly, with me still dangling twenty feet below the deck. The propellers whirled and the raft jerked forward.

I yelped as I trailed behind the speeding raft, dragged along by my tether.

What was going on? Were we running? From what?

I climbed my tether, hand over hand, swinging sideways as the raft turned in crazy angles. I reached the deck just in time to catch a glimpse of Bea vanishing into a hatch. At the wheel, Swedish handled the lumbering three-ballooned raft like a racing thopper, playing hide-and-seek behind white waves of Fog.

I climbed toward the crow's nest. "What's going—"

"Mutineers," Hazel said without lowering her spyglass.

Above us, the middle balloon creaked in protest as Swedish veered suddenly to the left.

"*What?*" I shivered in the sunlight. Not now, not with a diamond in my belt pouch. "Where?"

She nodded at the Fog. "On the far side of that peak."

"Did they see us?"

"I don't know. They came into sight a mile away and turned toward us. Maybe a coincidence, but . . ."

"They'll leave us alone, right?" I patted my pouch nervously. "I mean, mutineers hardly ever bother salvage rafts."

"*Hardly* ever," Hazel said.

When the mutineers revolted, they'd taken over the most distant mountaintop that belonged to the Rooftop. Port Oro was less than a quarter of the size of the Rooftop, but they'd beaten back every attack for decades. That was the good news. The bad news was that being outnumbered made the muties defensive and quick-tempered, so sometimes they shot first and asked questions later.

And by "sometimes," I meant "usually."

"Bring her lower," Hazel called to Swedish. "Along that ravine."

Swedish scowled at the wide, wispy crack in the Fog. "That's a tight fit."

I swallowed nervously. The raft was fueled by refined Fog, called "foggium," which didn't work inside the Fog itself. That's why machinery didn't run in the white. If the engine dipped below the surface, we'd lose power immediately. The foggium would stop heating the air inside the balloons, and we'd tumble hundreds of feet and crash.

"You've got a foot on either side," Hazel told him. "You can do this."

"I can kiss my butt good-bye," Swedish muttered, plunging the raft into the ravine.

The deck jerked as the middle balloon groaned, then hissed like an angry cat: the sound of a balloon about to pop.

I froze, straining to hear. Wind whistled through the rigging, and a valve released pressure with a *click-shhhht-click*. Nothing more from the middle balloon.

After a few seconds, I unclenched my hands from the rail. "The cargo netting's inside the Fog, Hazel. If it snags anything, we're dead."

"I *know* that," she snapped.

"Then why are we—"

"Mutineers never come this close to the Rooftop, Chess. Something's not right. I don't know why they're here, but if they don't see us, they won't sink us, so—"

A shadow fell over us from behind.

I turned and saw an airship with a zeppelin—a long cigar-shaped balloon—that dwarfed our three patched balloons completely. Whirling fans droned on cranes that sprouted from the airship like a water bug's legs, and run-off pipes spat clouds of exhaust.

It was a mutineer ship, with dull brass and predatory fins, her name gleaming on the prow: *Night Tide*.

A *war*ship. We were so dead.

10

A VOICE BOOMED FROM the mutineer ship. "Stop your props or we'll blow you from the sky!"

Hazel swung down from the rigging. "Do as he says, Swedish."

"*Muties*," Swedish mumbled as he slowed the raft to a halt. "Now they're after salvage rafts?"

"I've heard of the *Night Tide*," Bea said in a quavering voice. "I heard she opened fire on a trading post."

"That's a lie," I said, though I wasn't so sure. "Just the roof-troopers trying to make them sound bad."

Swedish snorted. "Did the roof-troopers make them threaten to blow us from the sky?"

"They're not driftsharks." Hazel took a shaky breath. "They're just people."

"People in a *warship*," Swedish said.

"They're from Port Oro."

"Which has been at war with the Rooftop for years," I reminded her.

"We'll get through this," she told me.

"Or we'll spiral down and die in the white," Swedish said with a shudder. "Our bodies eaten by dogs and—"

Bea squeaked in alarm, and Hazel said, "Swede!"

"Sorry," Swedish mumbled. "I'm just saying."

"Well, *stop*," Hazel said, inspecting the warship with her spyglass.

The voice boomed again from the mutineer ship. "Higher still, my poppets—up where we can see you!"

Another mutie shouted from the *Night Tide*: "Where we can shoot you!"

"Board you!" a different mutie called.

"Sink you!"

"Well, you were right, Hazel," Swedish muttered. "They sound like sweethearts."

"Take us up," Hazel told him.

"They'll kill us!" Bea cried.

"We'll be okay, honeybee," Hazel reassured her. "I have an idea."

I propped my goggles on my forehead with shaky hands and tugged my hair lower. After a few days on the raft, I almost forgot that I needed to hide my freak-eye. But the moment strangers approached, a hot flush of shame reminded me.

As I ducked my head, Swedish hunched at the wheel, Bea whispered to the foggium array, and Hazel stood at the prow, chin high and gaze steady.

On the upper deck of the mutineer airship, an almost elegant stretch of narrow railings was spiked with cannons and harpoons and lined with a dozen airsailors with sharp eyes and curved blades. A tall man with a scarred face lifted his hand, and silence fell. He strode to the quarterdeck, his cloak billowing behind him, revealing the cutlass and dagger at his belt. Ruby and emerald rings flashed on his fingers.

Looked like mutineering paid pretty well. Still, I didn't see any diamonds, so maybe bottom-feeding paid even better.

I patted my belt pouch to reassure myself that the diamond was still there, then quickly changed the gesture into a scratch. I didn't want to call any attention to myself. Not only because I hated being seen, but because I couldn't let them find the ring.

On the other hand . . . what if I just *gave* them the diamond? Would they take us to Port Oro? Maybe, but what about Mrs. E? We couldn't exactly ask them to pick her up in the slum. Plus, they were mutineers—outlaws and pirates. They'd probably just *take* the diamond.

"Is that an airship," the mutineer captain called, "or has a chunk of the junkyard floated away?"

A few mutineers jeered and one of them swiveled a harpoon toward me. My heart clenched, but a second later the mutie moved on, targeting the props instead.

"And what," the captain continued, frowning at the raft's balloons, "are *those*?"

"Our balloons, sir," Hazel called back.

"I mean the designs. Those paintings."

Hazel's eyes narrowed. "They're whales!"

"With fangs?"

"Those aren't fangs! They're smiling."

"They're enough to give *me* nightmares," the mutineer captain said. "And that's not easy. Who are you?"

"Just a salvage crew, sir, with some scrap metal and—" She cocked an eyebrow at me. "What else?"

I lowered my head. "Bricks and cash."

"Rusted iron, broken bricks, and toilet paper." Then, a little sarcastically, she continued: "A poor haul for such a grand ship as yours."

The mutineer captain frowned at her tone. "You're renting that trash heap from the junkyard bosses and you're mocking *my* ship?"

"Your aft propellers are off-kilter," Hazel told him with the barest tremor in her voice. "The *Night Tide* is waddling like a toddler in a diaper."

An angry murmur sounded from the warship, and I held my breath and clutched my belt pouch. You didn't mess with mutineers—you fled or you groveled. Was

Hazel *trying* to make them angry?

The scar-faced mutineer raised his telescope and swept our raft scornfully. "And *you* are the captain?" he asked Hazel.

"I am," she said.

"You look more like a dancing girl," he said. "Permission to board?"

"Permission denied," Hazel answered.

"Prepare to fire," he told his crew, and the clatter of harpoons filled the air, accompanied by the whistle of grappling hooks.

"On second thought," Hazel said, "we'd be honored if you'd pay us a visit."

"I thought you'd see it my way," he said.

The mutineer captain muttered a command, and a plank slid from the *Night Tide* and slammed onto our deck. The raft swayed when he crossed from his warship, and for a moment, I thought I heard that angry-cat hissing again from the middle balloon.

Three burly mutineers followed the mutineer captain across the plank, and the raft suddenly seemed even smaller and junkier than before.

Hazel curtsied. "Welcome aboard, Vidious."

I exhaled shakily. Figured that she'd know the mutineer's name.

"That's *Captain* Vidious," a red-haired mutie grunted.

Vidious just laughed. "You have the advantage of me, girl. What's your name?"

"Hazel."

"*Captain* Hazel," Swedish muttered.

The red-haired mutie shoved him. "Shut your yap."

Swedish raised a hand to shove back, and Hazel said, "No, Swedish. They're our guests."

"Plus," Bea added with a bright nervousness, "there's a hundred of them and only four of us, and our foggium array isn't feeling well."

I didn't say anything and tried to look small and boring. I had the crew's future in my belt pouch and couldn't give the mutineers any excuse to search me. This guy Vidious would definitely steal the diamond and leave us behind in the slum.

"Enough," Vidious told his airsailors. "If they touch you, teach them a lesson. Otherwise, don't bother. Now, then—" He eyed Hazel. "You're right that I don't care about salvage. I'm looking for reprisal against the Rooftop."

Hazel frowned. "Oh."

"What does that mean?" Bea asked in a small voice. "'Reprisal'?"

"Like revenge." Hazel eyed the mutineer captain. "Is that why you shot down our buoy?"

Bea gasped. "Poor Bumbleboy. . . ."

"We won't tolerate *any* Rooftop vessel at the moment." The quiet anger in Vidious's voice made me shiver. "Not even a buoy."

"Sorry!" Hazel said brightly. "Our mistake! We'll just be going now!"

"You're not going anywhere yet. You look like roof-trooper spies to me."

"We do?" she asked, her brow furrowing. "Don't we kind of look more like . . . slumkids?"

"Maybe you're both." He inspected us coldly. "And I'm going to make the roof-troopers pay for ambushing my sister."

"Well, what did you expect?" Hazel asked. "You're way too close to the Rooftop."

Vidious ran his hand along a frayed rope. "That's no excuse."

"But you're days from Port Oro. What're you doing this far from home?"

Vidious quirked an eyebrow. "Minding our own business, until a roof-trooper airship attacked us. And you're part of the Rooftop, aren't you?"

"Not really. We're from the slum."

"The slum of the Rooftop," he said, his voice sharp with accusation.

"Well, yes, but—"

"Cut their cargo tether!" Vidious called.

11

A HARPOON FLASHED FROM the *Night Tide* and sliced through the ropes holding the cargo netting. The bag of bricks and rusted iron gate tumbled away into the Fog, and the raft rocked violently. For a third time, I thought I heard a faint hiss from the middle balloon.

"We should take their geargirl, too," Vidious said as an afterthought. "If she can keep this junkpile in the air, she's some kind of genius."

"Over my dead body," Hazel said, and swung her fist at Vidious.

Swedish kneed one of the airsailors and shoved another before the red-haired mutineer smashed him in the head with the flat of his sword. As Swedish crumpled to the deck, Vidious sidestepped Hazel's punch and twirled her.

Almost like a dance, until he clamped her to his chest, his sword pricking her neck next to the seashell she wore on a leather cord.

My heart shrank three sizes. I froze, my hand on my belt pouch.

"I usually sink trespassers," Vidious purred into Hazel's ear, "even if my sister sulks for a week."

"We're not—" Hazel gulped. "We're not trespassers! We're in no-man's-land!"

"You're probably working for the roof-troopers. Still, I'll take the geargirl and leave the rest—"

"If you take Bea," Hazel said, her voice soft but strong, "I swear by the Fog that I'll find you. I'll claw my way back from the grave and haunt your dreams. I swear by the silence and the white that I'll ruin you and everyone you love. I swear by all the high places that—"

"Stop teasing her, Vid," a woman called from the *Night Tide*. "Let them go."

Jittery with nerves, I peeked at the warship and saw a woman on the quarterdeck, dressed in black with a pair of daggers at her hips. Her blond hair flowed down her back, and strings of beads looped around her neck.

Captain Vidious cocked his head. "Why should I do that, Nisha?"

"The girl is playing to *me*," the woman said. "She must've seen me with her spyglass. I gather she knows my reputation."

My fingers tightened on the belt pouch. Had Hazel seen the woman—Nisha—on deck? Is that why she'd tried to anger the captain?

"Besides," the woman continued, "none of my sailors were hurt, and the *Anvil Rose* is almost fixed. Plus, we *do* have more important tasks than reprisal."

"True enough," Vidious said, shoving Hazel away. "Though I'd still like to get my hands on Kodoc."

Hazel stumbled a few steps. "L-Lord Kodoc?"

"You've heard of him?" Vidious asked.

"Everyone in the slum knows his name," she said a little too quickly. "He's the leader of the roof-troopers. Is he . . . out here?"

Vidious gave a careless shrug. "Maybe."

I peered uneasily across the Fog. A few puffy clouds floated overhead, and I suddenly worried that Kodoc's airship was hiding inside them. What if I actually met Kodoc, face-to-face? Would he recognize me as his creation? Would he control me somehow, like a falconer controls his bird? Could I resist?

"Why do you care?" Vidious asked.

"They say he—" Hazel swallowed. "He works tether-kids to death. They say he experiments on them. They say he feeds kids to driftsharks to see what happens."

"He's a dangerous man."

Hazel tugged on a braid. "Um, there's one thing I don't get. . . ."

"Spit it out, poppet."

"Well, you just happened to be patrolling this close to the Rooftop?" Hazel asked too dubiously. "Minding your own business?"

"Exactly," Nisha said from the railing of the *Night Tide*.

Hazel nodded toward the warship's hull. "Then what are you doing with *that*?"

I followed her gaze and didn't see anything except a few exhaust vents and a row of lifeboats.

"Those are lifeboats," Nisha told her.

"I beg your pardon," Hazel said politely. "For a moment, I thought one of them was a cargo raft disguised as a lifeboat. My mistake."

An ache throbbed in my stomach when I looked closer. Hazel was right. One of the boats attached to the hull *was* a cargo raft: bigger, sturdier, and more maneuverable than a lifeboat.

Vidious scowled, and I silently begged Hazel to change the subject before he lost his temper completely—but Bea widened her eyes at the cargo raft.

"Ooh, he's got lovely turnbuckles!" she chirped. "Swede could fly him upside down through a gnat's eye!"

"Er," Hazel said quickly. "She means if it *wasn't* a lifeboat."

Vidious and Nisha exchanged a glance that seemed to chill the air, and I patted my belt pouch for reassurance. I definitely didn't want these two finding the diamond.

"But obviously it *is* a lifeboat." Hazel gave Bea a quick look. "Isn't that right, Bea?"

"Yes!" Bea squeaked, her cheeks flushing red. "Life-boat!"

Vidious touched the hilt of his dagger. "We should sink them," he told his sister.

"You're probably right," she agreed. "But we're not going to."

I wasn't exactly sure what was going on, but Hazel sounded frightened as she said, "Kodoc is no friend of ours. He's no friend of anyone in the slum, except the bosses."

Nisha leaned on the railing of the *Night Tide*, then vaulted overboard, her long hair streaming behind her. I gaped in shock, but she landed on the boarding plank that stretched between the warship and the raft.

"You remind me of myself at your age," she told Hazel, strolling closer.

"When you were her age," Vidious told his sister, "you couldn't have captained an empty boot, much less a sal-vage raft."

Nisha's mouth quirked. "Well, at her age *someone* got tangled in the rigging, and hung upside down for an hour."

"I was sick!" Vidious said.

"Of course you were," Nisha said mock soothingly.

"Why do you think Hazel mentioned the . . . odd-looking lifeboat to us?"

"Because she's a dumb kid."

"Look closer," Nisha told him. "This is a tight-run ship, even if it's patched together from junk. She's telling us she knows what we're after. She's offering to give us information."

Vidious narrowed his eyes at Hazel. "What are we after?"

"Um, you're smuggling something into the Rooftop?" Hazel gulped. "That's why you've got that cargo raft."

"You're half right." Vidious nodded to his sister. "Fine. Talk to her."

"Tell me about the roof-trooper patrols," Nisha told Hazel. "Do they search all rafts approaching the Rooftop?"

Hazel nodded. "But anyone can land on the *slum*. Well, if you find a dock or slipway."

"So getting into the slum is easy." Nisha absently rattled her beaded necklace. "How about going from the slum to the Rooftop?"

"Not easy at all," Hazel said. "You need a pass to cross the bridges, and there are armed guards watching everyone."

Nisha fired off a dozen questions about roof-trooper patrols, surface-to-air defenses, and pursuit strategies, and Hazel answered them all.

I gaped at her. How did she know all that?

Finally Nisha clapped Hazel on the shoulder in thanks and sauntered back across the boarding plank. "C'mon, Vid," she called over her shoulder. "We've learned as much as we're going to."

"Maybe you have," Vidious said. "But I still don't know why that tetherboy keeps patting his belt pouch."

12

A KNOT TIGHTENED IN my chest. I hadn't even *touched* the pouch! Well, maybe once or twice. But how had he noticed?

Vidious stalked toward me. "Hand it over."

"It's just—" I swallowed. "It's nothing."

"Don't test my patience," Vidious said.

My mouth went dry and I nervously shifted my weight. After a second, I grubbed around in my pants pocket for the wire goose "twisty" that Bea had made.

"This is, um, all I have," I said, my voice shaky.

Vidious narrowed his eyes. "Your belt pouch."

"I don't have anything!" I blurted. "Just a . . . a rose."

"Stop scaring the tetherboy," Nisha called from the boarding plank.

"Then you won't mind sharing," Vidious told me, ignoring his sister.

"Give it to him, Chess," Hazel said. "We're all friends here."

"No!" Whatever happened, I couldn't lose that diamond. "I dove for it, and I'm not going to—"

"Boy!" Vidious barked at me. "Give me the pouch."

When I shook my head, Vidious stepped toward me—and a sudden spurt of fear gave me strength.

I flicked the twisty goose into the air, and when Vidious followed it with his eyes, I vaulted off the deck. I dropped five feet, grabbed a rung of the boarding ladder, and swung under the raft. My heart pounding, I hauled myself past gears and rudders, then stopped below a hatch that opened to the deck and fiddled desperately with my pouches.

Ten seconds later, the hatch slammed open above me, and a rough hand yanked me onto the deck.

The red-haired airsailor tossed me across the raft. I landed hard on my elbow, and my goggles flew from my head. I moaned, lying in a heap at Vidious's feet.

"Let's see what you're hiding," Vidious said, slashing at my belt with his cutlass.

The tip of his blade flicked my pouch into the air. He caught it and pulled out a rose. That big peach blossom from the bush in the Fog.

"That's mine!" I whined, trying to hide my relief that

he hadn't found the diamond I'd just tucked into my boot pocket. "It's for . . . for Valentine's Day!"

"For *what*?"

"An old holiday," I said, trying to distract him with facts from my father's scrapbook. "When they used to wear green and say 'be mine' and kiss under a shamrock."

Vidious frowned. "Why?"

"They gave flowers to their sweethearts," I added, trying to look embarrassed.

Nisha's laughter sounded from the *Night Tide*. "The tetherboy is a romantic," she said. "I think I may swoon."

"Oh-ho, poppet!" Vidious said with a mocking smile. "Is this for your girlfriend?"

I glanced at Bea. "She's not my girlfriend."

"You brought me a rose!" Bea exclaimed, her eyes suddenly bright.

I wasn't sure if she was playing along or just excited to see the flower. No telling with Bea.

The mutineer captain looked from scrawny Bea to beautiful Hazel and his lip quirked. "You're giving the wrong girl flowers, tetherboy."

"Go fog your head," I muttered. "You garbo."

Vidious tapped me with the toe of his boot. "Mind your tongue."

"Don't tease the boy, Vid," Nisha said. "Young love is hard enough."

My head throbbed, my elbow burned, and they thought

I was in love with Bea—but I didn't care. I still had the diamond.

"You're lucky I'm in a good mood," Vidious said, and crushed the rose in his fist.

"If this is a good mood," I muttered, "I'd hate to see what you look like cranky."

He sprinkled the rose petals onto the deck, then strolled across the boarding plank. His three airsailors followed, and a moment later the plank vanished into a slot in the *Night Tide*.

"What do you think you're doing?" Hazel asked me, too softly for the muties to hear.

"Getting my butt kicked," I muttered, still splayed on the deck.

"In that case, you did a pretty good job."

"It's my special gift," I told her.

"Owww," Swedish groaned, waking up and rubbing his head. "Why aren't we dead yet?"

"Scurry back to the junkyard," Vidious shouted from the deck of the *Night Tide*. "And if I see you again, I'll drop you into the Fog."

The warship veered away, fins slicing the air. The back draft of its fans shook our balloons, and the deck jerked and swayed. I exhaled in relief but stayed still until the *Night Tide* disappeared behind a towering spray of Fog. Then a smile crept across my face—I still had the diamond!

"Got 'em!" Bea announced before I could say anything.

"Got what?" Swedish asked.

She showed him the crushed rose petals she'd collected from the deck. "These! They're so purple!"

"Looks more like pink to me."

"Not that kind of purple, Swede! And they're softer than silk."

"Chess!" Hazel said. "Would you tell me what—"

A slithery hissing sounded above us, louder than before, and the terrifying *put-put* of air escaping from a hole.

We all froze, staring up past the rigging. For an instant, I refused to believe my ears. Then the raft lurched, the deck slanted, and the middle balloon popped with a ter-rifying *bang*.

13

"SWEDISH, TAKE THE WHEEL!" Hazel shouted. "Chess, the balloons! Bea—we need altitude, *now!*"

Bea flung herself at the ballast tank as shreds of fabric cascaded around us. I raced into the rigging and wove my tether through the main lines: if I didn't hook the two remaining balloons together, they'd slip from the rigging and we'd fall from the sky.

While I tugged the lines closer, Bea crooned to the overtaxed engine.

Swedish muttered under his breath for three long minutes, then said, "Would someone tell me what happened?"

"Our balloon popped," I told him, "because you fly this thing like it's a racing thopper."

Which wasn't fair of me, but what can I say? Getting

tossed around by mutineers made me grumpy.

"I mean, how come we're still alive?" Swedish asked with a scowl in my direction. "What happened after I got knocked out?"

"Hazel saved us!" Bea called to him from the gyroscope. "She saw a lady on the mutie ship who she knew was nice, only they dumped our cargo and wanted to take me prisoner—I mean, they said I'm a good geargirl, and then Hazel saw a cargo raft and realized they're trying to smuggle something onto the Rooftop and—"

"The woman is Captain Nisha," Hazel called from the crow's nest. "She's Vidious's sister. They say she's three kinds of awesome, so I knew she wouldn't actually hurt us. Watch that Fog!"

The raft jerked sideways, avoiding a crest of Fog, and for the next few frenzied minutes, I tugged and jerked, forcing the lines closer, trying to secure the balloons.

"C'mon," I whispered to myself. "We're too rich to die."

"Get her five feet higher!" Hazel shouted beneath me. "*Now*, Bea!"

"She can't," Bea wailed. "She can't!"

"We're touching Fog," Hazel snarled. "You promised me five more feet."

"That was ten feet ago!"

"Give me five feet or we're dead."

"Fine!" Bea pulled a cable cutter from her belt and started apologizing to the raft.

Hazel gritted her teeth. "One notch to the left, Swedish."

Swedish frowned, his knuckles white on the wheel. "Poor Mrs. E. She's going to starve without us."

The raft swayed and bobbed, missing a ridge of Fog by inches. My arms ached from the effort of squeezing the lines tighter, and the bruise on my elbow throbbed. I gave one final heave, straining to pull the ropes together . . . and couldn't.

Hazel bellowed, "The aft balloon's slipping, Chess! Steady them *now*!"

"What do you think I'm doing?" I shouted, and threw my arms around the lines.

Linking the leather bracers on my wrists, I trapped the lines inside a desperate hug. The ropes chafed my arms, and the pain brought tears to my eyes, but the rigging started to steady. I wanted to call for help but closed my eyes instead. If Swedish moved the wheel an inch too far, the raft would overturn, if Bea didn't keep the fans spinning, we'd sink, and if Hazel didn't plot the shortest course, we'd shake apart in the air.

So I breathed slowly, trying to think of other things. Like switching the ring with the rose to trick the mutineers. Like selling the diamond to the bosses, then hiring coyotes to smuggle us into Port Oro. Finally we'd have more than a few scraps of food and a rickety shack. And we'd find a cure for Mrs. E.

For twelve years after saving me from the Fog, Mrs. E hadn't felt a twinge of fogsickness. Then last year, she'd started getting weaker. Only for a few hours, at first, but soon the sickness struck deeper. About six months ago, she'd spent two weeks straight sick in bed. Unable to stand, unable to feed herself. We'd known then that if we didn't find a cure, we'd lose her forever. That's when Hazel took me to meet the fogheads in the chamber under the platforms. And when they told us they couldn't help, we decided to smuggle Mrs. E—and all of us—into Port Oro.

We gathered in the kitchen and told her our plan. "We'll start scavenging farther from home," Hazel explained. "Until we raise enough money. There are places nobody's searched in a hundred years."

Mrs. E pursed her lips. "And there are dangers nobody's seen in that long, too. This is a foolish idea."

"There's no other way to get you to Port Oro," Hazel told her. "We need money. Lots of money."

"I forbid it!" Mrs. E said, her voice stronger than usual.

"Too bad." Swedish crossed his arms. "I'm not going to sit around and watch you die."

"Me neither," Bea said.

I wiped my face with my palm. "None of us are."

Hazel took Mrs. E's hand. "You fed us when we were hungry, you loved us when we were alone."

"And now it's *our* turn to take care of *you*," I said.

Mrs. E's eyes welled with tears. "The four of you . . . you're all I have. Every time you step onto that raft, I know I might never see you again. That's worse than fog-sickness."

"We'll always come back to you," Bea promised.

"And if Chess finds something big, we can hire smugglers no problem," Hazel said with an eager smile. "Heck, if he finds something *really* big, I'll haggle with the roof-toppers directly. Even Lord Kodoc himself might let us leave if we—"

Mrs. E jerked like she'd been bitten. "No! Not Kodoc. You stay away from Kodoc."

"I was just saying!" Hazel protested.

"Promise you'll stay away from him," Mrs. E demanded. "Promise me."

"Fine. I promise."

"I thought I could protect you, but now . . . I'm not so sure," Mrs. E said, her voice wavering but intense. "There's something I haven't told you."

"Something about Kodoc?" Hazel asked.

"Yes," Mrs. E said, her lips thinning. "If he ever finds us, he'll kidnap Chess and work him to death."

The walls tilted around me and I stared at Mrs. E, not quite believing my ears. That had been the first time I heard about the link between me and Kodoc.

"M-me?" I spluttered.

"He'll chain you to a tether, Chess, and he'll drag you

89

through the Fog, scraping you against rocks and ruins in his search for the ancient machines—."

"The machines that lower the Fog?" Bea interrupted.

"If they exist." Mrs. E took a trembling breath. "If Kodoc catches Chess, he'll kill him. He's killed dozens of tetherkids already, experimenting on them, keeping them in the Fog for days on end—"

Hazel frowned. "Does he know about Chess's eye?"

"He doesn't even know Chess is alive. But Chess wasn't the first child born with Fog in his eye. There are old stories of another child with the same white spots—"

"What stories?" I said. "I never heard any."

"Secret stories, Chess."

"You could've told me!"

Mrs. E raised a trembling hand. "It was safer this way."

Anger and confusion swirled in my head. I knew Mrs. E kept secrets, but not about *me*. Not about the one thing that shaped my whole life.

Hazel touched my arm. "Let her talk."

When I nodded, Mrs. E continued: "The stories say that a hundred years ago a child was born inside the Fog with white in her eye. A shifting, shimmering cloud of nanites. Like a pearly mist."

"But Chess wasn't born in the Fog," Bea said.

"Maybe he was," Hazel said.

"Lord Kodoc spent decades trying to create a baby like the girl in the story," Mrs. E said. "He thinks that any child born with nanites will have a special affinity for the Fog."

"What does that mean?" Bea asked. "Affinity?"

"A special connection to the Fog," Mrs. E explained. "Special abilities."

"Like how Chess doesn't get fogsick even though he dives way too much?"

Mrs. E nodded grimly. "Kodoc wanted to harness that power. So he locked pregnant women inside cages and lowered them into the Fog to give birth, hoping one child would be born with eyes of Fog." Grief deepened the furrows on her face. "But they were born with fogsickness instead. Every one of them died, until . . ."

"Until me." I touched the hair over my eye. "So *Kodoc* is the reason I'm like this?"

She nodded again. "When I was young, I worked with him. This is—"

"You *what*?"

"W-with Kodoc?" Bea stammered.

"No way," Swedish said. "How could you?"

A wistful expression flickered on Mrs. E's face. "We had big plans, big dreams. We were going to change the world, build shining cities on the mountaintops. Then I realized that his true goal was to turn the Fog into a weapon. I saw how cruel he was, how obsessed. He'd do anything to find the ancient machines." Mrs. E closed her eyes briefly. "Including experimenting on innocent people. I started to spy on him, looking for a way to stop him. But he found out. . . ."

She fell silent, and my anger and confusion gave way to curiosity. And respect. Mrs. E had been fighting this battle before I was born; she'd done things I couldn't even imagine.

"I had a friend named Tiara," she continued. "She was younger than me, and I used to dress her in silly costumes and braid her hair. We were like sisters." For a moment, Mrs. E seemed lost in her memories. "She met a man from the lower slopes. A poor man. A good man, Chess. They got married, and soon she was pregnant with you." Her dull eyes shone with unshed tears. "When Kodoc realized I'd been spying on him, he went after your mother. He forced her into the Fog with a dozen other women. And I lost my head. . . ."

Her voice faded, and she swayed. In a flash, Swedish was standing behind her, his hands on her shoulders to steady her.

"My mother," I said, blinking back tears of my own. "You went into the Fog after her."

"I waited until the middle of the night," Mrs. E replied in barely more than a whisper. "I snuck past Kodoc's guards. And I climbed down the chains leading to the cages."

My throat tightened as I thought about my mother,

trapped like an animal in a cage in the darkening Fog. She must've been so scared and alone.

"Most of the women were beyond help, but finally, *finally* I heard a noise. I must've only been a foot away—" She smiled sadly. "Or maybe you had really strong lungs. I heard you crying. You were so little that I managed to pull you between the bars. Your mother, though . . ."

She shook her head, and then I knew. My mother had died giving birth to me in the Fog.

"When Kodoc raised the cages the next day," she continued, "he must have thought you'd squirmed away."

"So you grabbed him," Bea said, biting her lower lip. "And brought him to his dad."

Mrs. E smiled softly at me. "You should've seen your father's face, Chess. He thought he'd lost both of you. He mourned your mother, but the way he took you in his arms . . . I knew from the first moment that he loved you."

I wanted to say something, but my throat felt tight and thick. That's why Mrs. E was sick: because she'd tried to save my mother and me. That's why I was a freak: because Kodoc had lowered my mother into the white. And that's why I loved the Fog, why I moved faster and saw farther than anyone: because I'd been born there.

"So that's when you got sick," Swedish said.

Mrs. E exhaled slowly. "By the time I carried Chess

93

from the Fog, it was almost dawn. I'd spent too many hours in the white."

For a moment, nobody spoke. Then Swedish said, "I don't get it. Why hasn't Kodoc been searching the slums for a kid with a Fog-eye?"

"He thought all the test subjects died," Mrs. E told him. "He thought his experiment failed. I burned his records, burned his entire estate to the ground. Then Chess's father and I disappeared into the junkyard. We kept our distance from each other, in case Kodoc caught one of us." She looked to me. "I didn't even know that he'd died until months afterward."

I nodded. I didn't blame her for that. I didn't blame her for anything, really. But my mind was still whirling. I hadn't known the truth about myself until that day. I didn't only *look* like a freak, I *was* one. The leader of the Rooftop had killed my mother and given me this eye so I'd lead him to these ancient machines? It was terrifying. But I also felt a wash of relief, like a darkness in my mind had brightened. Because I finally *knew* why I was like this. I finally knew that my connection to the Fog was real, not a crazy delusion.

"And Kodoc never heard about my eye?" I asked after a long moment.

"You know what the junkyard's like," Mrs. E said. "There are a thousand new rumors every day. A cloudy eye would've sounded like any other disfigurement."

"If he'd heard about you," Hazel said, "the bosses would've lined up every kid in the junkyard and checked our eyes."

"Indeed." Mrs. E started trembling. "And now I think you're right. You must go to Port Oro."

"Yes," Hazel said. "We'll find someone to cure you and—"

"For Chess!" Mrs. E said, her voice suddenly high and frightened. "Before Kodoc finds him!"

"Kodoc won't find him," Hazel assured her. "We'll dive for salvage and hire coyotes—"

Mrs. E slid sideways, almost toppling from the chair. Swedish steadied her, but she'd already slipped back into the sickness. She kept repeating "before Kodoc finds him" over and over as Swedish carried her to bed.

At first, I dismissed her fears about Kodoc finding me. After all, he hadn't found me in thirteen years. But a few weeks later, we caught wind of a rumor about a kid with a Fog-eye living on the Rooftop. We'd never heard anything like that before. Then a new rumor claimed that Lord Kodoc himself was searching for the Fog-eyed kid— which terrified us.

How had the rumors started? Who was spreading them? We didn't know. We just spent more time than ever on the raft, searching the Fog for our ticket to Port Oro.

Meanwhile, Mrs. E spent most days asleep. She'd wake for a few hours and talk loco, her clouded eyes wild. I hated that; the real Mrs. E was strong and fierce, not pathetic and weepy. But one time, she woke and was herself again, a skinny woman whose beak-like nose and sharp alertness reminded me of a hawk.

She eyed me. "How long have you been sitting there?"

"Not long," I said.

"Liar," she whispered with a smile.

"Well, not *that* long."

I would've sat there forever if I'd known she'd sound like this when she woke, instead of babbling nonsense like usual. The thought of her going mad was too much—I couldn't handle Mrs. E acting like a stranger.

She must've seen something in my face, because she suddenly took my hand. "It's not your fault, Chess."

I shrugged like I didn't know what she was talking about. "That you sleep so much?"

"That I'm fogsick."

I'd never told her that I blamed myself for her sickness, but somehow she knew. Still, I wasn't sure what to say. So I just sat there as the sound of a bootball game drifted through the wall, and the distant *thrip* of a rivet gun echoed from Bea's workshop.

After a while, I said, "I barely remember my dad. I guess I was too little when he died. But I remember the way he sang me to sleep, and how he read from his scrapbook. And one other thing."

"What's that?"

"A story he told me about a lady who risked her life trying to save me when I was a baby. Me and my mom."

A faraway smile rose on her face. "Oh, Chess, I still don't know how I found you in all that Fog."

I took a deep breath. "But you—you're dying, Mrs. E. There's no way to help, at least not on the Rooftop."

"Shhh," she said, her eyes closing. "Hush, Chess. . . ."

"We're not even sure *Port Oro* can heal you. The fogheads said so, but who knows if they're lying?"

"On the Port," she said, her voice faint, "many things are possible."

She fell asleep before saying more, and I watched her slow, steady breathing. Usually I hated when she slept, because it felt like she was already leaving us, already gone. But this time was different. This time I had hope.

14

Time limped past as I clung to the rigging beneath the leaking balloon. I drifted in a painful haze until Hazel swung down beside me, tied the main lines together with leather straps, and said, "You can let go now, Chess."

"Do I have to?" I gasped as I unhooked my bracers and sagged into the rigging. "I was just starting to enjoy myself."

She flashed an uneasy smile, then scanned the Fog with her spyglass.

I rubbed my aching arms and followed her gaze. Between Bea's frantic efforts with the engine and my painful grappling with the rigging, the raft could now fly with only two balloons. But not for long—we were still too low, and any strong gust of wind might shove us down into the white.

For hours, I waited for that deadly gust, yet our luck held. I wanted to tell them about the diamond, but Bea was busy with the engine, Swedish with the wheel, and Hazel scanning the Fog, plotting our route to the inch.

I decided to wait until things calmed down a little. And finally, squinting toward the setting sun, I caught a glimpse of the Rooftop, a jagged mountain range with foothill "islands" breaking through the Fog all around. Green fields seemed to glow in the high meadows, and distant waterfalls caught the fading sunlight. Fancy mansions dotted the high peaks, where Mrs. E had lived as a little girl, among the parks and estates of the upper slopes, with lakes full of catfish and forests full of deer. She said that a busy city rose on the third-highest peak, packed with shops selling fresh-baked naan, smoked sausages, and unrotten fruit.

We didn't completely believe her stories, but Hazel dreamed of flying over the Rooftop for a closer look. She ached to see the elegant clothes, to hear the fancy music, and maybe even to feel solid ground under her feet for the first time in her life. But the roof-troopers didn't let slum-dwellers onto—or even over—the mountain. Patrolling airships would've shot us from the sky.

Below the highest peaks, ramshackle buildings of salvaged alumina and concrete crowded the lower slopes, along with smoldering smokestacks and ratty windmill-blimps. Even lower, the junkyard surrounded the mountain, floating fifty feet above the Fog on dilapidated platforms. Trash and shacks covered every foot, except for a few sparse patches where the junkyard bosses had "ditched" a neighborhood by overturning a platform and dumping everything into the deadly Fog below. That was the punishment for not paying rent.

Still, as the raft sputtered closer to the slum, I felt myself smile. The junkyard was horrible, but it was still home.

"Sight for sore eyes?" Hazel asked.

"Sight for sore *everything*," I told her, rubbing my bruises.

She chewed her lower lip. "Do you think this whole thing is a mistake? I mean, trying to sneak onto Port Oro? Nobody ever makes it that far."

"Nah," I said. "Port Oro's going to be great. I hear apples grow on trees."

"And it rains *water*!" she said.

I laughed. "I'm just glad we made it back."

"We haven't yet," Swedish grumbled from the wheel. "We're going to crash and burn."

"Swede's right," Bea called from beside the condenser, a smudge of grease across her nose. "We're not going to reach our dock, not even close."

"How about the nearest slipway?" Hazel asked. "Can we reach that?"

Slipways were makeshift ramps with mooring masts and space for undercarriage engines. Not as safe as our dock, and farther from home, but better than dying.

"She might hold together that long." Bea nibbled her lower lip. "Barely."

"How barely?" Hazel asked.

"*Barely* barely," Bea said. "With only two balloons, she's flying on dreams and dandelions."

Hazel set a course, and Swedish threaded the wallowing raft through high crests of Fog, toward the outer edge of the junkyard, a fringe of welded scaffolding, rusty chains, and plastic bags woven into sheets.

"Speaking of dreams," I said, patting my boot pocket.

Hazel glanced at me, a curious glint in her eyes. "Yeah, what were you doing picking a fight over a flower?"

"Not that it wasn't a very *nice* flower," Bea called from under the raft.

"Probably poisonous," Swedish muttered, angling the raft toward the slipway.

A clank sounded from below. "It was not!"

"Would you two hush?" Hazel said. "Chess is trying to tell us something."

"Probably that it's dangerous to talk to muties about smuggling stuff onto the Rooftop," Swedish grumbled, adjusting the rudder to catch a breeze. "If the troopers capture them—"

"I found a diamond," I broke in.

Silence fell, and I laughed at the hope and disbelief flickering on their faces.

Bea popped from the hatch and everyone spoke at once:

"A *what*?" Hazel asked with a shocked laugh. "Are you sure?"

"A diamond?" Swedish said. "Probably fake. Probably *cursed*."

"Oooh," Bea said. "Can I see? Is it pretty?"

"Chess, if you found a real diamond—"

"Mrs. E says they sparkle like the stars."

"You know what *they* do with diamonds?" Swedish demanded. "Why nobody's allowed to own one?"

"What do they do?" I asked, widening my eyes in fake fascination.

"*They* are collecting diamonds to build a bomb—a mountain buster big enough to blow the whole Rooftop into gravel."

"Right," I scoffed. "Because that's what the rooftroopers want more than anything. Gravel."

"A diamond!" Hazel crowed. "You know what this means? We're halfway to Port Oro already."

"Let's see!" Bea said. "I want to see it! A real diam—"

The raft gave a violent shudder, and the engine coughed and spat.

"We're not home yet!" Hazel yelled. "Bea, keep her in the air. Chess, take the crow's nest."

As I climbed the rigging, she shouted, "And don't drop that rock!"

Hazel leaned over the prow of the raft like a figure-head, ready to call a warning if an outcropping of Fog threatened the engine. As we flew closer, the stink of the junkyard rose in the air and mixed with the sharp tang of the overheated engine.

A crowd watched us wheeze toward the slipway's mooring mast, a tottering tower of rusty automobile engines and bathroom fixtures. A stringy-haired vendor shouted her prices for rat kabobs, as a frenzy of trading started around her. Almost nobody used coins in the slums. Real money was tucked away for special occasions. Instead, we bartered lengths of wire for plasteel buttons, a bag of potting soil for a bone needle, a skewer of crab apples for some grilled squirrel.

At first, I didn't understand why they were trading. Then I almost laughed. "They're *gambling*," I called to the others. "They're betting about us reaching the slip-way."

"Wish *I* could throw down a little something," Swedish said.

"Me too!" Bea chirped. "We're going to get there for sure!"

Hazel grunted. "That's not how Swedish would bet, Bea."

"He'd bet *against* us?" Bea's voice sharpened. "Swedish, you're horrible!"

"Listen to the engine," he said, his fingers dancing over the steam organ keyboard. "The gears are snapping. There's no way we're staying in the air."

A series of loud pops shook the raft. Gray smoke puffed from an intake valve.

"We *will* reach that slipway," Bea said, her green eyes narrowing as she spliced cables together.

A hundred feet from the slipway, sparks started shooting from the propeller. Hazel's grip tightened on the prow and she leaned forward. "We can't sink now," she said. "Think of Port Oro!"

Seventy feet away, the forward balloon began flapping and hissing. "C'mon, c'mon," Hazel muttered. "Stay in the air."

At fifty feet, the deck was shaking like a rattlesnake's tail, and Hazel yelled, "Almost there, Bea! Almost there!"

Forty feet, and I grabbed a mooring strap and raced for the prow. I needed to hitch us to the mooring mast before the engine died.

Hazel shouted commands and Swedish muttered dire predictions. Bea clamped a valve shut with her foot and crooned to the engine, which answered with a screech. Catcalls sounded from the crowd, the odds of our survival falling fast.

Only I remained silent, twirling the mooring strap overhead. Not close enough. Not yet. . . .

"Bea!" Hazel yelled, running toward her. "Abandon ship, abandon ship!"

"No! She needs me!"

Hazel grabbed Bea's wrist and dragged her forward. "We have to jump! Swedish, *run*! Throw the strap, Chess."

"Not yet," I said.

The rear balloon exploded into scraps, and the deck tilted crazily. "Now!" Hazel shouted. "Now, now!"

"Not yet—"

"Throw it now!" she screamed, and I did.

15

THE STRAP SPUN IN the air, a loop of nylon and wire.

Time slowed, freezing the faces of the shouting crowd, freezing the snarl on Swedish's lips and Bea's horrified expression as Hazel shoved her toward the prow.

The mooring mast—the target of my throw—glowed in the light of the setting sun. The loop twirled closer and closer . . . and fell three feet short.

But one thing a tetherboy knew was *tethers*, and a strap wasn't all that different. Three feet short? No way.

I whipcracked the strap, and the loop flicked higher. It still missed the mooring hook, but it snagged a fender that jutted just below it. The fender was crimped and rusty, definitely not strong enough to keep the raft in the air. Still, it might hold the weight of the *crew*, so I screamed—"Grab the strap! Grab the strap!"—as I pulled the hacksaw from my leg sheath.

Ten feet away from landing safely on the slipway, the raft engine died.

The world moved in slow motion. The raft tumbled downward. The rigging snapped, the pistons screamed. The deck angled crazily as I furiously slashed and hacked at the strap.

The raft fell five feet. My breath caught and my boots scrambled for a foothold.

The raft fell ten feet, and fear built in my lungs. In seconds, the weight of the raft would tear that rusty fender from the mooring mast and we'd all die. Swedish, Hazel, Bea—

No. With one final, terrified slash, I sliced the strap from the raft's deck.

Through fear-widened eyes, I caught a glimpse of Hazel and the others above me clinging to the mooring line—now attached only to the fender, not the raft. The loop tightened around the fender, and they slammed into the mast, bruised and battered but dangling safely below the slipway.

Frantic and trembling, I hitched the line to my tether, and an instant later it jerked at my harness, stopping my fall. I swung like a pendulum and slammed into the slipway.

Ouch.

Below me, the raft dropped into the white and disap- peared. No crash sounded, no explosion flashed. The Fog simply swallowed the raft whole.

I dangled there, limp and aching and defeated. We'd come so far. We'd dived in uncharted territory and found a diamond, we'd survived mutineers and reached the junkyard—but we'd lost our raft to the Fog, and that ruined everything.

After a minute, I felt myself being dragged higher, until Swedish pulled me onto the slipway and gave me a fierce back-pounding hug, ignoring the groans of the people who'd wagered against us.

"Too small," Swedish said gruffly. "I should throw you back."

I brushed my hair over my freak-eye. "You sound like that mutineer captain."

"My poor raft," Bea sniffled.

"We got lucky, Bea!" Swedish said. "We crashed and didn't die. If Chess hadn't tossed that line, we'd be lumps of meat right now."

"*We* didn't crash," Bea said, removing her cap respect- fully. "*She* crashed. The raft gave her life for ours."

"And I lost my lucky bootball," Swedish grumbled.

He shouldered through the crowd, leading us toward the slipway owner, a skinny man eating his dinner in a darkened doorway.

"Who's going to pay for the damage to my slipway?"

the slipway owner barked at Swedish, digging in his bowl with chopsticks. "You bottom-feeders dented my mast—and you owe me docking fees. Either you pay, or I take the pretty one as a chambermaid."

Swedish cracked his knuckles. "Just *try*."

I took a breath and stepped beside him. I didn't like fighting, but I'd lived my whole life in the junkyard—I'd fight if I had to. Then a rough-looking woman in a stained sari appeared behind the owner, cradling a makeshift crossbow. We couldn't fight *that*.

"We'll pay," Hazel announced, stepping forward. "For the damage, the fees, *and* for salvage rights to our raft."

The slipway owner pointed his chopsticks at her. "Your raft is smashed into a thousand pieces."

"That's not your problem," she told him. "We'll dive from your slipway, salvage the wreckage, and rebuild."

Bea pulled me closer. "I can't rebuild the raft, not after *that* crash."

I shushed her. I didn't know what Hazel was doing, but I knew she was doing something. She was *always* doing something.

"You can't give this guy money," Swedish murmured. "We barely have enough for food."

"We don't have a choice," Hazel muttered back. "We crashed the raft, and we don't *own* the raft."

My stomach soured. That was the problem. We'd lost the junkyard bosses' raft, and they'd make us pay for a new one—with the diamond. Our only way of getting to Port Oro.

"There won't be much worth salvaging," Bea said in a small voice. "Not enough to rebuild—"

"Shut your mouth, Bea!" Hazel snarled between clenched teeth. "Do as you're told."

Bea's lips trembled. She pulled a wire from her pocket and started making a twisty—to keep herself from crying.

Hazel and the slipway owner bickered for a while; then she turned to me. "Give him the toilet paper."

I took the folded stack of "cash" from my pocket. "The thousands are softer than the hundreds," I told him.

He didn't seem to care. Maybe he knew it wasn't true. He kept telling Hazel that he needed more coin, and they haggled and argued until we finally set off for home along a trash-littered road skirting an open sewer.

Swedish scowled at Hazel. "You made Bea cry."

"I'll explain when we get home," she told him. "I wouldn't talk like that without a good reason."

Bea peered at her. "You—you didn't mean it?"

"You know better than that," Hazel said. I could tell her feelings were a little hurt that they'd thought she'd really lost her temper. "The both of you."

Swedish shot Hazel an apologetic look, then kicked at an imaginary bootball.

Bea said, "Sorry, Cap'n."

"Have some faith," I said, tapping her leather cap.

She wrinkled her nose at me and slipped the twisty she'd just made into her tool belt.

"What'd you make?" I asked.

"Nothing," she said.

"C'mon!" I said. "Let's see."

She scuffed her feet. "It's nothing."

"Hey, I told you about the goose."

She glared but handed it over. I angled the twisty to catch the moonlight and saw that she'd wrapped the wire into the shape of a sloppy face, with a big, open mouth and snakes instead of hair.

"What is it?" I asked.

Swedish peered closer. "A startled porcupine."

"Or a really angry mop," I said.

"It's Hazel," Bea said. "Yelling at me."

Hazel glanced at the twisty. "My hair doesn't do that."

"I can't believe we lost the raft!" Bea blurted. "Well, at least we still have the—"

"*Crew*," Hazel interrupted, before Bea could say *diamond*.

"What?" Bea asked.

"The crew," Hazel said, nodding toward the hostile faces watching us from shadowy doorways. "At least we have each other."

"Oh!" Bea flushed. "Right."

After that, we kept quiet as we headed through darkening passages and garbage-filled clearings. We didn't normally dock in the slipways, so none of us knew this neighborhood. Strange noises rose in the gloom—the grinding of unseen clockwork, the sickly wheeze of the fans keeping the slum aloft. Rats and roaches scuttled in the corners, and a baby cried out from a shadowy archway.

Then a hoarse voice shouted, "The world didn't end with a bang! It began with a slow rise of mist! The Fog is the healing breath of the Earth!"

"Fogheads," Swedish muttered. "They're all whacka-doo."

"Let's go around him," Hazel said.

I pointed toward a detour. "That way."

Swedish knew that Mrs. E called fogheads the "Subassembly," and that they'd been scientists working for the Five Families before Kodoc betrayed them and stole their research. But he insisted that they were complete lug nuts, always skulking around and muttering about the Fog.

Before we turned away, the foghead stepped from the shadows, a small man wearing a gray robe. "A thousand ticktocks will rise from the lowest Fog," he told us, "to cleanse and burn and purify!"

"Let's go," Hazel said, and headed off.

"They come not to bury us, but to warn us!" the man yelled, edging closer.

Bea and Swedish followed Hazel, but when I started after them, the foghead grabbed my wrist. My pulse rocketed and I raised my boot to stomp on his foot as he searched my face.

"Wait!" he blurted, releasing me. "Are you—are you him?"

Hunching my shoulders, I started to follow the others.

"The boy with Fog in his eye?"

My stomach dropped, and the night suddenly felt cold and unfriendly.

"I—I don't know what you're talking about," I said, ducking my head.

His gaze softened a little with recognition. "Your name is Chess, isn't it?"

"What do you want?"

"You're more important than you know," he said, sidling closer. "Your eye isn't a sign of shame, but hope."

Sharp needles of fear pricked my skin, but I didn't move. A stranger knew my secret. How did he know? It was impossible. And what did he mean, a sign of hope?

I swallowed. "Wh-what are you talking about?"

"You're marked by the Fog, Chess. You belong to the Fog, and maybe the Fog belongs to you. But you're in danger. Grave danger. And we are to blame."

"You are? Fogheads?"

He pursed his lips. "The Subassembly. You came to us for help, months ago—you and the girl."

My breath caught in my throat. "I—what if I did?"

"One of us saw your eye." The man bowed his head.

"And he mentioned it—in public. The rumors are our fault. . . ."

"Hey!" Swedish yelled, stepping from the alley. "Get away from him!"

"Kodoc knows," the foghead whispered to me. "Kodoc knows you're alive."

16

THE DARKNESS GATHERED AROUND me, and nausea rose in my stomach. *Kodoc.* The name sounded like a death sentence. I steadied myself on a dingy wall, dizzy with fear. One of the fogheads saw my eye? What else did they know about me? What other secrets had they spread—

"You!" Swedish roared, stepping closer. "Foghead! Back off!"

For a moment, the man stood there staring at me. Then Hazel joined Swedish, and he slunk away into the shadows.

"Are you okay?" Hazel asked me.

I swallowed. "Y-yeah."

"What was that about?"

"I don't know. That guy, he . . ." I shrugged, still jittery and afraid. "I don't know."

"What did he say?"

"Uh, he told me . . ." The truth caught in my throat. "He mostly rambled."

I ducked my head and slouched toward the alley. Why had I lied to them? If Kodoc really knew I'd survived the cage, I needed to tell the crew. But something strangled the words before I could speak them. Fear, I guess. Like if I said Kodoc's name out loud, I'd summon him. Like if he knew I was alive, he'd come and claim me.

His creation. His creature. His freak.

"Chess!" Hazel touched my arm. "What's wrong?"

"Nothing. He just . . . I guess he saw my freak-eye."

When I was younger, if anyone spotted my eye, I'd claim that the white shimmers were floating scars. Sometimes they'd still give me a thrashing, just for being ugly. It stopped happening when I'd gotten older and more careful, but the memories still hurt.

"Oh," Hazel said.

"I like your eye," Bea said loyally. "It's cool, like clouds reflected in a puddle."

"So now you're saying I'm a muddy puddle," I told her, trying to sound normal as we headed away.

"A *cool* muddy puddle," she insisted.

"Yeah," I muttered. "That's like an *awesome* toenail clipping."

"Fogheads." Swedish spat. "They give me the creeps. If they like the Fog so much, they ought to live there."

"They're not so bad," Hazel said. "You're just mad we lost the raft."

"There's no way we're getting to Port Oro now," he grumbled. "*They* saw to that. We have to use the . . . rock to repay the bosses for the raft."

Hazel shushed him. "Let's talk about that when we get home."

The slum shifted underfoot as a breeze swirled through the Fog, and the miles-wide patchwork of floats and balloons and hoverfans heaved and creaked and popped.

I didn't mention the foghead again, even though I knew I had to tell them what he'd said. *Kodoc knows you're alive.* Those weren't just rumors we'd been hearing, they were rumors about *me.* I kept trying to say the words aloud, but I couldn't. I was too scared. Sometimes I thought that when Kodoc had made me a freak, he'd also made me a coward.

So I kept my head down, feeling ashamed as we picked our way through a thicket of chains tethering balloons to the slum platforms. They clattered so loudly that we had no warning. We had just turned the corner when we found ourselves facing down a street gang playing boot-ball in the dusky light.

A boy missing his front teeth grabbed a sharp-edged

brick and snarled, "What're you doing here? This is *our* patch."

"Just passing through," Hazel said, her voice almost steady.

A scar-faced girl touched the pipe strapped to her leg. Gangs like this battled over food and turf and money. They fought over insults and respect, and sometimes just for fun. That was life in the slum—life and death.

I felt the others tense behind me. We were salvage rats, not street fighters, but I didn't see any way out of this without bloodshed. For once it didn't scare me—*anything* was better than worrying about Kodoc.

Even this.

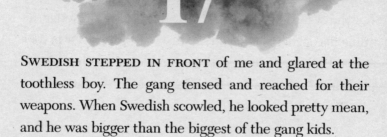

17

SWEDISH STEPPED IN FRONT of me and glared at the toothless boy. The gang tensed and reached for their weapons. When Swedish scowled, he looked pretty mean, and he was bigger than the biggest of the gang kids.

Then Swedish toed a bootball from the ground into the air, catching it on his foot.

He bobbled the ball from his foot to his knee, caught it with his ankle, then kicked it above his head. He hunched his shoulders, and the bootball landed on the back of his neck, balanced there for a second, then plopped to the ground.

The gang kids laughed, and relief bubbled through my chest.

Swedish popped the ball straight upward, then smacked

it with his forehead toward the goal.

The goalie swatted it away, and his team cheered.

"What do you play?" the scar-faced girl asked.

"Goalie," Swedish said. "Or fixo."

"You're kind of big for it."

"He used to be smaller," I told her.

Hazel gave a quick smile and nudged Swedish, "Well, we'll get out of your way," she told the gang kids, and started across the clearing.

"If you're ever looking for a game," the first guy called after Swedish, "you know where to find us."

Halfway down the next alley, Swedish started grinning like a goon. "Did you see that?" he said. "If everyone played bootball, there'd be no problems. No hunger, no fighting. Bootball—I'm telling you—it's the solution."

"To what?" Bea asked.

"To everything!"

"In the old days," I said, trying to take my mind off the foghead, "they played a game called 'golf.' You knocked a ball the size of an egg into a little hole in the ground, using a club."

Swedish cocked his head. "You couldn't use your feet?"

"No, just the club."

"What'd they call it?" Bea asked.

"Golf," I repeated.

"Not that," she said. "I mean, what'd they call the club?"

"Oh. Just a club, I think."

She giggled. "They did *not* call it a club! Might as well call it a cudgel or a beating stick."

"Well, that's what it says in the scrapbook."

"Huh," Swedish said, scratching his cheek. "So each team had a hole? It sounds too easy to guard. You just put your foot over the hole."

"Until the other team starts beating you with their clubs," Hazel said.

"Oh!" Swedish nodded, satisfied. "Yeah, that makes sense."

Bea made a face. "Golfball sounds pretty violent."

"And it's not just the other team you had to watch out for," I told her. "The field also had sand traps and hazards and windmills."

"Windmills?" Hazel asked, quirking an eyebrow.

"I'm not sure where those came in," I admitted.

"Maybe they milled grain while they played," she suggested. "Makes more sense than whacking an egg with a cudgel."

We started walking faster as we neared our neighborhood, following a trash-ridden trail around the Spew—the river of sludge that seeped from mounds of garbage, winding its way around the slum before cascading into the Fog.

Finally Bea sang out, "We're home!"

She disabled the booby trap we always set when we

left Mrs. E alone, then flung open the narrow door. The entryway was cluttered with splintery crate shelves and baskets of plastic bags from before the Fog. Whenever we weren't on salvage runs, we wove the bags into sheets and sold them for handfuls of rice flour or lambs' feet.

"I'll check if Mrs. E's awake," Bea said.

Swedish grunted. "Not likely."

"She was fine when we left!"

"That was yesterday," Swedish said. "And she wasn't *fine*, she was *awake*. There's a difference."

Bea glared at him. "Well, I'll check if she's—"

"Hold on a second," Hazel told her.

"What?"

"First we need to talk." Hazel rubbed her face. "We lost the raft. That's seriously bad news. We can't—"

Mrs. E's voice floated from the main room. "Children? Is that you?"

Bea squealed and shot into the shack, with Swedish close on her heels. Hazel and I exchanged a hopeful look. Mrs. E was awake and didn't even sound confused!

The main room was slightly higher than the cramped entryway, with a rickety table, a woodstove, and a catch barrel for rain. Chopsticks and plastic bowls cluttered the cabinet, along with what Mrs. E called a "milk jug." She insisted that people used to drink *cow's* milk, which always made Bea giggle.

Everyone knew that milk came from sheep and goats and camels.

Once I saw Mrs. E sitting at the table, I forgot all about the foghead. She almost never left her bedroom these days—she almost never left her *bed*—so I felt myself smile at the sight of her. The scent of the four slices of honey bread on the table didn't hurt, either.

"Mrs. E!" Bea hugged her fiercely. "We've got so much to tell you! The muties boarded us and they shot the cargo tether and—wait! First Chess went diving, and you'll never guess what he found!"

"Mutineers?" Mrs. E's clouded eyes narrowed. "They boarded the raft?"

"They wanted to kidnap me," Bea said, "but Hazel stopped them, and then a balloon popped, but we kept the raft afloat until—"

"Slow down, sweetie." Mrs. E smiled, her voice gentle. "Have a bite of honey bread. Swedish, where are you? I can't see you."

"I'm here." He took one of her frail hands. "How did you afford the bread? You know *they*'re watching us—"

"Stop fretting," she told him. "A friend brought it."

"Who? You don't have friends. You're afraid friends might . . ." Swedish trailed off, glancing at me. "Y'know."

"Expose our secrets," Hazel finished.

"He's a very old friend," Mrs. E said with a strange note in her voice. "He just found me again, after many years."

Hazel twisted a braid around her finger. "Is something wrong? What is it?"

"Stop *thinking* so much," Mrs. E scolded Hazel. "I'll tell you everything after we eat. Now where's Chess? Lurking in the background?"

"I don't lurk," I told her, stepping forward. "I skulk."

"Then we're all here," she said. "Now sit down and eat."

Swedish grabbed two slices. He gave one to Bea as I started wolfing down a third. The sweetness melted on my tongue and warmth spread in my stomach, but Hazel just toyed with her slice, eyeing Mrs. E.

"Did your friend tell you something?" she asked, taking a bite. "What happened?"

"He brought news."

"What kind of news?"

Mrs. E took a shaky breath. "Terrible news."

The sweet bread in my mouth turned to mud. "Is it . . . Kodoc?"

Mrs. E nodded. "Kodoc heard that one of his 'test subjects' survived the cages as an infant—he's on the hunt for Chess."

"How?" Swedish demanded while Hazel gasped, "No!"

"He's suspected for weeks," Mrs. E said, swaying in her seat. "Because of the rumors. He's been scouring the mountain, checking every child between the ages of ten and fifteen. And once he's done there . . ."

"After he finishes the Rooftop," Hazel said. "He'll start

124

searching in the slum."

"He'll find Chess," Mrs. E whispered, her face paling. "You need to hide, you need to run. . . ."

Her voice faded, her head dipped, and she slumped sideways, falling toward the floor.

18

Swedish caught Mrs. E as she fainted, and the rest of us jumped from our chairs.

"C'mon," Hazel told Swedish. "Bring her to bed."

She followed him through the traffic-sign door while I picked at a crack on the tabletop. I thought about Mrs. E climbing into the Fog to save me, about my mother dying, my father being handed a baby with one freakish eye. And about being Kodoc's creation: not just *born* a freak, but *made* a freak.

Now he was coming for me.

"At least we're already planning to leave," Bea said. "I mean, Kodoc knows about you, but that doesn't change anything."

"Except that there are a thousand roof-troopers hunting for us now."

"Other than that," she agreed. "But we were trying to get to Port Oro anyway."

"Which would be easy if we could sell the ring. But we owe the bosses for the raft, and they won't let us leave without paying. Our only way to pay is—"

"The diamond!" she blurted, brightening. "Show me, show me!"

I almost smiled at her enthusiasm. But when I reached to unsnap my boot pocket, Swedish and Hazel returned to the main room, looking grim.

"Is she okay?" Bea asked them, her brightness fading.

Hazel fiddled with her braid. "She's not great."

"Not *great*?" Swedish rubbed his face. "More like 'terrible.'"

"Yeah, well . . . at least she's sleeping comfortably."

"For now," Swedish said.

Hazel nodded. "Let's talk in the workshop, so we don't bother her."

We went into the front room, where Swedish opened a hatch in the floor. Inside, a rope ladder dangled down a shaft that led to the shadowy underside of the slum, beneath the platforms where fans roared and sludge dripped, fifty feet above the Fog.

The workshop was bolted under the platform, a square

room with telefoam poles for a frame, tightly woven cables for walls, and scraps of alumina drywall for a floor. It was where Bea tinkered, designing and building the thoppers that Swedish flew in drag races.

When she fiddled with a knob, a soft glow shone over dinged tools, scratched dials, and a battered foggium compressor. A workbench sat against one wall, with tidy racks of bolts, wire, and old lenses, and a large rectangular hole opened in the middle of the floor. The thopper—about the size of an overgrown camel, with three wings on each side and a wide fantail—dangled below, hanging from sturdy chains. There was nothing between the thopper and the Fog but empty air.

"We have lots to talk about—" Hazel started.

"Wait," I interrupted. "I need to say something."

"Stop talking and show us the diamond!" Bea said. "Let's see that purple rock!"

"Yeah," Swedish said with a tired smile. "We've been waiting for hours."

So I leaned against the workbench and pulled the box from my boot pocket. I waited a moment—enjoying their excitement—then lifted the lid. The diamond caught the dim light in the workshop and cast rainbow sparkles onto the wall.

Bea gasped, her big green eyes shining. "Is it really real?"

"Definitely fake," Swedish said in a soft, awed voice.

Hazel carefully lifted the ring from the box. Silence fell. That diamond was worth more than everything we owned, more than everything we'd *ever* owned.

"Give me your hand," she told Bea.

"Sure," Bea said. "Why?"

Hazel raised the ring toward her finger. "I want to see how it looks."

"Oh, no!" Bea squeaked, and stuck her hand behind her back. "*You* should wear it, not me!"

"Go on, Bea," I said.

I knew that for Hazel, the diamond was like a window into the world of the upper slopes, with silk dresses and rolling parks. And she didn't just dream of that life for herself, she dreamed of it for all of us—especially Bea.

After Hazel slipped the ring on her finger, Bea wrinkled her nose. "It looks dumb on my dirty hand."

"Nah," Swedish said. "Nothing goes better with a diamond than an honest smear of grease. Well, except roast goose. *Everything* goes better with roast goose."

I threw a rivet at him, then Bea climbed onto the workbench and locked the ring in a hidden compartment in the ceiling. "Why'd you promise that slipway guy money?" she asked Hazel, hopping down. "And why'd you tell me to shut up?"

"Hold on." I looked at my scuffed boots. "Let me go first."

"You're the Prince of Diamonds, Chess," Hazel said.

"You can say anything."

"Remember that foghead who grabbed me?"

"What did he say?" Bea asked.

I swallowed the lump in my throat. "Uh, he kind of told me why Kodoc knows I'm alive." I explained about a young foghead blurting the truth in public. "And that's how the rumors started."

"But you didn't say anything," Bea said, sounding confused. "You didn't tell us."

"Chess!" Hazel snapped. "He *recognized* you? What if he'd told the roof-troopers?"

"I—I didn't think—"

"What if they followed us home to Mrs. E? I know how you feel about your eye, but—"

"You don't know!" I snapped back, my face flaming. "You don't."

Her jaw clenched. "Having Fog in your eye doesn't mean you can lie to us."

"It means I spend every minute lying. That's all I ever do—I pretend I'm normal. My whole life is one big lie."

"Not to *us*!"

I glared at her. "I've got a billion machines in my brain, and . . . and Kodoc *customized* me, like Bea fixing an engine. No, like Bea building a weapon. You don't know what it's like, Hazel. He made me. He created me."

"So did your mom, and your dad, and Mrs. E." Hazel

returned my glare for a second, then sort of smiled. "And all of us."

I ducked my head. "I guess."

"We're crew," Hazel said. "You don't need to keep secrets from us."

My anger faded. "Sorry. I was . . . scared."

"Course you were," Swedish grunted. "I would've done the same."

I blinked at him. "You would?"

"Me too," Bea said. "*Everyone* would be scared of that." She peered at Hazel. "Well, almost everyone."

In a girly voice, Swedish said, "My name is Hazel, and I'm *soooo* brave."

"I eat roof-troopers for breakfast!" Bea chimed in as she did a gawky version of one of Hazel's ballerina spins. "And I dance with mutineers!"

"Oh, shut your valves," Hazel grumbled. "*Anyway*. I told you to keep quiet at the slipway, Bea, because you started saying that we can't salvage the raft."

"We can't! My poor raft is in a thousand pieces!"

"And if the bosses know that, they'll make us pay," Hazel said. "Or they'll ditch us into the Fog as an example."

Bea's forehead wrinkled. "So we have to give them the diamond?"

"But they *don't* know we can't fix the raft," I told Bea as I realized. "That's what Hazel was doing—buying us time."

"Time for what?" Swedish asked.

"For something sneaky," I said.

Hazel tucked a few braids behind her ear. "Forget the raft and forget the bosses. We're giving the diamond straight to a coyote, as payment for smuggling us to the Port."

My heart skipped a beat. "And we're not paying the bosses for crashing their raft?"

"That's right," she said.

Swedish whistled in awe. "You want to cheat the bosses?"

"Whoa," I said a little shakily. Nobody messed with the bosses—not if they wanted to live.

"It's the only way." Hazel exhaled. "Kodoc knows about Chess. We're running out of time."

"Are we . . ." Bea bit her lower lip. "Are we ready?"

"No," Hazel told her. "But this is it, honeybee. Either we cheat the bosses or we're finished."

The clockwork engines in the workshop ticked and tocked until I broke the silence, "Well, I'm not standing around picking my nose until Mrs. E dies. Let's do it."

"I'm in," Bea said, her eyes shining. "Port Oro, here we come!"

"We're going to regret this," Swedish grumbled. "When the bosses find out, they'll ditch us into the Fog. This is a stupid move. A huge mistake."

Nobody said anything.

"But," he continued, "you're my crew. Whatever huge mistakes we make, we make together."

"Always," Hazel said, her eyes clearer than any diamond. "Okay, first we'll talk to some coyotes I know, then we'll—"

A bell chimed faintly from above.

"That's Mrs. E!" Bea squealed, and scrambled up the rope ladder.

Hazel glanced at the ceiling, smiling. "I guess what we'll do," she said, "is plan our escape later."

19

I WAS THE LIGHTEST sleeper, so I bedded down near the front door, ready to raise the alarm if anything woke me. Swedish slept in the main room—the only place he could stretch in the morning without knocking holes in the ceiling. Hazel and Bea shared a lumpy acrylicloth mattress in a nook behind a beaded curtain. And Mrs. E had the only real room, a cramped space behind a door made of rusted traffic signs, the floor heaped with mildewed notebooks and smudged charts and my father's scrapbook on a special shelf against the wall.

I followed Bea into the room and found Mrs. E curled in bed, toying with the bell she'd rung.

When she'd first found me in the alleys, she'd seemed like a force of nature, striding along with her chin high and her spine straight. But now she was bent and wizened, with clouded eyes and clawed fingers. Still, she looked better than usual. At least she was awake.

"Hey, Mrs. E!" Bea chirped. "Do you need something?"

"How *very* kind of you to ask," Mrs. E told Bea in an almost girlish voice. "I want ices. Raspberry ices."

"Ices?" Bea repeated, the happiness draining from her face. "You mean, um—"

Mrs. E gasped. "You're not my governess!"

I wanted to cry at the confusion on Mrs. E's face. She'd recognized us twenty minutes earlier, but now she thought she was a child again, living in the upper slopes, surrounded by servants and sweets.

Bea hung her head. "I'll get her, ma'am."

"Why did she call me *ma'am*?" Mrs. E asked me, her fear fading into a pout. "You're the gardener's boy, aren't you? Would you like a glass of lemonade?"

I backed toward the door. I didn't know what to say, and I couldn't stand seeing her like this, so feeble and confused.

"My grandpapa says he once drank *real* lemonade as a child. He says *his* grandfather was alive when the Fog started rising. Just a fine dew on the ground, in the lowest places. Then it started rising an inch every week, then a foot. . . ." She widened her cloudy eyes at Hazel when she entered. "Where *is* that coachman? You promised me a ride in the camel cart."

"Not in this snow," Hazel said, her voice calm, even though I knew how much she hated playing along with the sickness. "I'll read you a story, instead."

"Read me one about the Fog!" Mrs. E grabbed a weathered notebook from the floor. "My favorite! *Gasiform Nanites and White Blood Cells: An Analogy.*"

Hazel grimaced. She read better than Swedish or me—Bea was still learning—but Mrs. E's technical notebooks were beyond her. So instead of reading, she sat on the bed and spoke in low, soothing tones.

I squared my shoulders and started collecting the dirty laundry while Swedish stood in the doorway, blinking away tears.

Hours later, I snuggled into my threadbare blanket on the floor, thinking about the dive, the diamond, and Hazel's desperate plan. We'd have to sell the ring to the coyotes without the bosses catching us, leave the Rooftop without Kodoc catching us, and then sneak into Port Oro without the mutineers catching us.

We sure were counting on a whole lot of people not catching us.

Getting there sounded impossible, but I still daydreamed about our new lives on Port Oro. Maybe we'd work as a shuttle crew. Maybe we'd buy a fishing airship. Or maybe, knowing Hazel, we'd join the mutineers ourselves. And of course we'd find a cure for Mrs. E.

Bare feet padded closer, then Hazel plopped down beside me.

"Can't sleep?" I asked.

"No," she said. "You?"

I shook my head. "My mind's racing like a thopper."

"Worried about selling the diamond?"

"That and, y'know, saving Mrs E."

"And avoiding Kodoc," she said. "But no pressure."

I smiled, then asked the question I'd been wondering about. "The bosses hear everything that happens in the slum. How can we hire a coyote without them finding out?"

"Carefully," she said.

I shot her a look. "Oh, good, thanks. Now I feel much better."

"I've been talking to coyotes for months, Chess. As long as nothing cockeyed happens, we're in good shape."

"You're telling *me* about cockeyed?"

She smiled at first; then two little lines appeared between her eyebrows. "Actually, I'm worried about everything." She looked toward where Swedish and Bea were sleeping. "What if something happens to one of them? To one of *you*."

I nudged her with my elbow. Sometimes I felt sorry for Hazel, like we all depended on her too much. She worried more about us than herself.

"To one of *us*," I corrected her.

137

"I know," she said, swallowing. "But I worry most about losing Bea."

"It'd be like losing our hearts." I said.

"Yeah."

"If we lost you," I told her, "it'd be like losing our dreams. And if we lost Swedish, it'd be like losing our—"

"Goalie," she said, and we laughed softly. "No," she said. "He's our anchor. He keeps us grounded."

"Yeah."

Hazel rested her head on my shoulder. "Our heart, our dreams, our anchor. . . . Do you know what *you* are?"

"Our killer instinct?" I asked. "Our deadly warrior?"

She raised her eyebrow at me and thumped my arm. "Our hope," she said.

We sat in silence, listening to the distant fans whirr. After a while, Hazel said, "On the raft today, at the slip-way?"

"Mm?"

"You threw that mooring strap, cut the line, and ran up the deck in two seconds."

"Well," I explained, "I was in a rush."

She smiled. "I've never seen you move that fast."

"I move a lot faster than that in the Fog."

Hazel stopped smiling. "Nobody else does."

"Yeah." I shrugged. "Well, I'm a frea—"

"*Different*," she interrupted. "And you weren't in the Fog when you cut the mooring line, Chess. What if the nanites are changing you? What if you're getting sick?"

"Fogsickness doesn't make you faster."

"You're not like everyone else."

"Yeah, I'm not just a freak, I'm an experiment."

"You're mostly a garbo."

"At least I don't look like a startled porcupine," I said, remembering Bea's twisty of an angry Hazel.

She gave me a shove. "Let me see your eye."

For most of my life, accidentally revealing my eye meant a beating, so the idea of showing it on purpose made me a little sick. But this was Hazel; she checked my eye after every long dive, to make sure it wasn't getting worse.

I wiped my hair off my forehead and she examined me. I watched her for signs of disgust but didn't see any. I never had, not from her.

"Bea's right," she finally said.

"It looks like a muddy puddle?"

"Like white clouds in a dark sky. It's kind of beautiful."

"Yeah, I'm gorgeous."

"You're scruffy as an old boot. But your eye is cool. Almost hypnotic."

"You're getting sleepy . . . ," I said in a dopey voice.

She laughed—a little. "At least it looks the same as always. I'm probably worrying for no reason."

"You always worry that I'm getting sick," I told her. "Now you're worrying that I'm not?"

She chewed on her lower lip. "Nobody spends that much time in the Fog and stays healthy, Chess."

"Don't be so impatient," I said, pretending to scold her. "Give me a few years."

"It's not funny. I have nightmares about you getting fogsick, but it's almost as scary that you haven't."

I tugged my hair over my eye. "I guess I must have an affinity."

"Mrs. E says the nanites won't protect you forever."

"It doesn't matter. Once you talk to a coyote, we're out of here. I won't need to dive after we get to the Port . . . as long as nothing cockeyed happens."

"Yeah," she said, but she still looked worried.

20

I WOKE TO THE scuffle of footsteps outside the shack.

They didn't sound like the sewer worker down the alley or the family with the rust stall. No, they sounded quick, purposeful, and dangerous. Like a gang closing in.

My pulse spiked, and I rolled to the side and threw a bootball at Swedish, who was snoring in the main room. He snorted awake. Without a word, I crawled behind the crate shelves, grabbed the lever that operated the trap-door, and waited.

Whispers sounded from the main room, and the beaded curtain rattled. I stayed hidden, my back to the wall, as the footsteps outside scuffed closer.

How many of them were there? Five? Ten? Did they

know about my eye? Had Kodoc sent them to grab me? Was this the end?

I couldn't do anything except take a shaky breath and try not to cry. So I did both as I watched Swedish grab a shovel and Hazel reach for Mrs. E's rapier. I squeezed the lever tight. The gang would burst inside, then stop at the sight of Swedish. If Hazel couldn't convince them to leave, I'd open the trapdoor beneath them.

At least, that was the plan.

Instead, I felt the prick of a knife in my back. Someone had cut a hole in the chickenwire-and-plastic wall and crept inside to wait for me.

"Hands off the lever," a girl whispered in my ear. "Don't yell! You'll scare Perry and he'll start breaking things."

"Loretta?" I gasped, recognizing the voice.

Loretta was a gang girl Swedish had a crush on. She was short and stocky, with spiky black hair and a tattooed face. Swede liked her gap-toothed smile, narrow eyes, and fearlessness. Hazel claimed she liked him back, but I'd never seen any sign of it. And her knife in my back wasn't exactly winning me over.

"Bosses' orders," she murmured, almost apologetic. "We ain't killing you, though. Well, as long as you don't open that trap."

My hand dropped from the lever. "What do they want? They sent Perry? He's the worst kneebreaker they've got—"

"Wake-wakey, bottom-feeders," a shrill voice called from outside. "And open this door!"

Hazel lowered her rapier. "Perry? Is that you?" She sounded scared, like she thought they'd come for me. "What do you want?"

Perry didn't answer. Instead, two thuds sounded. The door shuddered, then snapped from the hinges and crashed to the floor.

When I shifted closer to the lever, Loretta tapped me harder with her knife. I ignored her. I wasn't the bravest guy in the world, but you didn't need courage to protect your family. I'd open that trapdoor in a second if the thugs attacked, despite the fear bubbling up in my stomach.

Perry stomped inside, a pale creep with a lot of yellow hair. He worked for his uncle, one of the bosses who ran the junkyard for Kodoc, as an enforcer. Rumor was he'd ditched his own parents into the Fog, that he showed no mercy and felt no pain. His voice sounded like a five-year-old's, but he still scared the goggles off me.

"When I knock, you *run* to open your door," he squeaked at Hazel. "My uncle owns everything from here to the Spew, including your nasty little shack."

She narrowed her eyes. "That's why we pay him rent."

"Shut it, Hazel, or I'll break more than your door."

He glared as if daring her to speak, but she just lifted her chin and remained silent. I knew how scared she was, but she managed to look completely unafraid.

"I've got a message from the bosses," he said as two thugs stepped beside him.

My breath caught in my throat. A message? So they weren't here for me? Did that mean the bosses knew about the diamond?

"Pay up," Perry continued.

The shack tilted around me. They *did* know about the diamond!

"Give me your raft rent," Perry sneered. "Right now."

The shack stopped tilting. Wait a second. They only wanted raft rent? So they *didn't* know about the diamond! And they didn't know about me. I would've slumped in relief if I hadn't had a knife in my ribs.

"Rent's not due for five days, Perry," Hazel said. "And, um, you probably haven't heard. Our raft crashed."

"It's not your raft," he squeaked. "It's *our* raft. And of course I heard, that's why we're collecting early, as penalty for losing the raft."

"It's not lost. We're salvaging it. We'll be back on the Fog in no time."

"You ain't fixing that raft. Not even *your* geargirl can raise the dead."

"We'll see." Hazel smoothed her kimono. "In five days, we'll—"

"You don't get it." Perry kicked the basket of plastic bags. "You think you're so clever, but you don't know nothing. We've had orders from Lord Kodoc himself."

Hazel frowned. "From . . . from Kodoc?"

"That's right, you *should* look scared," Perry told her. "His lordship's hunting for some deformed kid in the junkyard."

"A what? Why? What kind of deformed kid?"

Perry shrugged. "They ain't told us yet. All you need to know is that my uncle's raising money for the search. That's why you're handing over your raft rent right now."

"We don't—"

"Hey!" Perry interrupted, his eyes narrowing. "You've got a deformed kid in your crew."

My heart stopped.

"I—what?" Hazel said.

"Yeah, your geargirl." Perry laughed scornfully. "All those freckles. Now get me that money, or we'll tear down the walls and stomp the roof flat as a cockroach."

Swedish grunted. "Cockroaches aren't flat."

"They are after you stomp 'em," Perry said in his high-pitched voice. His thugs laughed cruelly. "Draw your swords, boys, maybe we'll stick a few holes in the bootball player first."

Loretta stiffened behind me, but her knife stayed steady.

"Wait!" Hazel said. "Look around. We don't have anything worth taking."

"How about in that workshop?" Perry stomped a few times. "Under the floor? I'm betting you've got a hidey-hole

145

down there with some valuables."

"We're not hiding anything—" Swedish started.

Quick as a snake, Perry punched him in the stomach. "Don't mess with me, bottom-feeder."

"Chess," Swedish wheezed. "Show 'em."

That was my cue. I was supposed to threaten Perry with the trapdoor, but instead Loretta pushed me forward, showing everyone the knife at my back. I saw a tightening in Hazel's eyes.

"Loretta?" Swedish stared up at her in disbelief. "What're you doing?"

"Orders is orders," she said.

"You work for *Perry* now?"

"I work for whoever feeds me, don't I?"

He shot her a look of disgust. "I thought you were better than that."

"I guess I'm not," she said, and I heard a hitch in her voice.

Swedish curled his lip. "Don't need to *guess*."

"Shut up," Perry shouted at Swedish, "unless you want to tell me about your stash. Every crew has one. Maybe I'll ask that geargirl of yours."

A new voice cut through the shack. "You'll do no such thing!"

Mrs. E stepped into the main room, with one frail arm around Bea's shoulders for support. She looked wan and sickly, but her dull white eyes sparked with anger.

"I know your uncle, Periwinkle," she snapped at Perry. "I've seen him stare into the Fog and cry like a baby. Look around you, boy. Hazel runs the best salvage crew in the slum, worth a hundred times more than any raft. So why don't the bosses keep them under lock and key, make them work for free?"

"Because they're too ugly," Perry squeaked.

"Because the bosses need to keep *me* happy," Mrs. E said. "I've forgotten more about the upper slopes than they ever knew. Who do you think tells them how to deal with the Rooftop? How to hold a fork and ask a favor?" Her lips thinned. "Tell your bosses that Ekaterina says we have five days to pay our rent. Until then, you *will* leave us in peace."

The spark in Mrs. E's face seemed to kindle a blaze in Hazel. She suddenly looked a foot taller than Perry.

"Thank you, ma'am," she said to Mrs. E. Then she nodded to Bea, who helped Mrs. E back into the bedroom, and looked at me. "Chess, come here."

With a knife in my ribs, I was almost too scared to move, but Hazel's confidence gave me courage. I stepped forward on wobbly legs. A moment later, I was beside Swedish, my pulse pounding in my ears.

"We'll see you in five days," Hazel told Perry.

Perry sneered. "I ain't scared of a sick old lady."

"Of course not," she said soothingly. "Still, you should probably talk to your uncle."

"Maybe I will." He kicked the crates. "But there's one thing I've got to tell you first."

"What's that?"

"Don't even *think* about running. We start searching for this deformed kid tomorrow, but that doesn't mean you're off the hook. My uncle already spread the word, and there ain't a coyote in the junkyard who'll even talk to you, not anymore."

I almost whimpered, but Hazel just said, "Why would we want to talk to a coyote?"

Perry glared at her for a few seconds and then stomped away. His thugs swaggered after him, as Loretta faded into the shadows and a sharp-edged silence fell in the shack. Then Swedish exhaled and I leaned against the table to support my wobbly knees.

"Are you okay?" Hazel asked me.

"Not really. We can't hire a coyote now—we're dead."

"I was talking about the knife in your back."

"Oh. Yeah." I squinched up my face. "Sorry about that. Loretta's a sneaky one."

"She's a gutter rat," Swedish said, wiping his face with his hand. "I should've known. Can't trust a gang girl."

Hazel shot him a sympathetic look. "Can you believe Mrs. E, though? She was wonderful. She—"

"Come quick, something's wrong!" Bea cried, from inside the bedroom. "She's hot and shivery and can't hardly breathe."

21

I RUSHED INTO THE bedroom behind Hazel and saw Mrs. E lying on her back, her face flushed and her eyes blank. She raised her trembling hands like she was reaching for the ceiling, and her entire body started shivering.

"She's feverish," Hazel said, feeling her forehead. "Chess, soak a pair of socks in water."

I grabbed a pair of limp gray socks, ran into the main room, and shoved them into a bowl of water from the rain barrel. Then I rushed back into Mrs. E's room and stood there with the wet socks in my hands.

"Put them on her feet!" Hazel snapped, looking up from washing Mrs. E's face.

"How come I always get her feet?" I grumbled.

I wrestled the cold, wet socks onto Mrs. E's knobby

feet despite her pitiful whines. We bathed her hands with moist rags, massaged her scalp, and finally, by late morning, the fever subsided.

With the crisis over, we gathered, exhausted, in the main room. Suddenly famished, I emptied the last bag of dried locusts onto the table. Hazel sighed and Bea wrinkled her nose. Swedish offered to soak them for a while, then mash them into paste, but that only sounded worse.

"In the old days," I said, trying to distract them from the locusts, "people ate gross stuff, too. Like mud and string and sticks."

Swedish squinted at me. "They did not."

"They did! They just called it 'mud pie' and 'string cheese' and 'fish sticks.' Trying to make it sound better." I looked at the locust in my hand. "Maybe we should call these 'bug nuggets.'"

"Or sky candy," Swedish said.

"Candy doesn't have hairy legs," Bea grumbled, rubbing her eyes.

We crunched in silence until Hazel said, "She's dying. She can't survive another fever."

"How long does she have?" Swedish asked.

"Maybe a week," Hazel said. "And now I can't even talk to the coyotes."

Bea started crying. "So what're we going to do?"

Swedish wrapped his arm around her narrow shoulders,

and I asked, "How did the bosses know we were going to run?"

"They're mean," Hazel told me, "but they're clever. And tomorrow they'll get a description of the kid they're looking for. Even Perry might realize he's never seen Chess's eye."

"There are plenty of one-eyed kids," Bea said, wiping tears from her face.

"And they'll check them all," Hazel said. "We have to leave today."

"What?" Bea asked, sniffling. "Leave for where?"

"The Rooftop."

I choked on a locust leg. "Today?"

"This morning. We need to sneak onto the lower slopes, find a jeweler, and sell the diamond. The bosses scared off all the *junkyard* coyotes, so we need a *Rooftop* coyote to smuggle us to the Port."

"Why sell the diamond?" I asked. "Why not just give it to the coyote?"

"We'll need money when we reach the Port." Hazel rubbed her eyes. "The trouble is, I don't know any smugglers on the Rooftop."

"What about Mrs. E?" Bea asked.

"She'll sleep for days," Hazel said. "We'll come back for her once we hire a coyote."

"And, uh, how do we even get to the Rooftop without passes?"

"We bribe the guards," Hazel said with a sudden glint in her eyes.

Hazel loaded the leather cord of her necklace with dyed feathers, fused-glass gems, and colorful nanowire twistys. She tucked the diamond ring in the middle, hidden amid all the brightness and sparkle, and hung the whole thing around Bea's neck.

"*I* don't want it!" Bea said, her green eyes wide with alarm.

"It's safest there," Hazel told her. "You won't call any attention to yourself."

Plus it made sense to keep the two most precious things together: Bea and the diamond. Of course, nobody would notice Bea, not with Hazel wearing a shimmery tank top, flowing skirt, and gauzy half veil. And Swedish looked dangerous with his hair in a thuggish topknot.

I wore what I always wore: scuffed boots, patched cargo pants, and a worn jacket, but Hazel made Bea change into a patchwork dress and striped stockings.

"Dresses are stupid," Bea said, wrinkling her nose.

"You look more like a maid now," Hazel explained.

"How about me?" I asked. "Do I look okay?"

"Perfect. You're a natural."

"I am?"

"Yeah, you *always* look like a downtrodden servant." She laughed as she dodged the plastic carton I threw at her. "Bea, cut a hole in the wall so we can slip out without Perry seeing."

While Bea snipped the chicken wire, Hazel wrote a letter on a sheet of fancy paper she'd been saving for a special occasion. We checked on Mrs. E one last time, then squeezed through the hole into the garbage-strewn alley.

Bea glanced at the letter Hazel was tucking into her sleeve. "Is this going to work?"

"It'll get us killed," Swedish groused. "Kodoc's searching for Chess, and we're running *toward* him? I'm starting to think this whole thing's a—"

"Conspiracy?" I asked, slipping into the maze of alleys.

Swedish glared at me. "A bad idea."

"Of course it'll work!" Hazel told Bea. "We don't need the guards to believe what the letter says. We only need them to believe that their bosses will believe them."

"Oh." Bea wrinkled her nose. "What?"

Hazel shot me a sidelong look, amused by Bea's confusion. "The letter gives them an excuse to take the bribe, that's all."

We followed the alleys for a while, then skirted a hill of packed garbage, ignoring the squawks of seagulls and the mutters of the trash pickers.

As we passed a gloomy alley, a memory sparked in my mind. "Hey," I said, stopping. "That's where Mrs. E found me. Down there."

Bea peered into the darkness. "Yuck."

"She found me on the other side of the Spew," Hazel said, chewing on a braid.

Mrs. E had plucked Hazel from a crew of child soldiers, she'd snatched Swedish from a work gang, and she'd bought Bea from a factory. We'd all lost families before she adopted us. Swede's mom had gotten a job on the Rooftop and never come back for him. Bea's parents had had too many kids to feed and sold her to the factory. Hazel's dads had died in a refinery, after they couldn't pay rent. Mrs. E had done more than save our lives when she'd taken us in. She'd given us a reason to live—a family.

Twenty minutes later, we'd almost reached the Rooftop . . . but we couldn't just stroll from the junkyard to the mountains. A wide gap separated the floating slum platforms from solid ground, and roof-trooper checkpoints stood sentry at the bridges that spanned the distance.

None of us had ever set foot on the mountain, but between slum-dwellers who worked on the lower slopes and rich toughs who slummed in the junkyard, traffic flowed across the bridges pretty steadily. A marketplace had sprung up around the checkpoint, and when we got closer, I watched the crowd shuffle past bored-looking roof-troopers.

Bored looking, but heavily armed. I suppressed a shiver of worry. What if they were checking kids' eyes? Would a letter and bribe really work?

I watched for a few seconds, and didn't see any of the

troopers stopping kids. Maybe the search hadn't reached the slum yet—or maybe they didn't think I was stupid enough to head straight for a checkpoint.

Well, I'd show them. I was *plenty* stupid enough. "Chucklebutt" was my middle name.

"Something's wrong," Bea said suddenly.

"What?" I asked, scanning the street. "Where? Who?"

"It's the ground." Bea stomped on the floor. "It feels solid. It's all . . . weird."

"*You're* weird," I said, exhaling in relief.

Hazel laughed softly. "The slum platforms don't move much this close to the mountain, honeybee. That's what you're feeling, the lack of motion."

"Yeah!" Bea said, wrinkling her nose. "The ground's all stiff and funny."

"Because it's supported by stilts and columns," Hazel told her. "They run through the Fog into the ground."

"But there are balloons, too, right?" Bea looked worried until she spotted a blimp not too far away, attached to the slum with massive ropes. "Oh, there's one! I don't how anyone can sleep at night without balloons nearby."

"Soon," Hazel said, her brown eyes bright above the veil, "we'll sleep every night on solid ground—on the Port."

"I don't know," Bea said dubiously. "Solid ground is so . . . groundy."

Hazel took her arm and started toward the bridge.

"Once we get through the marketplace and past the checkpoints, we'll be fine."

"As long as nothing cockeyed happens," I muttered.

She shot me a look. "Everyone ready?"

"Ready to die," Swedish said.

"This is going to be so *purple*!" Bea squeaked a little nervously.

"Let's go," I said, and started across the road toward the marketplace.

"There they are!" a voice called out. "Get them!"

Five gang kids jogged toward us, with Loretta in front, leading the pack.

22

"Go!" Swedish barked at us. "Get out of here!"

Hazel and I exchanged a glance. "We're not leaving you," she said.

"There's five of them and three of us." I squared my shoulders. "We'll steam their butts."

"No, there's *four* of us!" Bea said, like she was going to start brawling.

"Do as I say," Swedish snarled, his eyes fierce. "*Now!* Get Bea out of here."

Without another word, Swedish stalked toward Loretta's gang. He looked so angry that pedestrians quickly stepped aside. I'm not much of a fighter, but I started to follow him, because win or lose, I had his back.

Then I felt Hazel's hand on my elbow. "He's right," she said. "We've got to go."

I tore my arm from her grip. "But he's *crew.*"

"Yeah," she said, her eyes angry, "so why don't you try trusting him?"

I glared at her but followed as she dragged Bea through the marketplace toward the bridge. Behind us, someone yelled: *"Hey! What're you kids doing?"*

A sick feeling coiled in my stomach. "We can't just leave him there. What if he needs us?"

"Now you know how we feel," Hazel told me, "every time you dive."

I stopped short. "I never thought of that."

"Because you're a dunderbunny," Bea explained.

She was kind of right. Whenever I dove, I left them on the raft to worry about me. "Okay," I said. "Well, let me take a peek, at least?"

"Quickly," Hazel said.

I clambered over a quilter's table in the marketplace, then pulled myself onto a rickety roof. I shaded my eyes, scanned the snarls of foot traffic, and—there!

Swedish was circling a gang kid in the middle of a crowd near a gambling tent. The mah-jongg players from inside had gathered to watch the fight. And gamble on it, of course. I couldn't see clearly, but the thug he was facing looked short and spiky-haired. Like Loretta.

"Is he okay?" Bea asked after I hopped down.

"I don't know, it looks like he and Loretta are *talking*."

"That doesn't sound right."

"Keep moving," Hazel said with a weak smile. "If Swede can't cross, we'll meet him at home later."

We trotted through the marketplace, and ten yards from the roof-trooper checkpoint, Hazel bowed her head. When she straightened, she looked different, with a soft smile and dull eyes. She strolled toward the checkpoint, while Bea and I trailed behind like drudges. I kept my head down and my hair over my freak-eye, suddenly thankful for all the years of practice.

One of the roof-trooper guards eyed Hazel. "Papers?"

"My pleasure, sir." Hazel handed him the letter. "We have jobs lined up."

The guard scanned the letter. "Says that this fellow needs a scullery maid, a shoeshine, a doorman, and an entertainer."

"That's right, sir," Hazel said in a breathy voice. "This is the maid and the shoeshine boy. And I'm—"

"The doorman?"

"Oh, no, sir!" Hazel fluttered her eyelashes, which almost made me laugh. "I'm the dancer!" She spun, and her skirt flared. "I dance."

"I mean, where's the doorman?"

"Oh! He's behind us. A tall boy with a topknot. Impossible to miss."

The guard scratched his cheek. "Is this all you have for me?"

"No, sir! I also have this."

Coins clinked as she handed the guard a pouch containing all the money we'd saved in the past three years. "Looks fine," he said, weighing it in his hand. "Go on, then."

"Thanks so much!" Hazel gushed. "And the doorman? You won't forget him?"

"We'll see," the guard said.

Hazel's jaw clenched, like she was going to argue, so I cleared my throat, still looking at my boots. After a tense moment, she exhaled. "Well, we can't keep our new boss waiting."

Hazel lowered her eyes demurely as she stepped onto the bridge. Bea bustled along, looking young and overwhelmed.

We paused in the middle of the bridge and glanced backward. Still no sign of Swedish. After a minute, Hazel shook her head.

We continued across the bridge, twenty or thirty feet above the terraced fields on the mountainside just over the fogline. The freshly plowed earth smelled so rich that it made my stomach rumble.

"Look at that," Bea gasped.

At first I thought she was staring at the stone building on the other end of the bridge, but then I realized she was looking at the *trees*. She dashed over to one that was growing alongside the bridge and strummed her fingers across the bark.

"It feels like a cat's tongue," she said, "but a thousand times rougher!" Her eyes shone. "Look at the leaves! There are so many of them, and they're all juicy and green and *purple*!"

She'd never seen a tree this close before. Sometimes I forgot that the others had never walked on the solid earth, never splashed in a stream or sat in the grass. So after we crossed the bridge, I took charge, leading Hazel and Bea past the stone building—another roof-trooper checkpoint—toward a neighborhood of cramped houses with plastic-thatched roofs. Chickens clucked, goats bleated, and pushcarts rattled across cobblestones.

A flush of triumph warmed me. We still needed Swedish, still needed to sell the diamond and hire a coyote, but we'd gotten this far. We'd made it to the Rooftop.

One step closer to Port Oro. Also one step closer to Lord Kodoc, and surrounded by thousands of roof-troopers. But we were on our way to finding a cure for Mrs. E. On our way to a new life and a new world, free from the shadow of fear.

23

THE HOUSES OF THE lower slope were bigger and sturdier than junkyard shacks. Some were built with timber and tin, some had clay-and-laptop walls—a few of them even had two stories. Camel carts heaved past them, laden with carrots and radishes, and a grimy boy walked along, eating a shiny apple.

My mouth watered. In the slum, a bigger kid would've snatched that apple in a second—and this was still the *poor* section of the Rooftop.

We wandered down the street, gaping at the sights, until Hazel stopped so suddenly that a pinch-faced woman almost crashed into her.

"Oh!" Hazel said. "Sorry."

The woman glared. "Watch where you're walking, miss

fancy-piece—and that goes for your urchins, too."

She bustled past, and Hazel nudged me. "See? I told you, people are the same everywhere."

"Yeah," I said. "Grumpy."

"We're *urchins*!" Bea told me proudly.

I couldn't tell if she knew what "urchins" meant, and I almost laughed. "We're really moving up in the world."

"Why'd you stop?" Bea asked Hazel.

"We need to stay at the bridge," she said. "So we'll see Swedish when he crosses."

"Oh, right." Keeping my head lowered, I scanned the area. "We can wait outside that glassblowing shop."

Bea brightened. "Glassblowing! Do you think they'll show me how?"

"No," I said. "And you can't ask."

"Why not?" she demanded. "I'll show them how to make twistys."

"They'd probably like it better if you showed them how to fix a foggium engine with a rusty bottle cap and a little chitchat."

She stuck her tongue out at me. "Why can't I at least talk to them?"

"Because we don't want to attract any attention while we wait."

"You're not waiting," Hazel told me.

"I'm not? What am I doing?"

"Finding us a jeweler."

I felt a tingle of excitement with an edge of fear. "Right now?"

She nodded. "I need to stay close in case Swedish has trouble crossing. And look at that. . . ."

Down the street, a patrol of roof-troopers marched through the crowd. They wore armored uniforms and carried swords and steam-bows. One plump woman didn't see them coming and was knocked to the ground. When the patrol disappeared into the guard station, the entire world breathed a sigh of relief.

"You can't stand around next to the guard stations," Hazel continued.

I took a deep breath. "Yeah, okay. So where should I look for a jeweler?"

"I don't know." Hazel unclasped the veil from her face. "Not this close to the slum. Look higher on the mountain, and meet us back at the bridge."

"Gotcha."

"Then we'll sell the diamond together," she told me. "That's not the kind of thing you want to do alone."

"Okay."

"And don't go chasing after coyotes. We'll find them once we get the money."

"All right."

"And Chess? If you get into trouble, just bow and grovel and run away."

"Sure."

She smoothed my hair farther over my eye. "One more thing."

"Yes, Admiral Bossy-pants?"

She poked me in the chest. "Don't steal any apples."

Bea giggled, and I took a ragged breath and left them. I slouched along the street, past chugging generators shooting sparks and street vendors bellowing prices. I couldn't believe how rich everyone was. Nobody fought over the pencil stub on the ground or the pile of soggy acrylicloth scraps—nobody even noticed them.

Swallowing my amazement, I followed a switchback trail uphill. I scanned the crowd for someone to ask about a jeweler, and a shadow fell across the street. When I looked upward, I saw a patrol airship swooping directly toward me.

"No," I gasped.

I froze, rooted to the spot as the ship angled closer . . . then flew past.

The troopers hadn't seen me, they were just patrolling. Dizzy with relief, I watched the guardship roar over the smokestacks and chimneys. And *whoa*, it was one sweet ship. I mean, Rooftop patrols flew over the slum sometimes, but never that low and slow, showing off every detail.

I hoped Bea had a good view.

When I looked back to the street, I spotted a skinny man with a friendly-looking face. "Uh, excuse me, sir?" I said, falling into step with him. "I'm looking for a jewelry store?"

To my surprise, he smiled at me. "Sure. Take a left at the mill, head up-mountain for a few minutes, and it's in the square past the hydrostatic station."

Five minutes later, I was lost in a junction of walkways and stairs near the mill. Five minutes after that, I was lost at a stone quarry. But five minutes after *that* I crossed a square and saw the sign: JEWELRY BOO-TEAK.

Strange name, but the shop itself looked perfect, with flowers blooming beside the door and thick iron bars on the windows. I turned in a circle to get my bearings, then headed down-mountain, back to the bridge.

Halfway there, I paused on a stairway beside a hillside airfield dotted with gearslinger workshops, oversized thoppers, and half-built frames. Looked like gearhead heaven. Bea would go peanuts over all the top-notch gear—and so would Swedish, if he got across.

The thought worried me. Had he made it? I rushed down the flight of wooden steps, then trotted toward the bridge in search of the crew. No sign of them. Not outside the glass shop, not under the white-barked trees.

Where *were* they? Had something happened?

I drifted toward a row of empty pushcarts, feeling an itch of fear. Then a hand clamped my mouth from behind, and a knife jabbed my ribs.

24

"SHUT YOUR FACE!" a voice breathed as the hand dragged me into an alley.

The attacker had struck without warning, like a coil of Fog thickening suddenly into a driftshark. At least this was just a person. Half blind with fear, I stomped with my heel, aiming for the knife wielder's foot.

I hit the cobblestones instead, and pain burst through my leg. So I lunged backward, but the attacker sidestepped and my head smacked the wall. I slumped sideways, seeing double. Two walls beside me, two skies above me, two Lorettas in front of me.

"L-Loretta?" I stammered, rubbing my aching head. "What are you doing here? Where's Perry? Where's Swedish?"

"What do you think I'm doing here?" She grinned crookedly. "I came to buy some pretty hijabs, like Hazel."

My fear edged into anger. I wasn't good at fighting, but I wasn't afraid of it, either. Especially after she put her knife away.

"Where *is* Hazel?" I demanded, stepping closer.

"Whoa, there." Loretta raised her hands in surrender, though her fingerless gloves only made her look even more thuggish. "Me and Swede came over together."

"Together?"

"Uh-huh."

I glared. "You and Swedish?"

"Yeah. And Perry's nowhere. Well, he's *some*where, but not here. He doesn't even know we're here, not yet."

"You came with Swedish? Why?"

"Well, I kind of, um . . ." Loretta toed the ground. "I got to thinking about what he said? About me being worse than he thought? And, um—yeah."

"Yeah, what? Last I saw, your thugs were trying to stomp him."

Her broad face broke into a smile. "You should've seen him, Chess! For a sweet guy, he really knows how to handle himself. He mowed down a couple of Perry's best hitters before you could say 'cockroach relish.'"

I rubbed my head again. "And then what?"

"Then I fought Swede down the block, and maybe I could've stabbed him in the knee, but I didn't." She

168

considered. "Of course, he could've broke my arm and *he* didn't, either. So I thought, you know, he still likes me."

I blinked at her. "Because he didn't break your arm?"

"Ain't that sweet?" she said, sighing.

"It's adorable," I said.

"And anyway, here we are."

"No," I said. "Here *you* are. Where's he?"

"With Hazel and Bea. They're hiding."

"What? Why?"

"You can't drop Hazel in a crowded street and think nobody's going to notice! Dressed like *that*? The boys started swarming like flies on a skinned rat."

"Oh. So they sent you to look for me?"

"That's right," she said with her gap-toothed smile. "Nobody notices me. I ain't pretty like Hazel, or big like Swede. Me and you, Chess, you know what stands out about *us*?"

"What?"

"Nothing."

"Yeah," I said.

"Except . . ." She peered at the hair falling over my face. "I bet your eye's messed up. I've never seen it."

"Good."

"What is it, an empty socket?"

"Maybe."

She made a disgusted face. "I bet it's gross."

169

"It's hypnotic," I told her. "Are you going to take me to Hazel?"

"Of course I am! What do you think? C'mon, stop wasting time."

She led me past a few round buildings with kangaroo-hide walls, and I felt a slow simmer of suspicion. I didn't trust Loretta. I hadn't trusted her last week or last year, and I sure didn't trust her after last night.

"How did you get past the guards?" I asked.

"I borrowed a pass," she said.

"Someone lent you a pass?"

She shrugged. "Well, me and my knife borrowed it."

"Oh."

"And I still had to knock the guy out." She shook her head sadly and stepped into a farm shack. "Some people, huh?"

"Right," I said, my suspicion rising as I followed her inside.

"Chess!" Bea bounded from the shadows. "You're okay!"

I yelped in surprise. "I'm fine! But what's Loretta doing here?"

"She's with us now," Hazel said. "Tell me you found a jeweler."

I frowned. What did that mean, *she's with us now*? What about my freak-eye? If Loretta joined the crew, I'd need to start hiding my eye in private, too. And this was my family. You don't run around inviting new people into your family, not without asking everyone first.

"What are you talking about?" I said, my voice rising. "Loretta's here—that doesn't mean she's *with* us."

"She is," Hazel told me. "She's crew."

"No," I said, clamping down on my anger. "We're crew. The four of us."

Hazel rubbed her eyes, then asked me very quietly, "Do you trust me?"

"Do you trust Loretta?" I shot back. "Do any of us trust her?"

"Far as I can throw her," Swedish said.

Bea cocked her head. "How far is that?"

"I don't know," Swedish said, glancing at Loretta. "I haven't tried yet."

Loretta toed the dirt again and for some reason looked almost pleased.

"She helped us, Chess," Hazel told me. "She got Swedish across the bridge, and she—"

"She mugged some poor slob for—"

"*And,*" Hazel interrupted, "she told the other thugs not to report us to the bosses."

"She did?"

"Uh-huh." Hazel nodded. "Loretta's friends won't even tell Perry we're on the Rooftop."

"Oh, they'll tell him," Loretta said. "They'll take their lazy time is all."

"How much time?" I asked.

"They'll probably wait till nightfall. The gangs are going to be busy searching for this kid Kodoc wants—"

"Yeah," I cut in. "Whoever *that* is."

"But once the bosses hear you ran," Loretta continued, "they'll make an example of you. They'll ditch your whole block into the Fog."

"They'll ditch your block, too," I said.

"I don't have a block, I don't have anything that matters except . . ." She glanced at Swedish. "Anyway, if Hazel's making a break for the Rooftop, she's got a plan. And you know what?"

"What?" Swedish asked.

"I don't want to die for the bosses, just another worthless slumgirl. I don't want to die fighting over a pair of rat-skin gloves. You four are different. You've got that gleam in your eyes—you always have. So whatever scam you're running, I want in. Plus you need a fighter."

"We never needed one before," I told her.

"After the bosses ditch your shack, they'll keep hunting you. They won't ever stop. They answer to Lord Kodoc himself. You know anything about him?"

I glanced at Hazel. "We've heard the name."

"Well, he's not a fellow who lets things slide. They'll keep coming until they toss you in the Fog."

"If they can find us."

"He's a Rooftop lord," Loretta said, "and we're slum

172

trash. My money's on him."

"You don't have any money," Swedish said.

Loretta's bold gaze flicked to Hazel. "You sent Chess for a jeweler?"

"Yeah," Hazel said.

"Why? You found some gold or something?"

Instead of answering, Hazel looked at me, like she was asking my permission to tell Loretta about the diamond. Because once we did that, she was part of the crew, like it or not. We'd have to tell her about everything else. Including my eye.

"If you're smart," I told Loretta, "you'll head back to the slum and forget all about this."

She scratched the burn scar on her arm. "Well, nobody ever accused me of being a deep thinker."

I frowned at the floor. Our lives were changing fast— too fast. Maybe that was scaring me more than telling Loretta our secrets. But some things never changed: of course I trusted Hazel. I trusted her more than I trusted *myself*.

So after a second, I nodded.

Hazel flicked a smile at me, then said, "We found a diamond."

Loretta gaped at her. "A di—a diam—no *way*."

"The purplest diamond you ever saw," Bea said.

"Like a . . . a *diamond* diamond?"

"Almost exactly," Swedish told her, his eyes crinkling.

"Now tell me you found a jeweler," Hazel said to me.

"Yep," I told her. "Fifteen minutes up the mountain."

"So we have until tonight to sell the diamond, hire a Rooftop coyote, and pick up Mrs. E."

"Coyote?" Loretta said. "What're you smuggling?"

"Us. Into Port Oro. After we sell the diamond."

"Port Oro," she breathed.

"*If* we sell the diamond," Swedish muttered.

Loretta scratched her nose. "Um, can I see it?"

"Maybe later," I said quickly. "It's in my boot pocket."

Loretta didn't need to know that it was actually on Bea's necklace. Maybe I'd learn to trust her eventually, but there was no reason to rush into things.

Swedish shot me a look. "Chess, you don't have to—"

"Time to go," Hazel interrupted.

Ha. Looked like Hazel wasn't so sure about Loretta either.

"Keep your eyes down and your hands to yourselves," Hazel continued. "Stay together. We'll meet here if we're separated. No fighting, no stealing, no shoving. No shouting, no swearing, no—"

"Fun," Loretta said.

25

I LED THEM UP the winding streets of the mountain toward the jeweler.

When we reached the stairway beside the airfield, Bea stared at the thoppers and babbled about pressure valves and rotation speeds. Then she stopped short, halfway up the hill. "That's a twelve-spark repeating tes-array!"

"Bea!" Hazel tugged her arm. "C'mon."

"But Cap'n, *look* at her." She pointed to a twin-hulled thopper with a gleaming engine and exposed gearworks. "She's purple as a mayfly!"

"As a *what*?" I said.

"She looks like a mayfly."

Actually, she looked like a thopper, but I knew better

than to argue. Once Bea gave an airship a nickname, she refused to budge.

Swedish nodded. "She's a beaut."

"Except for that condenser," Bea said.

Loretta said, "Huh?"

"The condenser," Bea explained. "He's grumpy as an upside-down sundial."

"You mean the pilot?"

"She means the condenser," Swedish told her.

"It's *grumpy*?"

I hunched my shoulders, disgusted at Loretta's confusion. How could she be a crew member if she didn't even understand Bea? "We're not far now," I said. "Let's go."

"One day," Bea announced, still gazing at the twin-hulled craft, "I'm going to build a thopper as pretty as that mayfly."

"Bea, come on! Does Swedish have to carry you?!" Hazel asked her.

"I'm coming, I'm coming!"

When we reached the square, we clustered under the awning of a general store and eyed the Jewelry Boo-Teak—and the bakery and blacksmith and a handful of vendors with pushcarts.

"Ooh," Bea said. "Look at all the shops!"

"Now you sound like Hazel," Swedish told her. "If you see any pretty skirts—"

"Shht!" Hazel hissed, staring across the square. "Look at that."

I followed her gaze toward a small crowd standing around a water pump. At first, I didn't see the problem. Then I realized that one of them was a bull-necked guy with armored plates on his chest and forearms, and a wooden cudgel at his hip.

A roof-trooper. He was only filling a jug of water from the pump, but what if he could tell we were slumkids? What if he checked our eyes?

"What do we do?" Bea whispered.

"Look natural," Hazel said. "He'll leave in a minute."

Bea started whistling, I ducked my head, Loretta cleaned her fingernails with her knife, and Swedish pretended he was kicking an invisible bootball.

"Stop it!" Hazel hissed. "Not like *that*! Just stay still!"

We all stopped exactly where we were.

"Don't *freeze*! Would you—" She gritted her teeth in frustration. "Loretta and Swede, pretend you're . . . into each other. Bea, show Chess one of your twistys."

Loretta grabbed one of Swedish's hands and beamed up at him. "Start being into me, big guy. I'm all ears."

He flushed. "Well, that's good, because your ears are as cute as berry pie."

I pretended to barf as Bea tugged my sleeve. She showed me a twisty in her palm, a jagged shape that looked like a rat crossed with a stepladder.

"What is it?" I asked, glancing at the bull-necked roof-trooper.

He was scanning the square as he chatted with a woman in overalls, so I quickly turned my attention to the twisty.

"A snapping turtle," Bea said. "I even made hinges on the shell."

I looked closer. "Um, I'm not sure the shell actually snaps."

"Of course it does! A snapping turtle is a turtle that snaps, like a bobcat is a cat that bobs. It says so in the name."

"Sure," I said. "And grizzly bears loooove to grizz."

"I bet they do," she told me. "Everyone loves to grizz."

"He's leaving!" Hazel whispered as she turned from the general store window. "Okay, let's sell this diamond. How should we— Swede?!"

Swedish was still chatting with Loretta, a few steps away. "Hm?" he asked.

"You can stop now."

"Oh." He dropped Loretta's hand and flushed again. "Um."

"He's a real sweet-talker," Loretta said with a wide grin.

"And so *cute*!" I said in a fake, gushy voice—then dodged Swede's fist.

Hazel took a shaky breath. "How should we do this? We've never sold anything on the mountain before.

Anyone have any ideas?"

I shrugged. "Not me."

"Just march in there," Loretta said. "Easy as pigeon potpie."

"I hope so." Hazel thought for a second. "Chess, come with me. Everyone else stay here. We don't want to spook the jeweler."

"Take Bea if you don't want to spook them," I said.

"Just keep your head down."

I nodded, figuring she didn't want to take Swedish because he was so big and didn't want to take Bea because it might get dangerous.

"Okay, Bea," she continued, "give me the ring."

Bea pulled the necklace off and fiddled with the trinkets, carefully removing the diamond from the strap.

Loretta glared at me. "You said it was in your boot pocket."

"I lied."

"I'm on your side now!"

"Someone once told me that you work for whoever feeds you. Hmm, who was that?" I paused for dramatic effect. "Oh, that's right, it was *you*."

"Jerk," she muttered.

"Maybe after you go a whole day without pulling your knife on me, I'll trust you."

"Ought to stick my knife *in* you."

"Not helping, 'Retta," Swedish told her.

"I don't like it here." She eyed the shoppers in the square. "It's too pretty."

"*They're* trying to lull us," Swedish said. "That's how *they* work."

"What does that even mean?" I asked.

Hazel slipped the ring into the little box. "You ready?" she asked me.

"Not even close."

"Then let's go," she said, and we started across the square.

26

A BELL JINGLED AS Hazel opened the jewelry shop door. I followed her inside, then stopped short: cabinets built from hubcaps and iSlates lined the wall, displaying rings, necklaces, and bracelets. I'd never seen so much wealth in one place before.

The jeweler flashed a fake smile at us. "Welcome, welcome! Looking to buy a trinket?"

I lowered my head and stayed behind Hazel, desperately hoping this would work. If the sale went smoothly, we'd have enough money to find a coyote and escape the Rooftop.

"Actually, sir," Hazel said, "we're looking to *sell* something."

"Is that so?" The smile vanished. "Wire jewelry you made? Bead earrings?"

The bell over the door jingled again before Hazel could answer, and when I turned to look, I almost whimpered. So much for this sale going smoothly.

The roof-trooper from the square stepped inside, his water jug in one hand and his cudgel in the other. "What are you kids doing here?" he barked.

"Oh! I beg your pardon, sir," Hazel said with a nervous little curtsy. "We'll, uh, we'll come back when you're done."

"I asked you a question!" the trooper snarled. "What're you doing here?"

"We—we came to sell some jewelry, sir."

"What're you doing on the *mountain*?" He set his clay jug down on the counter with a clunk. "Couple of slum-kids sneaking into a jewelry store? That's not right."

"They're from the junkyard?" The jeweler sniffed. "Well! I don't deal with filth like that."

"We have day passes, sir," Hazel told the trooper tightly. "For a job."

The trooper stuck his hand out, and Hazel gave him the letter she'd written.

He frowned at the letter and I studied the floor, trying to make myself invisible. *Let us go. Just read the letter and let us go. . . .*

"Huh," he finally said. "This looks okay."

"Yes, sir," Hazel said.

"Now get out of here," he said. "Back to work."

"Yes, sir," she said again, and stepped past him toward the door.

I followed—until the trooper blocked me with one thick arm.

"But first," he said, "let me have a look at you."

"At me?" I whispered, hanging my head even lower than normal.

"Um, is—is something wrong?" Hazel asked.

"He keeps his eye hidden," the trooper told her. "That's not allowed on the mountain. Not for a kid his age. Raise your head, boy."

"Okay," I said, but I didn't move.

I *couldn't*. The idea of exposing my freak-eye had always terrified me, and I always worried that the fear of calling attention to myself made me a coward. But this time, the threat was real.

"Please, sir," Hazel pleaded. "He's scarred and he's shy. Don't make him—"

"I ain't asking again!" The trooper grabbed my shoulders in a tight grip. "Show me your face or I'll—"

Crash!

Water splashed my cheeks, and the trooper howled. He shoved me away and spun toward Hazel, who was holding the shattered water jug in her hands.

She'd broken it over his head. Wow.

He lunged at Hazel and she dodged, her eyes wild and her braids flying everywhere. In her shimmery tank top and flowing skirt, she looked totally defenseless as the trooper swung his cudgel at her head.

A flush of rage rose in my chest. I wasn't going to let this guy hurt Hazel. I wasn't going to let him touch her.

I dove at his knees and slammed him hard, my shoulder jolting. He grunted and stumbled, his cudgel flying from his grip and clattering across the floor.

"Guards!" the jeweler screeched. "Help!"

"Run!" I yelled, wrapping my arms around the trooper's knees. "Hazel, *go!*"

The trooper jerked his legs, but I only clung tighter. The bell over the door jingled, and I knew Hazel was safe. My sense of relief was cut short when the trooper started punching one of my legs so hard that I almost screamed.

Instead, I sank my teeth into his thigh. What can I say? I fought like a slumkid.

"You little roach," he snarled, and boxed my ears.

My head spun, and he grabbed my hair and twisted. Pain shot through my scalp and tears sprang to my eyes—then the bell jingled again, and a loud crash came from across the room.

A second later, a meaty smack sounded, and the trooper collapsed beside me.

Loretta stood over him, his cudgel in her hand. She

started to hit him again, but Hazel said, "Enough," and caught her arm midswing.

With my head still throbbing, I pushed to my feet and saw Swedish standing over the groaning jeweler.

"Look at me!" Loretta cried, grabbing some jewelry from the floor. She held a bright blue earring to her nose. "I'm a princess!"

"People are coming," Bea squeaked from the doorway. "They heard the noise."

"Are you okay?" Hazel asked me. "Can you walk?"

"We can run." Swedish slung an arm around me. "C'mon, 'Retta! Leave the rest."

"Sure," she said, snatching another handful of pearls.

In the square, shoppers gawked as we dashed out of the jewelry shop. A deliverywoman shouted, "Stop them!" as a bald man yelled, "Guards!"

Swedish helped me as we raced along a row of rusting vans converted into homes, then skidded through a garage door into a factory. A deafening clatter filled the room, and my head pounded as we wove past tables where little kids were assembling flywheels. Then we burst from the other side of the factory into an open yard—and stopped short.

The throb of an approaching engine sounded above the clamor.

"What's that?" I asked.

"A roof-trooper guardship," Bea said, pointing overhead. "They've spotted us!"

"OVER THERE!" I POINTED across the yard. "Hide in that alley!"

We dashed into a narrow passageway as the growl of the airship engine became a roar. Clouds of dust billowed around us. My eyes watered, and I could barely see Hazel throwing herself at a flimsy door.

"Swede!" Hazel yelled. "Kick this down."

Swedish took two steps and slammed his foot beside the latch.

The door flung open and we tumbled into a yard where wet clothes dangled on the line. From there, we dashed into a neighborhood of cramped houses, slipping under crooked stairways and past smokestacks. We raced blindly until we turned a corner and almost crashed into a mariachi band playing to a packed crowd. We were in a clearing above a sheer thirty-foot drop. This whole neighborhood was built on a rise, and we'd reached the end. The *dead* end—a granite cliff side.

A flash of motion blurred above the band as a wide bronze hull sped through the air.

"The guardship!" I yelled, shading my eyes as the wind ripped through my hair.

Hazel tugged Bea into the alley. "Get back, before they see us!"

Too late. The ship swooped closer, and the troopers hopped to the ground, pulling swords and steam-bows as they chased us.

We dashed past a trash fire, then veered down a half-hidden stairway into a courtyard where old women sat on planks, coiling copper wire around spindles. Another dead end, with four high wooden walls and heavily shuttered windows.

"Oh, no!" Bea cried.

"Don't panic," I told her, trying to sound calm.

"Why not?" Loretta asked.

"Because if she panics," I said, "I'll freak out."

That got a trembling smile from Bea . . . but it didn't last long, as the shouts of the troopers grew closer.

"Let me think," Hazel muttered, tugging on a braid. "Let me think, let me think. . . ."

"Looks like you're in a spot of trouble," said one of the

old women, taking a corncob pipe from between her lips.

Hazel spun toward her. "Please, ma'am—please help us."

"You're polite for a slumgirl," the woman said.

"Listen, you old bat," Loretta snarled. "She asked you to help, not—"

A trooper shouted into the courtyard from the top of the stairs: "Halt! Hands on your heads or we'll fire!"

"That's it," Swedish muttered. "We're dead. *They* always win in the end."

The old woman pointed her pipe at a curtain on the courtyard wall. "Through there."

In a flash, Hazel grabbed Bea's hand and dragged her toward the curtain.

Boots sounded on the stairway, and the roar of the guardship engine grew louder. Someone whimpered— maybe me—as we raced toward the wall. I was two steps behind Hazel when she pulled back the curtain . . . and I suddenly wanted to cry.

There was nothing behind it but another plank-shuttered window.

Closed tight. No escape.

"On your knees!" a trooper shouted from the top of the stairway. "Down, now!"

28

As **THE TROOPERS THUNDERED** down the stairway toward us, the shutters behind the curtain flung open, slamming against the wall with a solid *thunk*.

"Come!" a voice whispered from inside the dark window. "Quickly now!"

"Bea, go!" Hazel boosted her through the opening. "Now you, Loretta! Inside! Chess, move!"

The minute Loretta disappeared, I dove headfirst through the window and landed with her elbow in my gut. She squirmed away, and Swedish fell on me like a bear.

I yelped and the roof-troopers sounded loud and close in the courtyard.

"There!" one yelled. "She's climbing in that window."

"Get her!" another yelled. "Grab her!"

The shutters slammed closed. They must've been three inches thick, and the room turned black as iron bolts slid shut, locking the soldiers out in the courtyard along with—

"No!" I gasped. "Hazel's still out there! Open it up!"

"I'm here," her voice said in the darkness.

I almost sobbed in relief. "Oh, thank the peaks."

"Save your thanks," said a rough whisper in the darkness. "And follow me."

As soldiers hammered on the other side of the shutters, a hooded lantern sprang to life in the gloom. A dingy light hovered in the air, and I caught a glimpse of a cloaked man.

"This whole thing stinks like a trap," Swedish muttered.

"What stinks," I said, shoving him off me, "is your armpit in my face."

"At least we're not dead," Hazel said. "Follow the light. Stay together."

The glow drifted from the room, and we trailed after the cloaked man along a mazelike hallway. When we heard the soldiers smash through the shutters behind us, Bea squeaked in the darkness and Loretta swore.

The man didn't react. He just led us through a sliding panel, then whispered, "Watch your step."

The sound of the soldiers faded as we followed a

stairway downward. A moist draft washed over us, and the lantern painted the rough-hewn stairs with a sickly light. We headed into a dirt-walled corridor, and the sound of dripping water echoed all around.

"Where are we?" Hazel asked, sounding as lost as I felt.

"In the mines," the voice whispered. "They won't find us here."

"How do you know?"

"This section was condemned as unsafe years ago."

"Oh, good," I muttered, glancing at the ceiling. "I feel much better now."

Swedish snorted. "Yeah, I always wanted to die in a cave-in."

"Holy goalie!" Bea blurted. "Are we *underground*?"

"Yes," the cloaked man whispered.

With a whoop, Bea started jumping up and down, stomping on the floor. "It's dirt! I never thought there was this much dirt in the whole world! Look at all this—"

I grabbed her arm. "Would you *stop* that?"

"What?"

"It's been condemned as unsafe!"

She peered down the dark hallway. "What does 'condemned' mean?"

"That it'll fall on our heads if you keep hopping around."

"Oops."

"It is pretty cool, though," I admitted. "I've never been underground before."

"Underground smells like camel butt," Loretta muttered.

"Shhh," the cloaked man said.

We climbed the uneven stone stairs in the gloom. Silence fell around us, except for the scuffing of our footsteps and the drips of water echoing through the stairwell.

Finally Hazel said, "Who are you?"

The cloaked figure stopped on a landing. "My name is Turning."

"Why did you help us?"

"Cover your eyes." He fiddled with a rusted gearwork mechanism on the wall. "We're stepping into the light."

A door opened and sunlight poured into the dark stairway. I squinted as I followed Loretta into a cluttered room. Not an ordinary room: more like a laboratory.

Cabinets lined the walls, and a workbench divided the room, littered with half-built instruments and strange devices. Rows of tools were sorted in racks, and a clockwork machine as big as Swedish hunched in one corner, half covered with a cloth. Charts filled a bookcase, and round windows, shining with bright sunlight, overlooked the lower slope and the slum.

Bea gasped, gazing at a huge scope tilted toward one window. "Look at that spyglass!"

"It's a telescope," Turning told her in his chilly whisper.

He lowered his hood, and I saw his face: tired eyes, a crooked nose, and a braided beard. Cloudy-white gems glinted in his earrings, the color of Fog.

"I never thought I'd see you so close," he said, surveying us. Then he frowned at Loretta. "And *you're* a surprise."

"We weren't exactly expecting *you*, either," she said.

Turning's laugh sounded like his whisper, scratchy and thin. "I suppose not, but—"

"You never thought you'd see us this *close*?" Hazel asked, frowning. "So you've seen us from afar?"

"Indeed I have," he said. "Through the telescope."

"He's been watching us." Swedish turned to me. "I *told* you someone was watching us."

"Yeah, well—" I couldn't think of a snappy reply. "You were right."

"Ha!" he crowed. "I knew it!"

"Oh, Mr. Turning, can I look in the telescope?" Bea pleaded. "Please? Pretty please?"

"Of course," he said.

She scampered across the room, greeted the telescope politely, then peeked through. "Ooh, everything looks so close! There's a waterwheel. Oh, there's the airfield with that mayfly! That is *such* a purple thopper!"

"Why have you been watching us?" Hazel asked Turning, her voice sharp. "How did you find us? Was that old lady in the courtyard expecting us?"

"We monitor the roof-troopers," Turning said. "We saw them chasing you."

I felt a chill of worry as I scanned the room. Who *was* this guy, with his secret passages and hidden laboratory?

"You monitor them?" Hazel asked. "Why?"

"For our own safety."

Hazel's eyes narrowed. "Who *are* you?"

"Look!" Bea squealed. "The slum's so close I could touch it."

"He's a foghead." I pointed to a charcoal sketch on an easel. "That's too freaky for anyone else."

"What—" Loretta made a face. "What is it?"

The drawing looked like an evil thopper with legs instead of wings, and a spiny shell of shattered bricks. I said, "A ticktock, I bet."

"Only in my imagination," Turning said with a slight smile. "I've never seen one. Nobody has. Not in a hundred years."

"So it's true?" Hazel asked Turning. "You're a foghead?"

"I suppose I am," Turning said, his scratchy voice calm. "Though that's not what we call ourselves. We are the Subassembly, and I'm a leader—a 'cog.' My full name is Cog Turning."

So he wasn't just a foghead, he was a foghead *boss*? And he'd brought us to his hidden lair, with illegal books and creepy drawings? We needed a coyote to take us to

Port Oro, and instead we got a mist-sniffing fog-freak. A sick sense of dread uncoiled inside me like a driftshark: we needed to get out of there. We needed to sell the diamond and get away from the Rooftop before everything fell apart.

29

LORETTA'S HAND DRIFTED TOWARD her knife, and Swedish stepped closer to Hazel. The room thickened with suspicion, everyone clenched and edgy. Well, everyone except Bea, who kept looking into the telescope, completely oblivious.

"Don't be afraid," Turning said, his voice calm. "I'm a friend."

Swedish scowled. "That's what *they* always say. You fogheads are the ones who started spreading rumors about Chess."

"I'm sorry about that," Turning said. "However, if the Assemblers you met in the junkyard hadn't foolishly spread those rumors, I never would've found Ekaterina. And I couldn't have saved you just now."

"Why *did* you save us?" Hazel asked. "How do you know Mrs. E? What do you want from us?"

"There's the market!" Bea called from the window. "Oooh! That's the watering hole. *Our* watering hole."

"I'll answer all your questions," Turning said, stroking his braided beard. "But would you like to eat first? I have cucumbers and chorizo stew."

Despite my fear, my mouth watered. I'd never even seen a whole cucumber, only the peels.

"You have meat?" Swedish asked.

"We're not hungry," Hazel lied. "Answer our questions."

"I'll do more than that," Turning said. "I'll help you reach Port Oro."

A chill silence fell. How did he know we were trying to reach Port Oro?

"Port Oro?" Hazel's eyes narrowed. "What makes you think we're trying to get to Port Oro? I don't know what game you're playing, but—"

He lifted his gnarled hand. "I've known Ekaterina for a very long time."

"You're her friend!" Hazel shook her head in surprise. "Her mysterious friend."

"No way," Swedish muttered. "This foghead?"

Turning arched a bushy eyebrow. "I'd offer you honey bread, but I'm fresh out."

"It *is* you!" I said. Nobody else would know about the honey bread.

197

"Indeed it is, Chess." He looked at me intently. "And I'd very much like to see your eye."

My stomach dropped. Of course he knew about my eye—it seemed like the entire Subassembly knew—but I still felt sick and scared, like I was naked in the middle of a crowd.

"What do you want to see his eye for?" Loretta asked. "I heard it's gross."

Turning smiled faintly but didn't answer her question. "I'd been looking for Ekaterina for a long time. She changed her name thirteen years ago—she wasn't born 'Ekaterina,' you know—and she vanished off the face of the Rooftop."

"This is so purple!" Bea announced from the telescope, totally unaware of the conversation. "I can see everything. Where's our house?"

"I thought she'd fled into the lower slopes," Turning continued, "or even Port Oro. Not the junkyard."

"There's no better hiding place on the Rooftop," Hazel said.

He nodded again. "When I tracked the rumors down, I finally realized where to look. But she was so sick. I—I hadn't expected that. She didn't even recognize me at first."

"She told us you're old friends," Hazel said.

A spark glinted in Turning's tired eyes. "The last time I saw her, years ago, she was standing at the edge of a fire-storm in the middle of the night."

"When she burned Kodoc's house down?" I asked.

"She's a remarkable woman." He steepled his fingers. "However, since Kodoc learned about the unexpected results of his long-ago experiment—"

"What experiment?" Loretta blurted. "What're you talking about?"

"A science experiment," I told her.

"What I'm trying to say," Turning continued, "is that while Kodoc's been searching for you, I've been arranging passage for you, to Port Oro."

"No!" Hazel said, her breath catching. "Truly?"

"Oh, look!" Bea suddenly called, from the telescope. "There's our alley! I bet I can find our shack."

"Truly," Turning told Hazel. "I sent a carrier pigeon last week and asked the Port to come pick up a package. The mutineers aren't overly fond of the Subassembly, but we still work together. They know that we understand the Fog better than anyone alive. And we find them quite useful."

"A package?" Swedish asked. "What kind of package?"

"The five of you." Turning eyed Loretta. "Six, now."

"Whoa," Hazel said. "A ship from the Port? For us?"

Turning nodded. "I think my message was lost, but fortunately I found a coyote willing to take you."

"You didn't!" Hazel said, her eyes dancing. "Get *out*! Really?"

"This foghead's too nice," Loretta muttered, scratching

199

the tattoo on her cheek. "Nobody's this nice without want-ing something."

"If he can heal Mrs. E's fogsickness," I told her, "I don't care about anything else."

"Hey, that's Perry!" Bea fiddled with the telescope's focus. "He's tiny, like an ant. I could crush him!"

"Can you really cure Mrs. E?" Hazel asked Turning.

"*I* can't, no." He smiled softly. "But for my friends on Port Oro, many things are possible."

"That's what she always says."

"She's right. You'll get to the Port, you'll cure Ekaterina, and you'll escape Kodoc."

"But why?" Hazel demanded. "Loretta's right. You must want something."

"What are they doing?" Bea asked the telescope. "That's weird. . . ."

"I want to help my old friend." Turning tugged at his earring. "And I will do anything to keep Kodoc from get-ting his hands on Chess."

Hazel's lips narrowed. "Why is that?"

"Because Chess is the only fog diver who can find the Compass."

"You want a compass?" Loretta asked. "*I* can find you a compass."

"Not a compass," Turning said. "*The* Compass. An ancient machine, buried in the Fog, that controls the nanites."

"Control the what knights?" Loretta had never heard Mrs. E's stories. "The naan knights? You fogheads are even dippier than I—"

"It doesn't matter now," Turning interrupted. "What matters is that I'll send word to the coyote and you'll leave for Port Oro tonight."

"Tonight?" Hazel's sudden smile brightened the room. "That soon?"

"We're really going!" I said, feeling a tingle of excitement. "After all this time—"

"Hazel!" Bea cried at the telescope. "They're ditching our block! They're ditching our shack, and Mrs. E is still inside!"

30

"THEY'RE DOING WHAT?" TURNING asked, sounding uncertain. "Ditching?"

I barely heard him over the blood thundering in my ears. If the bosses ditched our block, Mrs. E would fall into the Fog. This couldn't be happening, not now, not when we were so close to getting to Port Oro. No, no—

"No," Swedish gasped.

Hazel bent over the telescope, and I found myself standing beside her, watching her face. Hazel would say Bea was wrong, and we'd tease her for scaring us. Because she *was* wrong. She had to be.

But just then Hazel made a horrified sound. "They're prepping the platform to ditch. They're halfway done already," she said.

"How—how long do we have?" Bea asked.

"I don't know," Hazel said. "Thirty minutes?"

"We're too far away," Bea wailed. "What do we do? How do we stop them?"

Before I knew what I was doing, I shoved Loretta. She stumbled backward. "Hey!"

"Your friends did this!" I snarled at her. I'd told them we couldn't trust her. I'd told them, and now look what'd happened.

"I'm sorry," she said, her face falling. "I thought they'd wait till nightfall."

I shoved her again, dizzy with fury and fear. "I knew you were bad news. I knew it. If they ditch her, I swear by the Fog that I'll—"

A hand clamped my shoulder. "Please, Chess," Turning said. "Make no vows in anger."

I jerked away. "If anything happens to Mrs. E—"

"Quiet!" Hazel snapped. "Let me think."

I closed my mouth so fast that my teeth clicked. Anger drifted through me in a red haze, but I kept still. Hazel was our only chance.

Turning frowned. "Would someone please tell me what 'ditching'—"

"She said *quiet*," Swedish barked, slamming his palm on the workbench.

Hazel paced, chewing on a knuckle. I watched her. Swedish watched her. We all watched her.

She crossed the floor three times, then stopped and looked at Bea. "The mayfly!"

"The what?" Bea said, her eyes glossy with tears.

"That thopper you called a 'mayfly.' On the hillside airfield. You said you saw it through the telescope. Find it again. Hurry!"

Bea bent over the eyepiece, softly begging the scope for help.

"Ditching," Hazel told Turning, "is when the junkyard bosses flip a section of the slum, dropping everything into the Fog."

He frowned. "That sounds dangerous."

"That's the point," Swedish said.

"They do that on purpose?" Turning asked, a flash of horror in his eyes. "I've seen it, but I thought it was an accident. That's terrible—"

"We need your help," Hazel interrupted, and I'd never been happier to hear the bossy tone in her voice. "Bea's looking for an airfield we saw. Once she finds it, we need you to take us there—fast."

"An airfield? What are you going to do?"

"The same as always," Hazel told him. "Whatever we can."

"Found it!" Bea called.

Turning peered through the eyepieceand muttered fretfully. "Yes," he finally said. "I can get you there."

· · · ·

"But you *must* return." Cog Turning's voice echoed in the gloomy mine tunnel. "After you save Ekaterina, you must return to the Rooftop and find me."

"We will," Hazel told him.

"There's no other way to cure her, there's no other way to save yourselves. There's no other way to get Chess to Port Oro. Promise me you'll return." Turning hesitated at a dark junction. "I should bring you straight to the coyote and send you off."

My breath caught. If he let the bosses ditch Mrs. E, forget about Port Oro—I'd ditch *him*.

"But I can't do that to Ekaterina." Turning looked at each of us in turn. "Promise me you'll come back."

"We promise," Bea said.

Turning nodded, then led us up a rickety ladder into what he called a root cellar. At the far end, he opened a trapdoor in the planked wooden ceiling.

"Turn right on the street," he told us. "The thopper field is down the block."

"Thank you," Hazel told him. "We'll come back with Mrs. E."

I nodded uneasily. We'd snuck into the Rooftop once that day—I wasn't sure we'd get lucky twice.

"I'll speak to the coyote." Turning receded into the darkness. "Take care. You are more important than you know."

We climbed up through the trapdoor into an empty hut

that must've belonged to a farmer or laborer. As we clustered around the door to the street, Bea said, "What did *that* mean? More important than we know?"

"Because of Chess," Hazel said. "And this Compass machine."

"Because he's a fog-sniffing lug nut," Swedish said.

"Yeah," Loretta agreed. "He's as cracked as a glass trampoline."

"What's a trampoline?" Bea asked.

Loretta shrugged. "I don't know, but that guy is a cracked one."

"I like him." I told them over my shoulder. "Sure, that stuff about me is loco, but he said they'll cure Mrs. E."

"Yeah," Swedish said. "And he hired us a coyote."

"Let's go," Hazel said, grabbing Bea's hand.

She headed onto the bustling street, and Swedish and Loretta followed a second later. I patted my hair down, took a deep breath, then stepped into the sunlight.

"Is everyone clear on the plan?" Hazel asked.

Bea nodded. "I jump-start the mayfly."

"I bust heads," Loretta said.

"And we all go down in a blaze of glory," Swedish said as we jogged past a cobbler's shed.

I surprised myself with a laugh. "Our favorite kind of blaze."

Hazel glanced at me. I guess I'd surprised her, too.

Usually I stayed quiet in public, afraid that someone might notice my freak-eye. But even though I was scared for Mrs. E, I was also excited: we finally had a real chance to get to Port Oro.

We brushed past workers hauling crates and clambered over a fence onto the hillside airfield. A few of the gearslingers fiddling with engines and steam organs glanced at us, but nobody raised an alarm. We looked harmless, I guess, just a bunch of kids playing around.

But we weren't playing.. We were fighting for Mrs. E's life.

Bea and Hazel jogged toward the mayfly—that sleek thopper—while the rest of us ambled along behind. In the tool-cluttered outdoor workshop, two gearheads tinkered with the mayfly engine, and a woman in a fancy coat stood nearby, watching with a sour expression.

"She's lovely," Hazel said when she got close enough. "Is she fit to fly?"

"We're fine-tuning the piston array," one of the gearheads told her.

Hazel cocked her head. "Does she *fly*, though?"

"Oh, yes," the woman in the fancy coat said. "She's quite—"

"She flies!" Hazel called, and everyone sprang into action.

Loretta touched her knife to the woman's throat,

whispering threats, and a thump sounded from the other side of the thopper as Swedish clobbered one of the gearheads. I put my arm around the other one and said, "My friends have nasty tempers. Let's keep this quiet."

"You're s-stealing the thopper?" the gearhead stammered. "That's crazy! The guardships will shoot you down. There's nowhere to go."

"In that case," I told him, "there's no reason to make a fuss."

Bea monkeyed with the pistons while Swedish ran his fingers over the controls—then the engine roared to life. Hazel swung into position, Loretta grabbed for a boarding strap, and I scrambled on deck.

"Help!" the woman in the fancy coat screamed. "Somebody, help!"

With a blast of air, the thopper lifted off—and Loretta shouted, "Wait, wait!"

Sure, she could slink through shadows like a hunting cat, but she didn't know anything about boarding airships. She was still dangling halfway off the deck, her boots scrabbling against the hull, trying to get a toehold.

The thopper rose, and I looked down at Loretta and froze. We needed to save Mrs. E, not Loretta. We couldn't even trust her not to stab us.

"Chess!" Hazel snapped. "Get her. Now."

So I hooked my boots into the railing and snagged

Loretta as she started to slip off the hull. I didn't *really* want her to break any bones.

"Climb me like a ladder," I told her.

She grabbed a handful of my jacket, then my pants, pulling herself upward until Hazel heaved her on board. I lay there for a moment, draped over the edge, watching the hillside blur beneath us, praying that Mrs. E was still okay.

After I grabbed the railing and hopped on deck, I found Loretta sitting with her arms around her knees. "Th-thanks," she told me.

"It's nothing," I said, trying to ignore Hazel's dirty look.

"No, I mean it." Loretta swallowed. "I don't like heights. And I know you don't trust me, so—thanks."

"Sure," I said, then turned away to stare anxiously toward the junkyard.

I couldn't spot our neighborhood in the endless sprawl, and my jaw clenched as I pictured Mrs. E drowsing in her bed before the walls started collapsing around her. *We're coming, Mrs. E. Stay safe for three more minutes.*

"Hang on," Hazel called, grabbing a strap behind Swedish. "We've got company."

"C-company?" Loretta gulped.

"A guardship." Hazel grabbed Swedish's shoulder. "Swede, they're behind that rise."

I scanned the sky and saw a guardship veering toward us, a sleek craft with jointed fins, coming fast. There was nowhere to hide.

"We can't outrun *that*," I said.

31

"HE'S FAST, BUT HE can't turn," Swedish told me, yanking a lever. "No rooftop puddle-jumper is keeping me away from Mrs. E."

He swung the mayfly into the air, rising toward the clouds. As we climbed higher, the guardship drew closer. Loretta moaned while Bea danced around the engine, adjusting gears. Swedish hammered a soundless tune on the steam organ keyboard, his fingers a blur, and Hazel stood behind him, her braids flying.

"The shack's three wisps to your left, Swede," she shouted. "The guardship's five hundred yards and closing."

"That's what he thinks," Swedish said, aiming the thopper higher and higher.

Flying slower and slower as we rose.

"Four hundred yards," Hazel said, and shot me a look.

Sometimes with Hazel there was no need for words. "Bea!" I yelled. "Fasten down, this is going to get bumpy!"

Loretta looked at me with frightened eyes, so I unspooled a jack line and handed it to her, saying "Wrap this around yourself."

"Three hundred fifty yards!" Hazel shouted.

"Wh-why?" Loretta asked me.

"Because any second now," I said, "Swedish is going to start *flying* this thing."

"What's he doing now?" she moaned, and started winding the rope around her arm.

"Three hundred!"

I yanked the rope from Loretta's hands and strapped her down properly. The wind whipped my hair from my face, and she gasped. "Your *eye*! It's full of Fog—and it's *moving*. That's freaky!"

"Yeah," I said.

"*Totally* freaky!"

"Yup," I said.

"Dude," she said. "You're a Fog-eye."

"I know!"

"Wait, *you're* the kid Kodoc is looking for! You're the most wanted person in the entire Rooft—" she shrieked as the mayfly jerked.

"Two hundred yards!" Hazel shouted. "Swede, they've got harpoons cocked."

The deck was almost vertical. I tugged my hair into place, wedged myself against a boiler vent, and watched the guardship climbing after us, my heart thundering.

"One fifty!" Hazel shouted. "Swede, stop showing off!"

Swedish laughed and flicked a valve open.

The engine sputtered, and stalled. Then stopped.

A weightless silence surrounded us. No pistons pumped, no foggium flowed. We hung motionless in the air, aimed almost directly upward.

Then the pneumatic *pop-pop* of harpoons sounded behind us. Airtroopers shouted, and the mayfly dropped like a stone. The harpoons missed us by five feet. Wind lashed the hulls, and through my fear I felt a tug of excitement: it reminded me of diving into the Fog.

When the guardship roared past, our little mayfly rocked in its wake. In five seconds, the airship was a hundred yards above us, and heading away, while we were still plummeting toward the lower slope.

Swedish wrestled the wheel, and Bea stepped on a hose to adjust the flow of foggium. Loretta screamed, Hazel whooped, and the engine roared to life. The rudders caught the wind and we swooped toward the slum, ten feet over the rooftops. The bridge whirred past, then shacks and alleys blurred beneath us.

"Swedish did that on *purpose*," Loretta said, through chattering teeth. "If we live, I'm going to kill him."

Then a terrible wrenching noise overtook us: the sound of a junkyard neighborhood being ditched. Cracks appeared along the edges of a platform and all the shanties and trash—and Mrs. E, still in her bedroom—started sliding downhill. I leaned forward, urging the mayfly on.

I scanned the slum, my heart clenched in my chest. A hill of garbage sped past beneath us. A flock of startled seagulls screamed around us. I spotted the clearing where we'd stumbled onto gang kids playing bootball—but the cluster of balloons was gone. The bosses weren't trying to keep this part of the slum aloft, not anymore.

My throat dried and sweat stung my eyes. I saw the water hole, the alley stalls . . . then our half-collapsed block came into view, and the shack was still standing! I exhaled in relief—and saw a shadow flickering on the roofs beneath us.

I glanced over my shoulder and gasped.

The guardship was a hundred yards behind us, closing fast. Two cannon ports slid open along the prow.

"Cannons behind us!" I screamed. "The guardship, they're firing *now*!"

Swedish hammered the keyboard and the thopper rolled to the left so hard that a rudder snapped. A second later, the cannons roared like a thunderclap. The barrage slammed into the slum, blasting tents into scraps . . . and one cannonball clipped the mayfly.

Behind me, Bea gave an agonized shout that turned my blood to ice.

Despite the wild wobbling of the deck, I spun and staggered toward her. But she didn't look hurt. As I got closer, I saw that she hadn't yelled from pain. She'd yelled because the engine was on fire. Orange flames spewed from a broken hose, and smoke poured behind the mayfly like a black river.

"How bad is it?" I yelled.

"She's dead!" Bea called back. "We're going down!"

32

"SWEDE," I SHOUTED, TURNING toward the cockpit. "The engine's dead!"

Trash tumbled along the alleys below us as the slum platform tilted. The slimy river of the Spew changed course, sweeping away a cluster of stalls.

"Crash-land at home," Hazel bellowed to Swedish.

"Are you peanuts?" Loretta asked. "That whole block's going to ditch!"

"Mrs. E's in there," I told her.

"Everyone up front!" Hazel yelled, above the sound of the shrieking engine. "Bea, quick!"

With the deck shuddering beneath me, I dragged Loretta to the prow. When Bea arrived a second later, I swung her between me and Hazel, so we'd cushion her when we crashed.

Plumes of dust rose from collapsing shanties, twenty feet below the thopper.

Ten feet.

Five feet.

When the rooftops were two feet below us, Swedish veered into an alley like it was a landing strip. Trash flew everywhere, shacks started falling like dominos, and we hit the platform so hard that my knees buckled. We slid fifty feet, spun twice, and stopped.

For a long moment, nobody spoke, as the neighborhood shook apart around us.

"That wasn't so bad," Hazel said.

Bea giggled a little hysterically.

"You all," Loretta moaned, "are insane."

"At least the roof-troopers are writing us off as dead," I said, my voice oddly steady as I watched the guardship returning to the Rooftop.

"Look at that," Swedish said, swinging to the ground. "Twenty feet from the shack, and she landed sweet as berry pie."

"Let's go!" Hazel called. "We've got to get to Mrs. E."

She and Bea hopped down from the thopper, stumbling on the tilting platform.

"C'mon," I said, giving Loretta my hand.

She swung to the quaking ground, then looked up at my face. "Your eye's not *that* freaky," she said apologetically.

"Sure," I said. "Everyone's got one."

"Those white swirls are kind of neat," she said as we started trotting toward the shack. "Like, um, snowballs."

"Snowballs?"

She flashed a gap-toothed smile. "Except totally freaky."

I gave a huff of laughter; then a wall buckled nearby and we jumped away. Debris tumbled along the tilting platform as we scrambled after Hazel and the others. An avalanche of noise surrounded us—buildings collapsing, metal screaming—and trash battered us until we shoved into the shack.

Swedish staggered from the bedroom with a limp Mrs. E in his arms.

"How is she?" I yelled.

"Sleeping!" he grunted.

She was only half asleep, actually. She peered around the crumbling room and mumbled, "Look at this mess—no dessert for you!" then closed her eyes.

"Well, we're here," Loretta said as she wiped blood from her split lip. "Now what?"

Swedish plowed toward the entryway. "C'mon!"

"Hurry!" Hazel followed Swedish, struggling uphill as the shack floor tilted. "C'mon!"

"What are we doing?" Loretta asked, grabbing the table for support.

"Going to the thopper," I said.

"The thopper crashed."

I pushed her after Hazel. "Not *that* thopper."

Loretta took off, but I hesitated. I wanted to run into Mrs. E's room and grab my dad's scrapbook from the shelf. I couldn't leave it behind. But the platform jerked so hard that the rain barrel jounced across the room, and I knew I was out of luck—the entire shack was about to collapse. I scrambled after Loretta into the entryway. Plastic jugs and broken crates tumbled everywhere as we helped Swedish lower Mrs. E through the hatch into the workshop under the shaking platform.

The slum gave another sharp shudder and I slammed against the wall, then slid to the ground in a painful daze. Groaning, I crawled back to the hatch and wriggled through, into Bea's workshop. The floor was at a steep diagonal. Tools cascaded off the workbench. The foggium compressor rolled into the hole where the thopper dangled by heavy chains, then disappeared into the Fog below.

A racing thopper didn't have room for passengers, so Swedish was hunched in the cockpit with Bea on his lap and Mrs. E squeezed beside them. Hazel straddled the forward hull, holding the butterfly valve. On the far side of the thopper, Loretta desperately wound an inner tube around her wrist, strapping herself to a pump vent.

The ticking and whirring of the thopper engine grew louder. The wings spread to catch the wind, and foggium flowed through ignition chambers.

"Chess!" Hazel shouted. "Jump!"

I scrambled toward the hole in the floor—or what *used* to be the floor. I balanced on the edge, aimed for the fattest part of the thopper—

And Hazel screamed, "*Wait!* Stop!"

33

MY ARMS WINDMILLED, AND I barely caught myself. A shower of tiny springs ricocheted past my head and tumbled through the hole into the Fog.

"The chain!" Hazel pointed to the rear of the thopper. "The chain's stuck!"

Usually Swedish released the support chains from inside the cockpit, but with the platform slanting, the rear chain had snagged in an ugly snarl of metal. And if the thopper was stuck, we'd be ditched into the Fog in just a few seconds.

I blocked out the roar of the demolition and jumped. I caught the chain, slid down, and stomped at the snarl. It unraveled immediately, and I felt a flash of satisfaction. Ha! Can't beat a tetherboy!

Then it hit me: I'd just freed the chain from the thopper, but I was still *hanging from* the chain.

Huh. Maybe I should've thought that through.

Before the chain swung me too far away, I dropped. I hit the thopper near the fantail and couldn't get a grip. Rivets fell from the workshop and jabbed my face as I slid backward, digging my fingernails into a seam in the metal. Just when I started to fall, Swedish rolled the thopper sideways, which lifted me upward until the hull was beneath me.

I grabbed a hitch and tried not to faint as a downpour of trash roared into the Fog a few feet behind me. Bea had designed the thopper for speed and handling, but it was a one-person craft. Weighed down by six of us, it wallowed beneath the wildly tilting platform.

With a grind of protest, the thopper started lumbering forward, and soon we were flying just under the slum, in the fifty-foot gap above the white froth of Fog. Slime dripped from the platforms overhead, and huge fans whirred as I straddled the rear section of the hull. My head throbbed, and my shoulders and hands burned.

A prop crew stopped working as we flew past, and shouted jeers at us. One girl started climbing a ladder— probably to tell the bosses she'd seen us—and fear squeezed my heart like a fist. If we didn't move fast, the bosses would toss nets over the edges of the platforms to trap us. That way they could ditch us personally.

Did the roof-troopers know that the kids from the jewelry store were the same ones who'd swooped over the junkyard? Had Kodoc found out my name yet? Did he know my face and my crew? I could barely breathe until we emerged from the shadow of the junkyard.

Then I slumped in relief—we'd made it! Except for the fact that we were stuck on the Fog, in an overloaded thopper, without anywhere to land.

I looked over my shoulder and watched the slum recede into the distance. The only home I'd ever known had been tossed like garbage into the Fog. My neighborhood was gone forever—the clearing where I'd played bootball, the corner where Mrs. E once kissed my scraped elbow. My bracers were gone, my harness and my bedroll. So was the table where we ate, where we'd laughed and talked and argued. And my father's scrapbook.

Everything was gone. I didn't have a home anymore. None of us did.

"When I was a girl," Mrs. E said suddenly, "everyone called me Kat. Short for Katherine."

Hazel leaned toward her. "Yes, Mrs. E?"

"Don't interrupt! Everyone called me Kat, but I also *had* a cat. I called my cat Me."

I glanced at Bea. We hadn't heard that one before.

"So we were Kat and Me," Mrs. E said. "Except I was Kat and the cat was Me. Her real name was Meow."

"That's sweet," Hazel said. "Now stay still and—"

"Back then," Mrs. E said, "the Subassembly and the roof-troopers worked together. Not like today."

"The fogheads worked with the army?" Loretta asked.

"The roof-troopers are more than just an army," Hazel told her. "They do everything for the Five Families. They're in charge of schools, banks—"

"Some are scientists," Mrs. E interrupted in a lilting tone that sounded nothing like her normal voice. "Trying to find a way to control the Fog. In the old days, they wanted to harness the power of the Fog into engines and machines."

"You mean foggium?" Loretta asked.

Mrs. E giggled, which made my stomach sink. I hated when she started acting like a little girl. It felt like the fogsickness was mocking her.

"The Subassembly discovered foggium," she said, "but the roof-troopers built the refineries. Did I ever tell you about my cat?"

"Her name was Me," Hazel said.

"Don't be silly!" Mrs. E snapped. "Her name was Petunia. Now stop your chattering. I'm sleepy."

An uncomfortable silence fell over us. None of us wanted to face the fact that Mrs. E was slipping away. Swedish wiped his eyes, Hazel gazed into the distance, and I clung to the thopper, trying to keep my mind blank as we soared over the Fog, the valves clicking and the wings heaving us through the air.

Heading where? Nowhere.

The thought chilled me. "How much fuel do we have?" I asked.

"An hour's worth," Hazel told me. "Maybe two, with a tailwind."

"Shouldn't we head back?" Loretta asked, her face buried in her arms.

"Back to what?"

"The slum?"

"The bosses would kill us."

Bea bit her lip. "How about the Rooftop? We can find Mr. Turning again."

"The guardships would kill us." Hazel rested her palm on Mrs. E's forehead, checking for a fever. "And then Kodoc would kill us all over again."

"Yeah," I said. "But if we stay out here, the crash will kill us first."

34

NOBODY SAID ANYTHING FOR a long time. The quiet felt ominous.

"Okay," Hazel finally said. "I've got a plan."

"What kind of plan?" I asked.

"The regular kind."

"You mean desperate and loco?"

"Not necessarily," Swedish told me. "She could mean risky and doomed."

"You're both right!" Hazel said, brushing braids from her face. "This one is desperate *and* risky."

"In that case," I said, "I'm in."

Swedish snorted. "Yeah. What's the worst that could happen?"

"*This* is the worst that could happen." Loretta raised

her head and looked faintly green behind her tattoos. "I'd sell my nose for a block of solid slum."

For some reason, her misery cheered me. At least I wasn't turning green. "Maybe not a *whole* block, Loretta—your nose is pretty small."

She glared at me, then dropped her head again, wrapped in her private despair.

I scooted forward. "What's the plan, Hazel? We all grow wings?"

"We'll be angels soon enough," Swedish muttered, "once we crash."

"We're not crashing," Hazel said. "We're heading for the shipping lanes."

I steadied myself. "You mean the lanes that Mrs. E always told us to stay away from, because the merchants might report us to Lord Kodoc?"

She nodded. "Exactly."

"That whole 'let's grow wings' thing is sounding better and better," Swedish said.

"Don't worry," Hazel said. "We'll keep out of sight until we can intercept a merchant ship."

I gaped at her. "Until we can *what*?"

"Intercept a merchant ship," she repeated. "We'll offer them the diamond in exchange for passage back to the Rooftop."

"You want to swoop down on a merchant convoy? And before they open fire, you'll start *haggling*?"

"That's right."

"Then they'll bring us back to the Rooftop? To find Cog Turning?"

"Yup. And he'll bring us to his coyote friend."

"Wow," I said. "There's a word for that."

"Deranged?" Loretta asked. "Suicidal?"

"Brilliant," I said, and Hazel's laugh rang out across the Fog.

"I thought you'd like it," she said.

A gust of wind rocked the thopper, and the gyroscopes whirred. Bea worried that the clockwork sounded draggy, so I held her legs as she dangled overboard, fiddling with the torsion cables and grousing about the dress Hazel had made her wear. The breeze calmed as Swedish angled the thopper around a crooked pillar of Fog and we drifted over a misty white ravine.

"Slow her down, Swede," Hazel finally said. "This is the shipping lane."

"How does she know?" Loretta asked me. "Fog all looks the same to me."

"She knows Fog like you know fighting," I told her. "If Hazel says we're here, we're here."

Loretta scratched the scar on her arm. "When do we run out of fuel?"

I shrugged. "Forty minutes? Maybe an hour."

"That's all we've got?"

"No," I said. "We've also got Hazel."

"That's why she's the captain," Bea told Loretta, clasping my arm and pulling herself upright. "She'll get us out of this."

Twenty minutes later, though, even Bea looked nervous, scanning a thick cloud bank—of real clouds, not Fog—hoping for a glimpse of a merchant convoy. We drifted in aimless circles, but there were no airships anywhere.

"I wonder what a cucumber tastes like," I said to break the silence.

"Watermelon rind," Swedish immediately answered. "Except sour."

"Nah," Bea said. "I bet it's more like pigeon."

"Pigeon?" Loretta asked.

"Sure. Everything tastes like pigeon."

"But pigeon's a bird, and cucumber's a fruit."

"Cucumber's not a fruit," Swedish said. "Now *berry* is a fruit."

"I'm pretty sure cucumber's a fruit," Bea said.

"Hey, Swede," Loretta said. "Have you ever tasted a berry pie?"

"I saw one once," he told her, "when I was a kid. Some rooftoppers came around with free food. Mostly slop, but right there in the middle . . . a berry pie."

"You get a taste?"

"Well, the neighborhood boss had sent me begging, y'know? So I grabbed the pie and ran it back to him."

"Did he give you a bite?"

"Gave me a smack," Swedish said. "But I still remember how it smelled."

"There!" Hazel pointed into the thick mist. "A merchant ship!"

A dark speck grew in the cloud bank, then turned into a sweeping airship with a massive cylindrical balloon. Cannons and portholes dotted the hull, nanofiber propellers shone in the sunlight, and two smaller airships prowled alongside—armored gunships with chain guns and flamethrowers.

"That's no merchant ship," Swedish said. "Check out the diving platform."

I shaded my eyes and looked closer. Underneath the ship, a dozen tethers and winches were spaced across a massive scaffolding, like hundreds of ladders lashed together.

"That's the ultimate salvage raft," I said.

"What?" Loretta asked. "I can't see anything."

"They've got ten or fifteen tetherkids diving at once," I told her. "Look at all those winches."

"Diving for salvage?" she asked.

"I guess," I said. "They must be looking for something *big*."

"She looks like a Five Family ship," Hazel said, her voice tight.

"Who cares?" Loretta said. "Either they help us or we crash."

"At least she's not a warship." Hazel twisted one of her

braids. "Approach them slowly, Swede. Everyone look desperate and harmless."

"We *are* desperate and harmless," I reminded her.

"Then it'll be easy."

Swedish swung the thopper toward the convoy, and I read the name on the big ship's hull: *Teardrop.*

"Weird name," I said.

"Maybe they're merchants and that's their motto." Loretta deepened her voice. "'On the *Teardrop*, we're crying for a sale.'"

"'Prices so low,'" I intoned, "'you'll weep with joy.'"

"Would you two shut up?" Hazel said.

One of the armored gunships swooped forward, and Hazel waved her veil like a white flag and shouted, "We're a salvage crew!"

The gunship heaved to alongside us. Sheets of riveted metal blurred closer, and fumes seeped from brass nozzles. The wind from the gunship's gearwork fans rocked the thopper, and armored panels slid open to reveal airtroopers pointing weapons at us.

"We're a salvage crew," Hazel repeated. "Don't shoot!"

"That's no salvage raft," said a grizzled woman in an officer's jacket. She peered closer. "And what're you doing with that old lady?"

"Um, we lost our raft, ma'am, but—"

"On second thought, I don't care about your sad story," the woman said. "All I care about is that you're interrupting

Lord Kodoc's search."

My breath caught and my heart clamped tight. *Kodoc.* This was Kodoc's ship.

Darkness crept in at the edges of my vision, and the day turned murky. I felt dizzy and doomed, like in nightmares when I couldn't escape from a monster. Bea whimpered and Hazel went speechless for a long horrifying moment. Even Loretta fell silent.

The grizzled woman didn't seem to notice. "I'll give you thirty seconds to start running. Then we'll open fire."

35

"WE'RE ALMOST OUT OF fuel!" Loretta cried. "We can't reach the slum!"

"Too bad," the woman said. "His lordship's time is more important than your lives."

"Wait, ma'am." Hazel straightened up, trying to look official while perched on the wobbly thopper. "We, um, have something to sell."

"Hazel, no!" Bea whispered. "Not to *Kodoc*."

"We don't have a choice," I croaked.

One of the airtroopers laughed at Hazel. "What are slumkids selling? A handful of rust?"

"A ring," Hazel said. "A diamond."

The woman paused. "Show me," she said. "Come closer."

Hazel glanced at me, biting her lower lip. If Kodoc and his troops didn't buy the diamond, we'd crash. But what if Kodoc saw us? He might recognize Mrs. E—though she was so frail that she hardly looked like herself. Or worse—he might check my eye.

Mrs. E's words of warning echoed in my mind: *he'll kidnap Chess and work him to death.* He'd drop me in the white, in an endless search for some ancient machine that might not exist, and I'd never see the light of day again. Even if I succeeded, Kodoc would toss me overboard when he was through with me. But we had to take the chance. I'd rather become one of Kodoc's lab rats than lose my whole family to the Fog.

"Go on, Swede." I exhaled shakily. "She can't see the ring, not this far away."

Swedish edged the thopper nearer to the gunship, and when Hazel opened the lid of the box, the diamond glinted in the sun.

The officer muttered to her soldiers. "Keep still," she told Hazel. "We'll tow you to his lordship."

"Let's do this here," Hazel said tightly. "I'll give you the diamond, you bring us to the Rooftop. No need to bother his lordship."

"You'd trust me with your diamond?"

Hazel bowed her head. "Only because I don't have a choice."

"Slumgirl's got spirit," an airtrooper laughed.

"I don't have a choice, either," the officer told Hazel before turning to a soldier. "Heliograph his lordship and inform him of the situation."

A moment later, a polished copper plate—the heliograph—flashed a pattern of reflected sunlight at the bigger ship, passing the message along.

The thopper trembled beneath me, and I trembled right back. We were trapped on the Fog, with Lord Kodoc only a hundred feet away. The engine coughed, and I wondered how long we had before we ran out of fuel. Ten minutes? Twenty?

Then a light flashed from the *Teardrop*, and the officer said, "This is your lucky day. Lord Kodoc will grant you an audience."

"Great," Hazel said.

"Watch your tongue, though. You don't want to make him angry."

I cringed at the thought. A perfectly happy Kodoc scared me to death—I didn't even want to *think* about an angry one.

Swedish glanced at Hazel, as if he expected her to tell him to fly away. But she only nodded, so he angled the thopper toward the *Teardrop*. The big airship was already rising below us, like one of Hazel's drawings of a whale breaching the surface of the ocean.

First the massive steel-ribbed balloon loomed into sight, then came the mainsails, and after that an endless sweep of rigging. A few seconds later, the quarterdeck drew level with us, and I gasped at its grandeur. Polished floorboards gleamed in the sun, tidy sailors adjusted shining valves, and tables laden with charts and food scattered the deck.

A man with a long face stepped to the railing. His fancy green jacket shone in the sunlight. His glossy hair sparkled, and even his skin shone. He was the cleanest thing I'd ever seen, and when he inspected us through a monocle, I felt like a dirty ant on the wrong side of a magnifying glass.

Hazel gave a weird seated curtsy and whispered, "Bow! Everyone, heads down!"

I bowed, happy for an excuse to hide my face. Of course, there was no way that Kodoc would recognize me. He'd never seen me, not even as a baby. And I knew he wouldn't *personally* check the eyes of every kid he met—he'd leave that to his troopers. Definitely. No question about it. I wasn't scared of being discovered, my skin wasn't clammy, and my mind wasn't blanking. No, I was trembling for completely different reasons.

Sure I was.

Then he spoke. "Am I to understand that you—of all people—have in your possession a diamond?"

"Yes, Lord Kodoc," Hazel said, straightening from her curtsy.

"And you expect me to purchase it?"

"We hope you will, your lordship."

"You're hardly in a position to bargain, girl." His cold gaze flicked toward Mrs. E's slumped form, and he cocked an eyebrow. "If you keep the diamond, you'll be committing a crime punishable by death."

"That's why we flew into the Fog, your lordship. With, um, our grandmother. To sell the diamond to a person of good standing, a nobleman who'd treat us fairly, instead of a lower-slope—"

"Yes, yes, I take your point," Lord Kodoc said, a hint of cold amusement in his voice. "So you wish to sell a diamond. In exchange for what consideration?"

I didn't know what "consideration" meant, but Hazel said, "We beg safe passage to the Rooftop, your lordship, and permission to remain on the lower slopes."

Lord Kodoc laughed, a slithery sound. "*That* is your dream? To live on the lower slopes, packed together like animals?"

"Yes, your lordship."

Lord Kodoc swept us with his monocle. "Very well. Consider the diamond sold. I will drop you in the lower slopes."

"Thank you!" Hazel gushed. "Thank you, your lord—"

"Now bring that pathetic ship to the landing dock," Kodoc interrupted, turning away to grab a wineglass from a tray.

"See, Loretta?" Bea said. "I told you Hazel would save us."

Swedish swiveled the thopper toward the landing dock, and I clenched the hull so hard that my hands ached. "Save us"? Docking on Kodoc's ship was like a mouse hiding inside a cat's mouth.

"Wait!" Lord Kodoc said as he turned to inspect us. "You're a salvage crew? Which one's the tetherkid?"

After a terrified second, I raised my hand.

"I lost a diver yesterday." He swirled the wine in his glass. "Fifth one this month. You'll take her place."

"Yes, sir," I said in a tiny voice.

"Junkyard tetherkids are worthless until my people train them," he observed, "but an empty harness is even worse than an incompetent diver—"

He stopped suddenly, staring at me. Like he saw past my hair, straight to my eye. No, like he saw past my *face*, straight into my *thoughts*.

My throat clenched and my skin felt too small for my body. Seconds ticked past. I hunched my shoulders, listening to the engines, feeling the chill wind of the propellers.

Then Kodoc called, "Helmsman! Bring me closer!"

The big airship swept toward the thopper, like a massive hand swatting at a fly. The hull stopped ten feet away, and Lord Kodoc's slithery voice said, "Look at me when I talk to you, boy."

My stomach dropped, but I lifted my head a bit. "Sorry."

"Higher," Kodoc told me.

I moved my chin an inch.

"I know you," he said, almost too softly for me to hear.

"I—I don't think so, my lord."

"You're him." His gaze sharpened. "You're mine. You *survived*."

The world narrowed into a tunnel between Kodoc and me. Nothing else existed. My mind screamed, *You don't know me, you don't know anything about me!* but my mouth refused to form words, and I just sat there, silent and frozen.

"Show me your right eye," Kodoc said.

"No," I breathed.

Lord Kodoc smashed his wineglass against the deck. "Show me the eye that I gave you!"

Bea made a frightened noise that I barely heard over the rush of blood in my ears. I couldn't help myself: with a shaking hand, I brushed the hair from my freak-eye.

For a terrible second, Kodoc stared at me. His face burned with a feverish hunger as he whispered, "You. You're finally mine."

My arms started trembling, and I swallowed hard, too scared to speak.

"I'd hoped to intercept some mutineers who'd been pestering me," he said offhandedly, though his glittering eyes never left my face. "I never dreamed you'd fly out here to meet me. What a cooperative boy. What is your name?"

I swallowed again. "Ch-Chess."

"No." His smile made me shiver. "Your name is whatever I call you."

I trembled harder, so scared that all I could say was "Yes, s-sir."

"Bring that thopper to the landing dock," Kodoc ordered Swedish. "*Now!*"

36

SWEDISH GLANCED AT HAZEL for instructions. She bit her lip, and I saw in her face that she'd run out of ideas, which scared me as much as Kodoc . . . almost.

"Do what he says," she told him.

"No way," Swedish snarled. "I'd rather crash."

"Me, too—but we're not going to lose Bea."

"Don't blame me!" Bea squeaked. "*I'd* rather crash."

"I wouldn't," Loretta muttered.

"You don't get a vote," I told Bea shakily. "Head for the landing dock, Swedish."

He started to answer, and a blast of cannon fire roared so loud that my ears rang. Wood splintered, metal shrieked. Airtroopers screamed in pain and fear.

241

"We're under attack!" a trooper shouted. "*Mutineers!* Return fire, return fire!"

"Grab those slumkids!" Lord Kodoc snarled. "Get me that thopper!"

"I can't bring her around, m'lord," the helmsman answered. "Not with mutineers attacking."

"No excuses!" Lord Kodoc ordered. "I want that boy!"

"Dive!" Hazel screamed at Swedish. "Dive!"

That was the best idea I'd heard all year. "Now!" I yelled. "Go-go-*go*!"

Bea hugged Mrs. E to keep her steady, and the thopper plunged downward. A ripple of flame shot through the air where we'd been a moment before. Chains whirled and harpoons hissed, and Lord Kodoc shouted commands as the *Teardrop* swung closer, almost batting the thopper from the sky.

Two airtroopers on a lower deck hurled grappling hooks at us, but they missed when Swedish corkscrewed into a cloud of cannon smoke. Voices cried, hoses hissed, and splinters rained around us. I hugged the hull as we swooped lower. Hazel screamed at Swedish, and Bea screamed at the engine, and Loretta just screamed.

The thopper shuddered, then leveled out. With the noise behind us, I lifted my head and saw that we were skimming along the jagged surface of the Fog. The battle still raged, but all I heard were Kodoc's words: *you're finally mine.*

He scared me more than Perry, more than the junkyard bosses. Maybe even more than driftsharks. He'd looked at me like I was an object, a *thing*. Something in his eyes made me shrivel, made my bones turn to twigs. Something in his voice when he'd shouted, *I want that boy!*

My mind stuttered over my fears until a *boom* made me look upward.

I scanned the smoke and flame, then spotted a mutineer warship that must've slunk into attack range while the roof-trooper ships were surrounding us. Looking closer, I recognized the cigar-shaped zeppelin of the mutineer airship, and the armored bronze bands.

"It's Vidious!" I said, not quite believing my eyes. "It's the *Night Tide!*"

Swedish glanced higher. "What's he doing?"

"Probably calling Kodoc a 'poppet.'"

"He's not alone." Hazel pointed to the sun shining above the battle. "There's Captain Nisha."

I squinted into the light but didn't see anything. Then a shadow detached from the sun—and a second mutineer warship dropped from the sky to blast the *Teardrop* from above.

"Never thought I'd be glad to see mutineer warships," I said.

Kodoc's ship was quick for her size, but not quick enough. Cannon fire pocked her quarterdeck and harpoons stabbed the steel-ribbed balloon that kept her aloft.

The armored gunships returned fire, but a few mutie airsailors still slid down the harpoon lines from Nisha's warship, almost like tetherkids, and landed on the *Tear-drop*'s balloon.

Hazel shaded her eyes and looked up in awe. "Nisha's flying the *Anvil Rose*. Now *that's* a beautiful ship—"

"I hate to interrupt," Swedish said, his voice tight, "but we're into the dregs of the foggium."

Loretta gasped, and I said, "How long've we got?"

"Five minutes."

Hazel closed her eyes. Three seconds passed. Then ten. Then she opened her eyes and said, "Turn around and head back to the battle."

Back to the battle? I gulped. That meant back to Kodoc.

Loretta groaned and Bea's eyes widened, but Swedish just tilted the thopper into a curve and started climbing toward the noise and smoke and danger.

"His fancy lordship wants Chess," Loretta told Hazel. "What are you going to do, hand him over?"

"You *can't!*" Bea said.

"It's okay," I said, despite the lump in my throat. "We don't have a choice. We're running out of fuel."

"We're not flying to Kodoc." Hazel nudged Swedish. "Head higher, toward the *Anvil Rose*."

For a moment, nobody spoke. Then Loretta asked, her voice faint, "You want to start chatting with mutineers in the middle of a sky battle?"

"No," I said, suddenly awed. "She wants to sell them a diamond."

"It's worth a try," Hazel said. "We're not letting that creep get his hands on Chess."

I looked away from the fiery combat to stare at Hazel, because she was even more impressive than a flying death match.

She never panicked. When *I* got scared, my mind blanked and I froze. Not Hazel. Instead, she accepted every new problem and immediately calculated the best response. Maybe we'd only have a 50 percent chance of success, maybe only 10. Heck, if we only had a *1* percent chance of survival, she'd just grit her teeth and grab at that tiny sliver of hope.

I'd dived into uncharted Fog for three years and seen things nobody else had even imagined, but I'd never seen anything like Hazel.

37

AN UGLY RIPPING SOUND yanked my attention back to the battle. Mutineers and roof-troopers fought hand to hand on the *Teardrop*'s ribbed balloon, and through the smoke I glimpsed figures tossing buckets of sand on the flames. As Vidious blasted the big warship, Nisha poured fire at the escorting gunships. War chains whirled, harpoons spiderwebbed the sky . . . and the *Teardrop* spun and retreated.

A cheer rang out from the mutineer ships.

"Kodoc's running!" Loretta said. "The muties must've hit something important."

"But they didn't," Bea said, a worried note in her voice.

"Then why's he taking off?"

"It doesn't make sense," Bea told Loretta. "What's he doing, Cap'n?"

"I don't know." Hazel wiped her braids away from her face. "But there's no way he's giving up. You heard how much he wants Chess."

"Yeah, I've got a few questions about that," Loretta said.

"I'll tell you all about it," Swedish said, "if we're still alive in five minutes."

The thopper engine sputtered as we sped higher, watching the Rooftop ships retreat toward the cloud bank. Repair crews swarmed the mutineer warships, and everything ran so smoothly that I couldn't help feeling a spark of admiration. But mostly I was afraid that our five minutes of fuel were already down to a few seconds.

As we approached the *Anvil Rose*, a few mutineers glanced at the thopper, but nobody said anything until Vidious noticed us.

"Oy, Nisha!" he called to his sister's airship. "Look what washed up on our shore!"

"Who are they?" she yelled back.

"That salvage crew from yesterday. They're flying a thopper now, clinging to the hull like fleas on a dog."

"We're in our thopper," Hazel told Vidious as we hovered beside his airship, "because we had a spot of trouble with one of our balloons."

"Did you hear, Nisha? 'A spot of trouble' with that junky

raft." Vidious laughed. "Now, my poppets, you find me on the horns of a dilemma. On the one hand—" He stopped abruptly, and told his sister, "The little one is staring at my forehead, looking for horns."

"Sorry," Bea mumbled.

"The 'horns of a dilemma' means having two bad choices, poppet. On the one hand—"

The thopper jerked as a piston misfired, and Swedish muttered, "We're running out of time. . . ."

"On the one hand," Vidious repeated, "I'm in a generous mood, as we just repaid Kodoc for attacking my sister. And we needed to chase him off, in any case. To keep him from getting in the way while we take care of our . . . real task."

Nisha swung onto the railing of the *Anvil Rose*, her blond hair wild in the wind. "Those slumkids helped us win, Vid," she called. "With their well-timed distraction."

"On the other hand," Vidious said, ignoring his sister, "I recall saying that if I saw you again, I'd send you crashing into the Fog."

"That was before the whole 'well-timed distraction' thing!" I reminded him.

"True," he said. "But I hate to go back on my word."

"If you drop us," Hazel told him, lifting her left hand, "you drop *this*, too."

She twirled her wrist, and the ring glinted on her finger.

I held my breath as the captains exchanged a glance, and felt a glimmer of hope. Maybe we would actually pull this off. Then the thopper engine gasped, and my hope was replaced by anxiety. *Hurry up!*

"So *that's* what the tetherboy was hiding yesterday," Nisha said, raking me with her gaze.

"Give me the diamond," Vidious told Hazel, "and I'll refrain from sinking you."

"The diamond is yours," Hazel said, "if you'll take us to Port Oro."

Nisha laughed, a silvery sound. "You want to switch sides? Join the mutineers?"

"Yes, ma'am," Hazel told her.

The thopper trembled again, and I saw Swedish wince. We were running on fumes.

"I'll bring you to the Port, poppet, when we're done here," Vidious called to Hazel, rubbing the scar on his cheek. "But if the diamond's fake, I'll toss you overboard. Is that a deal?"

"No," Hazel told him. "If the diamond's fake, Captain *Nisha* will throw us overboard. I'm not bringing my crew onto the *Night Tide*."

"Your engine is gasping," Vidious said. "You're not in a position to—"

"Permission to come aboard?" Hazel asked Nisha.

"You seem to have a talent for infuriating my brother,"

249

Nisha told her. "I like that in a girl. Of course you're welcome aboard."

Hazel immediately said, "Go, Swede, *now*!"

When Swedish tapped the keyboard, the thopper sputtered forward.

Then, just twenty feet from the *Anvil Rose*, the wings twitched.

Vapor spat from the vents.

The clockwork engine squealed.

Our fuel ran out, and we fell from the sky.

38

THE THOPPER PLUMMETED. I gasped, and Bea grabbed my hand. I wanted to tell everyone that I was sorry. Sorry for finding the diamond too late, sorry for not curing Mrs. E. Sorry for the Fog in my eye. I wanted to tell them that they weren't just my crew, they were my family.

And . . . *WHAM!*

A silver bolt slammed into the hull.

The thopper bucked, and I squeezed Bea's hand. Loretta screamed and flew overboard—and kept screaming as she dangled from her inner-tube-knotted wrist.

Swedish yelled, "'Retta!" and we stopped falling. The silver bolt was a harpoon. The *Anvil Rose* had speared us from above.

After the mutineers heaved the thopper onto the war-ship's deck, Hazel hopped down from her perch as I untied Loretta with trembling fingers. Swedish checked Mrs. E—still somehow asleep in the cockpit—and Bea stared around the *Anvil Rose* in awe.

I guess I did the same, once my heart stopped pound-ing. I'd never been on a warship before. Everything slotted smoothly together, the gyroscopes and gunwales, the sky sails and the airsailors swarming the ship.

"This," Bea whispered, "is the *purplest*."

"Doesn't get any purpler," I agreed.

She giggled. "That's not a word!"

"Oh, but everyone says 'purplest.'"

She stuck her tongue out at me. "Listen to that engine, Chess! She's ticking as strong as a metal monkey."

We were so busy gaping at the rigging and wheelhouse that I almost missed Hazel curtsying to Captain Nisha, then thanking her for such a well-timed—and accurate—harpoon shot.

Hazel looked overwhelmed, so I lowered my head and crossed the deck to stand beside her. She tugged the ring from her finger and eyed the diamond for a minute, like she didn't want to say good-bye. Then she took a breath and handed it to the captain.

"I've never seen one so big," Nisha purred, holding the

diamond to the light. "But I'll give you a choice."

"What's that, ma'am?" Hazel asked.

"You can pay for the trip with the ring, or you can work for your passage and keep it. A diamond will come in handy when we reach the Port."

"We can keep it?" Hazel's smile looked like sunshine. "Wow. Yes, please. Yes. Thanks!"

"I warn you, I'm a demanding boss," the captain said, returning the diamond.

"We're a working crew, ma'am. In the slum, if you don't work, you don't eat. Oh, except for Mrs. E. She's fogsick, so one of us needs to stay with her."

"She slept through the air battle?" Nisha toyed with her string of beads. "That's not a good sign."

I felt a flash of worry, but Hazel said more mildly than ever, "Yes, Captain."

Nisha cocked an eyebrow at her. "I'm starting to suspect that there's more to you than a bunch of junkyard bottom-feeders."

"Of course, ma'am," Hazel said. "We're *mutineer* bottom-feeders now."

The captain laughed softly. "In that case, the old lady can have a cot in the surgery. You must bring her to the healers on the Port as soon as we land."

"Whoa!" Loretta called, stepping toward a harpoon. "Check it out, Swedish! This is one serious pig-sticker."

Swedish looked up from Mrs. E. "That'll come in handy . . . when pigs fly."

"What are you talking about?" Loretta asked, patting the gleaming brass.

"It's a saying from Chess's old scrapbook," Swedish told her. "It means something impossible, like 'a bunch of slumkids will escape from Lord Kodoc when pigs fly.'"

"But pigs *don't* fly."

"That's the point!"

"Your point is that pigs don't fly?" Loretta shot him a look. "How about gerbils? Do they dance?"

"Gerbils will dance when pigs fly."

"Now you're just messing with me."

"Um, Captain?" I said as they happily bickered.

Nisha looked at me with her too-blue eyes. "Yes?"

"Uh, well . . ." I wanted to ask if Kodoc was really beaten. I wanted to ask if she knew he was hunting me. But all I said was "Um, about that diving platform on the bottom of Kodoc's airship . . ."

Hazel came to my rescue. "We're wondering what Lord Kodoc is looking for with all those tetherkids."

Captain Nisha's lips thinned. "A fairy tale."

"You mean like 'Hairy Otter'?" Loretta asked, looking up from the harpoon. "Or 'Little Red Gliding Hood'?"

"I mean a story about an impossible machine, hidden in the Fog, that Kodoc calls the Compass."

I ducked my head. Did *everyone* know about that? Well, of course the mutineers knew—the fogheads must've told them. But what else did they know?

"Kodoc is obsessed with finding it," Nisha continued. "And terrified that the Subassembly will get there first. Whoever finds the Compass controls the Fog . . . and whoever controls the Fog rules the world. Kodoc thinks he's close. He just needs divers."

I didn't want Nisha thinking about Fog divers, so I jumped in, "He sounds as cracked as a trampoline."

"Huh?" she asked.

"Wait, that's not right. Um . . . glass! Cracked as a *glass* trampoline."

"What's a trampoline?" Captain Nisha asked.

"I'm not sure," I said. "But Kodoc is a cracked one."

She looked at me oddly, then turned back to Hazel. "I'll have one of the sailors show you around."

"Sheesh," I muttered. "It was funny when Loretta said it."

"Cap'n?" Bea called from the railing, her voice squeaking.

"Yes?" Hazel and Nisha said at the same time.

"Over there." Bea pointed over the Fog. "Look at Kodoc's airship."

I followed them to the railing and squinted toward the *Teardrop*, which was hovering just inside the cloud bank.

She didn't seem any different. Airtroopers bustled around repairing damage from the fight, the propellers twirled, and the sails billowed.

"Looks like they're securing the deck." Hazel frowned. "Bolting everything down."

"That's not all they're doing," Bea said.

Captain Nisha peered at Kodoc's ship through her spyglass. "Hm. They're engaging some kind of mechanism. . . . What *is* that? He's diverting the power of the engine into . . ." She gasped. "The—the hull is cracking in half."

Hazel shaded her eyes. "The propellers are separating."

"Vidious!" Nisha shouted, still watching through her glass. "Look to the *Teardrop*!"

"Maybe he's sinking," I said hopefully. "Maybe you damaged him worse than you thought."

"The ship's not sinking," Bea told me with a hint of awe in her voice. "She's *changing*."

"What are you talking about?"

"The props are unfolding, the hull's getting sleeker and longer. The balloon's the same, but the rigging is moving. Kodoc's bringing armor to bear and the guns—are those guns? I can't see."

"Those are guns," Captain Nisha said tightly. "Big guns. The geargirl's right, he's changing that ship into a . . ."

"A warship," Bea said.

"I've never seen one so big," Hazel breathed.

"Even the name is changing," Nisha said. "The letters are shifting around."

"The letters of *Teardrop*?" I asked.

"Yes," Nisha said. "Now they spell *Predator*."

39

HAZEL TURNED TO BEA. "How long before the ship is done changing?"

"Five or six hours," Bea said.

Nisha cocked an eyebrow. "How would you know?"

"I—um." Bea blushed a bright pink. "I can sort of tell."

"How fast is she?" Hazel asked. "Can Kodoc catch us?"

Bea wrinkled her nose. "These mutie ships—" She flushed again, glancing to the captain. "I mean, these *mutineer* ships are pretty fast, but with those props and that hull? The *Predator* is faster."

"We'll see about that." Nisha turned to her brother and called, "Looks like we're racing that warship back to the Port!"

"Not until we get the package!" Vidious replied from the deck of his ship.

"We can't beat *that.*" She gestured at the *Predator* with her spyglass. "Check out those guns!"

Vidious shook his head. "We need the package."

"The package?" Hazel asked, her brow furrowing. "You're not smuggling anything *to* the Rooftop, you're smuggling a package *from* the Rooftop?"

"We're trying to," Nisha said. "Why?"

A crazy thought occurred to me. "No way!" I blurted, turning to Hazel. "It can't be."

"Ten strips of kangaroo jerky says I'm right." Hazel looked at the captain. "Um, does the name Cog Turning mean anything to you?"

Nisha narrowed her eyes. "You know Turning? If you know Turning . . ." She fell silent for a moment, then slowly turned to me, a smile curling at her mouth. "Wait. You always keep your eye hidden. . . ."

I ducked my head.

"Are you the kid?" she asked, a hint of wonder in her voice. "You are! You're the package!"

"Um," I said, caught between my fear of admitting anything and my relief that the mutineers actually wanted to help us.

"But you're a *boy*," she said, sounding disappointed.

"Ye-es," I said. "Um. Sorry?"

She reached into her vest and tossed a pouch to Hazel. "A message came, ripped into shreds, mostly unreadable. Something about a girl with a . . . special eye. On the highest slopes. Cog Turning asked for a ship to bring her to the Port."

"You're the ship!" Bea said, clapping her hands. "You're the ship coming to smuggle us!"

Hazel nodded. "That's why they've been hanging around. I don't understand about this 'girl,' though."

"Cog Turning must've meant Mrs. E." I turned to the captain. "He helped us because he wants to cure her."

"She might be one reason," Nisha said. "But you're the other. We must keep you out of Kodoc's hands . . . if you truly are the child."

I hunched a shoulder. "I guess."

"May I see it?" she asked. "The mark?"

A flush of humiliation rose in my chest and I looked at my scuffed boots. I hated showing strangers my freak-eye.

"Chess." Hazel put a hand on my arm. "Just this once."

I kept my head down. My stomach soured at the thought of letting Nisha see my darkest secret, my deepest shame.

"Pretend she's me," Hazel said softly.

Neither of them spoke for a few seconds, and I took a

deep breath. Just this once. No big deal. Maybe I was a coward, but I could do this.

I took a breath, then raised my head and brushed my hair from my face.

When Captain Nisha saw the mark, surprise flashed on her face, mixed with disgust and maybe fascination. The Fog that had killed billions, the Fog that blanketed the earth, the Fog that swirled in an ocean of whiteness also glimmered inside my eye.

"You're *him*," she said, a strange hitch in her voice. "Born in the Fog."

The shame thickened in my throat as I tugged my hair back into place.

"Yes, ma'am." Hazel stepped closer to me. "And we appreciate everything you're doing but, um, could you ask that sailor to show us around now? And could you not tell anyone about Chess?"

"Only my brother," Nisha promised. "He needs to know that we got the package."

"But Captain Nisha?" Bea said, slipping beside Hazel. "What're we going to do? We can't beat the *Predator* to Port Oro."

"Of course we can," Nisha said.

Bea blinked her big green eyes at Nisha.

"Okay, the *Predator*'s faster," Nisha admitted. "But if we get close enough to the Port, other mutineers will help us fight Kodoc."

"Can we get close enough?" Hazel asked.

"If I push the *Rose* faster than she's ever flown?" Nisha said. "Maybe."

40

THE MUTINEER WARSHIP WAS divided into four levels, with engine rooms, cargo holds, an armory, a surgery, and workshops for the mechanics and carpenters. Narrow barracks lined both sides of the hull, and a steamy kitchen huddled in the stern, where massive engines rattled the pots and pans.

A grizzled sailor brought us to a cramped hallway in the bowels of the ship. The *whir-tick* of the props sounded through the floor as he opened a wooden chest and rasped, "After nightfall, you can string these hammocks across the corridor for beds."

"Are there any regular bunks?" Loretta asked, biting her lower lip. "I mean, that don't swing around?"

"You're on an airship now, girl," he cackled.

"Don't worry," I told her. "You'll get the *hang* of it pretty soon."

Bea giggled and told Loretta, "It's kind of fun, actually."

"Come along," the sailor said. "The quartermaster will assign you jobs."

"How come we've got to work?" Swedish grumbled as we followed the sailor across the ship.

"They let us keep the rock," Hazel told him.

"But they were looking for us anyway. We saved them a trip to the Rooftop."

Loretta scratched her cheek. "I guess that Cog Turning guy really called in some favors."

"Yeah," I said. "I guess."

"Except . . . how much of this is about you?"

I hunched a shoulder. That part made me nervous. "Not sure."

"Can I see your eye again?"

"No."

"I'll show you the scar on my butt."

"Ew," I said.

"They should at least let me fly this heap," Swedish muttered.

"Just do your job," Hazel told him, and headed into the quartermaster's office.

Inside, a bald guy with brown teeth sat behind a cluttered desk, reading a ledger. He flipped a page. Then another. Finally, he looked up and inspected us. He didn't seem impressed.

"You. Big fella." He glowered at Swedish. "What's your name?"

"Swedish."

"Are you as strong as you look? Find the master carpenter. They're fixing some damage—you'll fetch and carry." He eyed Loretta. "Are you good for anything?"

"I'm awesome at harpooning," she told him.

He quirked an eyebrow. "Have you ever touched one?"

"Sure."

"Before today?"

"Well, no." She sighed. "I'm good with a knife, though."

"Fine. Then you're on kitchen duty."

Loretta grumbled.

"How about you, little one?" he asked Bea. "I hear you're quite the geargirl."

"She's staying with Mrs. E," Hazel said brusquely. Then she softened her tone. "If you please, sir."

The quartermaster frowned at Bea. "We could use you in the engine shaft—some of the valves are hard to reach for anyone bigger'n a chipmunk. And you've never seen a sweeter clockwork than the one driving the *Anvil Rose*."

Bea shot a pleading look at Hazel. "Can I, please? Pretty please?"

"Mrs. E needs you," Hazel told her.

Bea sighed and said, "No, thank you, sir."

The quartermaster scowled at Hazel. "Fancy yourself

in charge, do you? You like giving orders? I bet you're expecting I'll put you to work as a first lieutenant."

"I'm fairly good with a needle," Hazel told him. "And a glue gun."

"Oh, you're a clever girl," he grumbled. "Not getting above yourself. Fine, to the sailmakers with you." He turned to me. "You're a tetherboy?"

"Yup," I said. "I mean, yes, sir."

"A little old for it, ain't you?"

"Only because I haven't died yet."

I hadn't meant it as a joke, but the quartermaster laughed. "You'll work for the riggers, then."

So Swedish wandered off to haul planks while Hazel disappeared into the sailmakers' workshop. A toothless sailor helped Bea bring Mrs. E to the surgeon, while Loretta headed for the kitchen and I returned to the deck.

Shading my eyes against the sudden brightness, I scanned the distance behind us. A few clouds smudged the blue horizon . . . and a black dot hung in the air like a splinter in the sky. The *Predator*. She was so far back, I couldn't see her propellers or guns. But she was still there, still changing. Getting ready for the chase.

With a shaky breath, I turned away. I found the rigging crew easily enough, because they all looked like me, compact and wiry. The rigging master was a swarthy woman of about my height, even though she must've been twenty or something.

"You're Chess?" she asked, eying me dubiously. "What're you, a bottom-feeder?"

"I prefer 'salvage engineer.'"

She didn't smile. "You scavenge in the Fog?"

"Yes, ma'am," I said.

"Well, if you find yourself in the Fog in this job, it means you slipped off your rig and you ain't *never* coming back."

"I'll try not to—"

"It would serve you right," she said. "It's your fault we've got Kodoc after us, you and that crew of yours."

I wanted to stick up for my crew, but I just ducked my head. Afraid to act, afraid to call attention to myself. Worrying that maybe Kodoc hadn't just given me nanites, he'd also given me cowardice.

The rigging master glared toward the distant speck. "I know riggings, boy, and that ship's rigged to catch us. Just a matter of time."

Then she sent me overboard in a harness to clean exhaust vents, andI spent the rest of the day scrubbing.

After a dinner of tortilla and kimchi with the rigging crew, I checked the sky. The little black dot was twice as big, and as I watched, the setting sun glinted off the *Predator*'s armor plating.

Coming closer.

When I returned to the hallway, I found Hazel mending clothes, and everyone else gently swinging in their hammocks. Bea was fiddling with wire, making a twisty, while Loretta and Swedish held hands as they rocked. Part of me wanted to talk about Kodoc and the *Predator*, but more of me wanted a break, wanted to pretend that my life wasn't a total mess.

So I flopped down beside Hazel and loosened my boot-straps. "You want a hand? You know I sew better than you."

"You're good with a glue gun, too," she said.

Swedish snorted a laugh.

"What?" Loretta asked.

"A couple years ago," Swedish told her, "Chess glued his thumb to his face."

"I was a little kid! I fell asleep holding a glue gun." I threw my boot at Swedish, then asked Bea, "How's Mrs. E?"

She wrinkled her nose. "The same."

"Was she rambling again?" Hazel asked.

"No," Bea said. "She slept all afternoon."

I rubbed my face. "Can we see her?"

"The doctor says she needs peace and quiet. No visitors."

"Maybe tomorrow," Hazel told me.

"There's no reason for me to sit there!" Bea blurted. "She's always sleeping, and I want to see the engine. I want to *do* something."

"I'm sorry," Hazel said. "But no."

"It's not fair! Just because I'm the littlest, you don't let me do anything! I won't hurt myself, I promise."

"I'm not afraid you'll hurt yourself," Hazel said, looking up from her sewing. "I'm afraid they'll see how good you are and never let you leave."

"Captain Nisha would never do that."

She was probably right, but I knew the real reason Hazel wouldn't let her work on the engine. We'd almost died 287 times in the past few days, and Kodoc was still behind us, madder than ever. The last thing we needed was to put Bea in any more danger.

"And anyway," Bea continued, "I'm not *that* good."

"You're worth more than the diamond," Hazel told her.

"Worth almost as much as berry pie," Swedish said. "With berries on top."

"Plus," I added, "you're completely whackadoo. Talking to engines all the time. They'd probably lock you up."

"Fine!" Bea scowled. "I'll stay at the surgery."

After a short pause, Hazel said, "How about you, Loretta? How was the kitchen?"

Loretta sighed. "I spent all afternoon grinding fish bones into powder, then mixing the powder into paste." She scratched her scarred arm morosely. "Do you know what they've got in the kitchen?"

"Fish paste?" Swedish guessed.

"*Food.*" Loretta flashed her gap-toothed smile. "Oh, it's like a beautiful dream, Swede! You've never seen so much food."

Hazel and I climbed into our hammocks as Loretta described mounds of pickled eel, stacks of roti, and simmering pots of Chungking pigeon. When she finished, we listened to the distant shanties of the airsailors celebrating their victory over Kodoc.

Then, after a lull, a voice carried to us: ". . . until that *Predator* swoops down and kills every last sailor on board. Don't kid yourself, she'll catch us easy, long before we reach the Port. . . ."

The voice faded, but the air in the hallway suddenly felt thick and itchy. The sailor was right: the mutie warships were fast, and fighting for every bit of speed, but the *Predator* looked even faster.

"Tell us a story, Chess," Bea said in a small voice. "From the scrapbook."

"What's a scrapbook?" Loretta asked.

"My dad collected notes from the time before the Fog," I told her. "Any information he could find. I guess . . . I guess it's gone now."

For a second, I wanted to cry. Not only was Kodoc closing in, but the scrapbook—my only real link to my father—had been ditched along with the shack. It was in the Fog now, lost forever.

"You memorized the whole thing anyway," Swedish said.

I took a breath. "Mostly."

"Tell us the one about the sailor," Hazel said in the darkness.

I swayed in my hammock as I tried to remember. It was better than thinking about Kodoc. "Okay. This is from a diary."

"A what?" Loretta asked.

"Like a logbook. The guy who wrote it said, 'In the town where I was born, there lived a man who sailed the seas. He lived beneath the waves in a yellow submarine.' Then there's a bit about tangerine trees and marmalade skies and a girl with colliding scope eyes."

"What's marmalade?" Loretta asked.

"Some kind of poison?" I guessed. "Like the Fog? Maybe that's why they lived beneath the sea."

She eyed me in disgust. "You don't believe that, do you?"

"Well, it's possible."

"There's no such thing as a 'sea.' There's never been that much water."

"Yeah," Bea agreed. "That part's silly."

"There *were* seas," Hazel told them. "Full of whales and squids and squarepants."

We'd had this argument a hundred times, so I changed the subject. I told them how in the old days, people searched "the googol" for answers to their questions.

"So the googol was a fortune-teller?" Loretta asked.

"Like palm reading?"

"The googol is a number," I told her. "A one with a hundred zeros after it."

"One zero zero zero zero . . . a hundred times?"

I nodded. "They wrote down the googol and stared at it until they found the answer they needed."

"Didn't work for you," Swedish said.

"You tried it?" Loretta asked me.

"Once," I said. "But the only thing I found was a headache."

Hazel turned down the lantern a few minutes later, and I closed my eyes and listened to the unfamiliar whir of the mutie propellers. Every time I started to drift off, I imagined the *Predator* sweeping through the night like a driftshark through Fog.

Finally Bea said, "I can't sleep. Tell me the story."

"Not again!" Swedish grumbled from the darkness.

"Please?" Bea pleaded. "Pretty please with pickled eels?"

"What story?" Loretta asked.

"The secret history of the world," Bea told her. "Mrs. E told us."

"Before the Fog rose," I started, "there was something called the Smog, which covered the whole earth and made *everything* sick. Not just people. . . ."

When I finished, Bea made Hazel tell the story of the red-caped hero named Superbowl, who leaped mountains in a single bound and threw pigskins.

Then a new mutie song started above us, softer and slower than the others, and we listened in silence. We were in the depths of a warship, heading to an unknown city, fleeing from Kodoc and trying to save Mrs. E. We didn't have the raft or the shack—or even the slum. But we still had each other. And, as we swayed in the dark hallway, that thought lulled me to sleep.

41

THE NEXT MORNING I woke before dawn. I swayed in my hammock and heard a faint metallic whine. The gears were straining for speed, the pistons firing hot and fast. Captain Nisha was pushing the *Anvil Rose* hard, trying to stay ahead of Kodoc.

Maybe too hard. If the engine failed, we were dead in the air.

I rolled from my hammock and crept away barefoot so I wouldn't wake the others. Around the corner, I tugged my boots onto my feet, then crossed the ship and slipped into the surgery.

The doctor snored in her hammock, bottles of medicine rattled in racks, and Mrs. E slept in a cot with high railings to keep her from falling out. Her skin was an unhealthy white, with red smudges on her cheeks. I stood there for a long time, watching her sleep. She'd given me everything I'd ever loved, everything good in my life since my dad died, and I still needed her. We all needed her.

When I returned to the hammocks, Hazel and Bea were lying on their stomachs in the middle of the hallway. Heads together, chatting softly, with dozens of scraps of paper scattered on the floor between them.

"What're those?" I asked.

"They're bits of the message that Turning sent to the Port," Hazel told me.

"Ripped into a hundred pieces," Loretta said from her hammock. "Looks like a hawk caught the carrier pigeon."

"Sounds tasty." Swedish yawned. "Lucky hawk."

"Look at this, Chess." Hazel pointed to an uneven rectangle of paper scraps. "This is the part they already deciphered."

The paper was crumpled and dirty, with a few splotches of what must've been pigeon blood. Still, some of the words were clear:

> . . . *found the child with . . . eye. Kodoc in pursuit . . . girl, on the highest slopes. . . . Send a ship to bring . . . to the Port . . . igh alert.*

"Turning said I was a girl?" I rubbed the back of my neck. "I thought he knew all about me."

"Yeah," Hazel said. "I don't know how he got that wrong."

Swedish squatted beside Bea. "Maybe he didn't."

"You mean Chess really is a girl?" Loretta asked.

I ignored her as a spark of hope ignited in my chest. "He means there might be *two* of us! *Another* kid with a freak-eye!"

That'd be awesome. If some upper slopes girl had a Fog-eye, I wouldn't be such a freak.

"We'll find out tonight," Hazel said, "when we put the rest of the pieces together."

"Wait a second." Swedish messed with the bits of paper. "I'm good at puzzles."

"Bea and I have been at this since we woke up, Swede," Hazel said. "You're not going to figure it out before breakfast."

"So, uh, you all know how to read, huh?" Loretta scratched the tattoo on her cheek. "Like, whole words and everything?"

"They do," Bea said. "I'm still learning."

Loretta glowered. "Reading is stupid."

"You can learn with me, if you want," Bea told her. "Swedish will teach us together."

Loretta squinted at Swedish, who was shuffling scraps

of paper on the floor. "He will?"

"Course he will," Bea said.

"That way you can read his love notes," I teased.

Loretta scowled, but I could tell she liked the idea. "You really think I can learn?"

"Sure you can," I said.

"It's easier than piecing together a hundred scraps of paper," Hazel told her. "C'mon, Swede, let's go."

"I'm almost done," he told her, moving one last piece of paper into place. "There!"

He looked at the message on the floor and read aloud:

> . . . *found the child with the eye. Kodoc in pursuit . . . he doesn't even know if the child is a boy or girl, on the highest slopes or . . . lowest. Send a ship to bring . . . to the Port. Find me. I'll lead you . . . nd take care. Kodoc on high alert. Noti . . .*

"Oh," Bea said. "He was saying that *Kodoc* didn't know if Chess was a girl."

Hazel gaped at Swedish. "How did you do that?"

"Everything fits together," Swedish loftily informed her, "if you know how to look."

"So I guess I'm the only freak," I muttered unhappily.

"You're not the only freak." Loretta elbowed me.

"Did you see Swedish solve that puzzle? Now *that* was freaky."

As I unstrung my hammock, I thought about the message. Bits were still missing, but it looked like Cog Turning hadn't even mentioned Mrs. E. He'd only told them about me. Why did the Port care so much? Did they just want to keep me out of Kodoc's hands, so he couldn't find the Compass? Or did they want the Compass for themselves?

"C'mon!" Bea said. "We'll miss breakfast."

We headed to the sweep deck, where the rising sun brushed the Fog with yellow fire and the breeze blew fresh and cold. I shivered, then opened my jacket so I could wrap Bea in half of it. We tore into the bread that Loretta had swiped the previous day and eyed the black smear hanging in the air. The *Predator* looked bigger than a thumbnail this morning. More like a fist.

"Kodoc's getting closer," I said.

"Only a little," Loretta said. "Maybe he's not as fast as you think."

"He's even faster-er now," Bea said.

Swedish eyed her. "What do you mean, 'now'?"

"Listen to the engine, Swede." Bea's lower lip trembled. "She's all trembly and overheated. She can't keep up this speed."

Hazel put a hand on Bea's shoulder. "She'll be okay,

Bea. The captain knows what she's doing."

"She's trying to get away from Kodoc." Bea's voice soft-ened into a whisper. "But even pushing the *Rose* this hard, she can't."

42

I spent the rest of the morning dangling over the edge of the warship, scrubbing vents. Waves of vaporous Fog swirled and rippled beneath me, and part of me wanted to dive—but the other part enjoyed the break. Scrubbing at splattered insects wasn't exactly *fun*, but at least it was easy.

At lunchtime, I unhitched my harness and headed for the sailmakers to find Hazel.

Halfway there, I heard a shout from the other side of the ship: Loretta's shout. *Uh-oh.* I trotted across the side deck, raced around a corner . . . and skidded to a halt.

Loretta was standing at the harpoon with a huge gap-toothed smile on her face.

"That's enough for today." Captain Nisha clapped her on the back. "Off to the kitchen with you."

Loretta saluted a few times, then jogged over to me. "The captain's showing me how to fire the harpoon!"

"Why?" I asked in horror. "You're bad enough with a knife."

"Hazel asked her to!" Loretta beamed. "She's the best."

"Sometimes I wish she'd mind her own business."

"You should see the captain shoot!" Loretta said, scratching her spiky hair. "She can put a harpoon through a goose's eye at a hundred yards."

"Don't say that in front of Chess," Swedish told her, falling into step with us. "He loves geese."

"Swede!" Loretta grabbed his hand, her face shining with excitement. "Captain says I'm really good for a beginner. She's says I've got the eye for it."

"Oh, great," I muttered. "Now *everyone* wants the eye."

Swedish snorted a laugh, and we headed belowdecks as Loretta babbled about her harpoon lessons. We met Hazel and Bea at the foggium tanks and waited in line behind a couple of welders for bowls of oxtail stew. We spent five minutes stuffing our faces, then another five chatting about the name. Why call it "oxtail stew"? Everyone knew it was made from camel tails.

After we licked our bowls clean, we headed outside and

scanned the sky. An uneasy silence fell, but nobody spotted the *Predator.*

"Where is he?" Bea asked, frowning into the distance.

For some reason, not seeing Kodoc at all was even scarier than watching him get closer.

"He's doing something." Swedish scowled. "He's *planning* something."

"Maybe we lost him," Loretta said.

"Sure, I'll believe that when gerbils dance."

Hazel nodded toward the crow's nest at the top of the rigging. "The captain's got two lookouts on duty. They'll spot Kodoc when he gets close."

"When he gets *too* close," Bea said, wrinkling her nose. "And . . . and I can't stand it!"

"We're all scared, honeybee." Hazel gave Bea a squeeze. "Knowing he's coming, even though we can't see him—"

"Not that! I mean the engine. Listen to the *Rose*—she's crying. She's too hot. She's sweating and crying and she needs help."

"Captain Nisha knows what she's doing."

Bea clamped her jaw. "I know what *I'm* doing, too."

"You're looking after Mrs. E."

"Would you tell her?" Bea demanded, turning to me. "Tell Hazel I should help with the engine."

But I barely heard her. I just kept looking into the distance, where I'd last seen Kodoc's ship. Thinking of his face when he'd said, *Your name is whatever I call you.*

And the tremor in my voice when I'd replied, *Yes, sir.*

At sunset, I met the crew in the surgery and we watched Mrs. E sleep. She looked so weak that a lump rose in my throat. The surgeon treated Mrs. E kindly and promised she'd keep her alive until we reached Port Oro, but she didn't *know* Mrs. E. All she saw was a tiny, helpless old lady. She didn't know that Mrs. E was a giant. She didn't know Mrs. E was the biggest thing in our lives.

An hour later, we swayed in our hammocks in the dark hallway, but I couldn't sleep. My mind whirled with worries and questions.

Finally I spoke. "How did Kodoc recognize me?"

Nobody answered.

Then Bea's soft voice said, "He knew your mom and dad, I guess."

I pulled my blanket tighter. "He said he knew me."

"Well, you have to remember," Swedish said, "he's whackadoo."

"He probably noticed you hiding your face," Bea said.

"What's the story with your eye?" Loretta asked me. "I mean, Swedish told me about Mrs. E saving you, but . . . can you feel the white gunk in there?"

"'Retta," Swedish said warningly. "He doesn't like talking about it."

"No, that's okay." I turned toward the dark shape of Loretta's hammock. "It feels just like my normal eye."

"Can you see out of it?"

"Yeah, I don't even notice the white gunk."

"The gunk isn't so bad, but the way it moves around like it's alive . . ." Loretta's voice trailed off, and I could almost hear her shudder. "*Gross.*"

"Yeah," I said.

"It works, though," she said. "That's all that matters."

Like that settled it. Like my freak-eye wasn't worth talking about. Sure, I had clouds of Fog drifting around my pupil, but so what? I found myself smiling in the darkness. Only Loretta could call you gross and make you feel better at the same time.

"At least I don't have a scar on my butt," I said.

"That's the most important lesson I ever learned," she said. "*Never sit on a barbed-wire fence.*" A wind buffeted the airship, and she groaned. "Well, that and *stay away from hammocks.*"

Swedish said, "I still don't understand why Kodoc wants Chess in the first place."

"For his search," Loretta said. "For this fog-machine."

"But he's already got tetherkids," Bea said. "Chess isn't *that* much better."

"Yeah, he is," Hazel said, her voice rough in the darkness. "When Kodoc forced his mom to give birth in the Fog, he gave Chess powers, he made Chess into—"

"His freak." I frowned in the darkness. "I'm, like, his creation."

"Well," Swedish said, "Kodoc can scream all he wants that you're his—"

"But you're not," Hazel finished. "You're *ours*."

43

OUR THIRD DAY ON the *Anvil Rose* dawned gray and misty. Life on the warship was starting to feel almost normal, and I contentedly cleaned vents for hours, until the rigging master told me to scrub the lifeboats lashed to the hull.

Three of them were fastened to each side of the airship, stripped-down craft attached to foggium tanks for emergency inflation. Except one was different. One was a disguised cargo raft, just like on the *Night Tide*.

I swung over for a closer look. Then I whistled. It was totally sweet, like a one-balloon version of our salvage raft, but built for speed and stealth—for smuggling.

For smuggling *me*. For snatching me from the Rooftop to the safety of Port Oro.

"Which is weird," I muttered.

I'd always known I was a freak, but I'd never suspected I was an *important* freak. Still, at least life on the warship was pretty good. I scrubbed, Hazel sewed, Swedish hauled, Loretta washed pots and fired harpoons. And Bea sat with Mrs. E and made dozens of twistys.

Before lunch that day, the rest of us joined Bea in the cramped surgery and gathered around Mrs. E.

"How's she doing?" Hazel asked the surgeon.

"She's getting worse. She needs the Subassembly."

"They can really help her?" Swedish asked.

"You heard Cog Turning," Bea told him.

"Yeah, but he's a foghead. They *always* talk loco."

"They know the sickness better than anyone," the surgeon said. "You need to bring her straight to them when we reach the Port."

"We will," I promised.

"*If* we reach the Port," the surgeon muttered under her breath.

Mrs. E tossed fitfully and made a whimpering sound. "Chess . . . ?"

Leaning closer, I took her cool hand. "I'm right here."

"Under my . . . pillow," she whispered, then drifted back to sleep.

"What'd she say?" Bea asked.

I eased my hand under the pillow and felt a hard edge. "There's something here. . . ."

When I pulled out my scrapbook, my breath caught. I opened the first page and saw my mother's name, and my father's, and mine. Written in my dad's handwriting. I blinked a few times, fighting back tears.

"She must've hidden it in her coat," Bea said, her voice soft.

I cleared my throat. "We've got to get her to Port Oro."

"We will," Hazel promised me.

"Unless Kodoc stops us," Swedish said.

"We'll get there," Hazel said, glaring at him, "But for now, we just keep our heads down and do our jobs."

Keeping my head down sounded smart. Not only because I *always* kept my head down, but also because the mutineers were scary. Even the friendly ones didn't enjoy being hunted by Lord Kodoc, and some of the less friendly ones blamed us outright.

After we grabbed bowls of stockfish and rice for lunch, a big sailor shouldered Swedish—hard. Swedish's face flushed, but he kept walking.

The big sailor shoved him again. "Watch where you're going, roof rat."

"I don't want any trouble," Swedish mumbled.

"Neither did we, but thanks to you we've got a death-ship chasing us across the sky."

"We'll reach Port Oro in time—"

"We *won't!*" the sailor snarled. "Listen to the *Anvil Rose*—she's breaking apart. The captain's melting the

288

engine into slag to save your sorry hides."

"Then talk to her," Swedish said, turning away. "Not me."

The sailor shoved Swedish from behind, sending him sprawling to the ground. "I'll melt *you* into slag."

The other mutineers jeered, eager for a fight, and I tugged my hair lower. *Okay, then.* I wasn't much of a brawler, but I'd rather get stomped than sit there and watch some guy beat up Swedish.

"Chess," Hazel hissed. "Stay put. He doesn't need your help."

I frowned in surprise. Usually she'd throw herself into a fight if anyone messed with one of us. But I stayed put.

The big sailor loomed over him. "Get up, bottom-feeder."

"The reason he doesn't want to fight," Loretta called, pushing to her feet, "is because we're here as guests."

"Mind your own business, girl," the big sailor growled.

"See, we don't want to offend the captain." Loretta strolled toward him, though the top of her head didn't even reach his chin. "Which might happen if we beat one of her dogs."

The big sailor glared. "You calling me a dog?"

"Nah," she told him. "Up close you look more like a cockroach."

"Are you blind? I'm twice as big as you."

Loretta put her hands in her pockets and shrugged. "You're bigger, I'll give you that."

"I'm twice as strong."

"Lots stronger," she agreed.

"And twice as mean," he said.

Loretta flashed her gap-tooth smile, pulled her hands from her pockets and threw a fistful of crushed fishbones into the sailor's eyes.

When he grabbed his face, she slipped to the side and kicked him in the knee with her metal-toed boot. The sailor grunted and collapsed to the deck—and Loretta slammed his ear with her forehead, then punched him in the neck.

As she lunged forward again, Swedish grabbed her arm to stop her.

An uneasy silence fell on the deck, broken only by the gasping of the injured sailor. Then the other mutineers muttered angrily, and I felt a flutter of fear.

"You think that's bad?" Hazel asked, her voice cutting through the silence. "You should see her *cook*!"

When one of the soldiers laughed, the tension faded. Two other airsailors helped the big guy limp to the surgery, and everyone else returned to their meals.

I was still hunched nervously over my bowl five minutes later when a metallic shriek sounded. Then voices shouted, boots tromped against the deck, and a cloud of stinking exhaust surrounded us.

Hazel touched my arm and glanced toward Bea, who

was gripping her bowl so tightly that her fingers were white. That shriek must've sounded like a cry of agony to her.

I knew what Hazel wanted. "Come on, Bea," I said, pushing to my feet. "Let's find the captain."

Bea's wide green gaze cut to Hazel. "Really?"

Hazel nodded. "The *Rose* needs you."

The three of us headed below, past a dozen frantic gearslingers, and found Nisha in a smoky corridor outside the engine room. "Captain," Hazel said, "I think you might—"

"Not now!" Nisha snapped, her face sweaty and her blond hair limp. "I've got flywheels tearing my ship apart."

"Bea can fix this," Hazel said.

"She's a child. Get out of here before I—"

"She knows engines the way Chess knows Fog," Hazel told Nisha. "I swear to you, by the wind and the water, that if Bea cannot fix this, it cannot be fixed."

Nisha eyed Hazel for two seconds, then looked at Bea. "Get in there and prove your captain right."

Bea scampered into the engine room, Nisha followed, and I stared at Hazel.

"'By the wind and the water?'" I asked, disbelieving. "How do you come up with these things?"

"I don't know," she said, flashing a grin. "It just came out."

When we returned to the deck, the *Night Tide* was

hovering alongside the *Anvil Rose*. "You can't evacuate onto my ship," Vidious was yelling to one of Nisha's officers. "My clockwork's ready to blow, too. I can't keep up this speed much longer."

The clatter of gears from the engine room drowned out the officer's reply.

"Either we slow down and let Kodoc catch us," Vidious answered, "or we think of a way to cool the engine that I've never seen before!"

An explosion shook the air.

A hole ripped through the side of the *Anvil Rose*, splintering the wood and belching gray smoke. I rushed to the railing through a crowd of shocked airsailors, and a little voice came from the cloud of exhaust.

"Sorry!" Bea called. "I had to move things around a little!"

Two seconds later, the grind of the engine softened. The clockwork ticked smoothly, and the unhealthy whine of overheated machinery quieted. The *Anvil Rose* was running cool again.

"Well, *that's* something I've never seen before," Vidious said, a lopsided grin on his scarred face. "Send that gear-girl to blow holes in my ship when she's done over there."

Bea fixed the *Night Tide* after she finished with the *Rose*—then the airsailors on both ships cheered her, and she flushed as red as a beet.

We told the story of her gearslinging triumph to a sleeping Mrs. E, then retold it twice after dinner, embarrassing Bea a little more each time. So we reenacted the whole thing, with me playing Bea and Swedish and Loretta playing the airships.

Finally, we stopped teasing her and settled into our hammocks. Bea swayed contentedly, and I eyed Hazel.

"What?" Hazel asked.

"At lunchtime? You *wanted* Loretta to fight that big mutineer."

Her bright brown gaze flicked toward me. "Why did I want that?"

"Because they think Loretta's just a pint-sized kid. So losing to her is worse than losing to Swede. Now they won't bother us again."

Hazel tied a ribbon around one of her braids. "She's like Bea. Easy to underestimate."

"Ain't that the truth!" Loretta crowed.

"But you cheated!" Bea told her. "Throwing that powder in his face."

"Look who's talking. You blew a hole in the ship."

"I had to! You cheated on purpose."

"Of course I did," Loretta said scornfully. "I never could've beat him in a *fair* fight."

44

ON THE MORNING OF the fourth day, excitement buzzed through the ship. Snatches of cheerful shanties sounded from passing airsailors, and the cook heaped extra eel in our bowls. Nisha and Vidious started flying side by side, with the *Night Tide* almost close enough to touch. The crews shouted to each other, friendly jeers and rude taunts—and more laughter than I'd ever imagined on a mutineer warship.

Not only were the ships flying fast and strong, thanks to Bea's fixes, but today we'd reach Port Oro. And the *Predator* still hadn't reappeared.

Dangling in my harness beside the hull, I found myself smiling. A cure for Mrs. E, freedom from Kodoc, and a big honking diamond: life didn't get any better than that.

The wind fluttered my hair, and the Fog pooled and rippled fifty yards below me. After four days in a warship, I missed diving. It was stupid and dangerous but I longed for the freedom, the speed, and the thrill.

I pulled the scrapbook from inside my jacket and ran my hand over the cover, thinking about my father. Then my fingers snagged on a curl of plastic sticking between two pages, like a bookmark.

Huh. Had Mrs. E left that for me?

I opened to the marked page, and found the scraps about "Skywalker Trek." I knew the whole thing was just a story . . . but sometimes, late at night, I still prayed that a fleet of spaceships would rescue us. They'd send the *X-Wing Enterprise* to gather everyone who'd survived the Fog and bring us to a lush, green world where clear land stretched to the horizon.

I'd told Mrs. E about that once, as we'd sat outside the shack. We'd watched the starry sky for a long time, and then she'd said, "What if the *X-Wing Enterprise* already landed? What if the rescue party is already here?"

"Swedish is totally a Klingon," I said, "and nobody's more Princess Solo than Hazel."

She'd ruffled my hair. "And you're my young Fog-walker."

Smiling to myself, I tucked the scrapbook away. I missed Mrs. E. And now that we were just a few hours away from Port Oro, the fogheads would heal her, and we'd be a family again.

A sharp cry cut into my reverie: "Ship on the horizon! The *Predator*'s closing fast, Captain!"

My smile died. Not *now*. Not when we were so close. My skin prickled and I felt Kodoc across the miles. His hot, hungry breath touched my neck like a jaguar about to sink its teeth into a jackrabbit.

I spun in my harness, my breath ragged. Without a spyglass, I couldn't see anything except Fog and storm clouds, so I just slumped there, limp and shivering.

"Tetherboy?" the rigging master called down. "I'm bringing you topside!"

My mouth was too dry to answer.

"Tetherboy?" she shouted again.

I licked my lips. "R-ready!"

"Lose the harness," she said after winching me up. "Captain Nisha's looking for you."

"What does she want?"

"Whatever she wants, you say 'yes, ma'am.'"

"Yes, ma'am," I said, trying to cover my fear with humor.

"You're not bad, for a bottom-feeder. Now get moving."

Numb and frightened, I trotted along the gangway. I stumbled down the steps from the spar deck and found the crew clustered around the captain.

I slunk into place beside Bea, my shoulders hunched.

"Have a look," Captain Nisha was saying, handing her spyglass to Hazel. "Do you see him?"

Hazel scanned the distance. "No."

"Neither did I. Look higher."

Hazel tilted the spyglass upward. "Where?"

"Higher."

Hazel gasped. "Oh, *no*."

"That's why we haven't spotted him," Nisha told us. "Kodoc camouflaged the underside of his ship, then spent the last few days climbing. Higher and higher, into the air that's almost too thin to breathe. Then all through last night . . ."

"He dove like a bird of prey." The spyglass trembled in Hazel's hand. "Like a peregrine falcon."

My breath caught. That was a fact from the scrapbook. A peregrine falcon normally flies at fifty miles per hour, but when it dives for the kill? It reaches two *hundred* miles per hour.

Hazel didn't say anything for a few terrible seconds. "He'll hit us in an hour. Two hours if you overcrank the props. But your engine's still weak. . . ."

Nisha tapped the hilt of her dagger. "You're a born air-sailor, Hazel. I'd offer to make you a lieutenant when we reach the Port—"

"*If* we reach it," Swedish muttered.

"—but you'd say no, wouldn't you?" Nisha finished.

Hazel nodded. "Yes, ma'am."

"Because you already have a crew." Nisha glanced at the rest of us.

"Born to bottom-feed," Loretta said.

Swedish nudged her. "Doomed to dive."

The captain ignored them. "I *am* overcranking the props, Hazel. I'm pouring everything into speed and hoping we don't melt down. He'll still hit us in two hours."

"How far are we from the Port?"

"Three hours." Nisha jerked her thumb toward the opposite railing. "Maybe a little less. You see that smoke on the horizon? That's the Port."

My heart started racing. Three hours from Port Oro! We'd come so *close.* . . .

"Um," Bea said in a little voice. "So we're three hours from the Port, and Kodoc is only two hours from us?"

Captain Nisha nodded. "He'll catch us an hour from home."

"Will your friends help?" Bea asked.

"She means the mutineer navy," Hazel said. "Can't they fly out to stop Kodoc?"

"They're too far away," Captain Nisha said, her blond hair half covering her face. "By the time they realize what's happening, Kodoc will be on us."

"And they're too timid, poppet," Vidious called to Hazel. "You might as well ask a turtle to leave his shell."

"They'll try to help," Nisha insisted. "I'll signal them. But there's no way they'll reach us in time."

"So what are we gonna do?" Loretta asked.

"There's only one thing *to* do," Vidious told his sister.

Nisha went completely motionless. Her stillness and silence made me nervous. What was Vidious talking about? Fighting? Surrendering? Handing me over?

"We could split up," she said.

"He's fast enough to catch us both," Vidious said. "And you've got the package."

"Don't do anything stupid, Vid."

"Stupid is our only choice." Vidious raised a hand to his pilot, and his airship swerved away from the *Anvil Rose*. "Take care, little sister!"

"We're twins, you idiot!" Nisha shouted after Vidious. "You're older by ten minutes!"

Vidious's laugh reached us faintly as he stalked to the prow of his ship, his cloak billowing behind him.

"What are they talking about?" Swedish asked Hazel. "What's going on?"

"He's going to attack the *Predator*," she said.

"The *Night Tide* can't beat Kodoc," Bea said, her green eyes wide. "Not even close."

"He's not trying to beat him," Hazel explained. "He's trying to buy us time."

45

"My brother's tough," Captain Nisha said, her worried gaze on the *Night Tide*. "He'll come through."

Hazel rubbed her face with her hand. "But Kodoc won't waste his time on the *Night Tide*. He'll stop her, then come for us."

"Well, *that's* comforting," Loretta muttered.

Captain Nisha eyed Hazel. "I hope you're worth all this trouble." She glanced at me. "I hope *he* is."

"I—we'll try to be." Hazel offered the spyglass back. "Thank you. For everything."

"Keep the spyglass," Nisha said, crossing toward the prow. "And keep your crew out of my way . . . *Captain* Hazel."

Despite the danger, a spark of pleasure glowed in

Hazel's eyes. She seemed to stand straighter as the wind tugged at her braids. She tightened her lips, trying not to smile, but I knew her too well: being called "Captain" by Nisha made her want to spin and shout.

"C'mon," Hazel said, heading toward the stern.

"Captain Nisha's awesome," Bea announced as she followed.

"Yeah," Swedish said. "But scary."

"Like a snake," Loretta agreed. "With claws."

"Snakes don't have claws," Bea told Loretta, starting down a ladder.

"Some do," Loretta said. "The kind *they* don't want you to know about."

Swedish gave her a look like he wanted to kiss her— then the deck started trembling as the airship accelerated.

When we reached the sweep deck, Bea frowned. "We're on the wrong side of the ship—we can't see the *Predator* from here."

"Doesn't matter." Hazel lifted her new spyglass to her eye. "We can't do anything about Kodoc anyway."

While she scanned the Fog, Bea and Swedish and I looked at one another. What did that mean? *Hazel* could always do something.

"Shouldn't we, y'know . . ." I gestured feebly. "Spring into action?"

"What action?" Hazel said. "Vidious is already trying to stop Kodoc, and Nisha is already flying at top speed."

"But Kodoc's ship is faster." Bea cocked her head, listening to the engine. "He'll win."

Hazel nodded curtly. "I know."

Bea's lower lip started trembling, so I grabbed her hand. Loretta sidled beside Swede and wrapped his arm around her shoulders. When Bea started shivering, I looked down at her sweet face, usually so bright and hopeful, and saw nothing but dismay.

I glanced at Hazel over Bea's tousled head, and she met my gaze. I saw that she felt just as dismayed as Bea, just as hopeless. She also felt responsible, like she'd failed us. I looked back at her and tried to tell her with my eyes that whatever happened next, I was proud of her. We were all proud of her.

She bowed her head and scanned the distance with her spyglass. Nobody spoke for a long time. Twenty minutes, thirty, forty. . . . The *Anvil Rose* trembled beneath us. Foggium hissed through hoses, and the props strained for speed.

Finally Hazel said, "There she is. Port Oro."

I trotted to the railing and shaded my eyes. A million peaks of whiteness caught the light of the sun and the wide blue sky. In the distance, a tumble of puffy clouds mixed with the mist of the Fog . . . and I spotted a dot on the horizon, a jagged green-and-gold crown rising through the vapor.

"We did it!" I said, feeling a dumb grin spread across

my face. "We actually did it."

"Except for the whole Kodoc-blowing-us-from-the-sky thing," Swedish grumbled.

Bea fidgeted beside me. "I'm scared."

After a moment, Hazel said, "We're all scared, but . . . do you know what they're calling us, back in the slum?"

"Dead meat?" Swedish asked.

"*Legends,*" Hazel told him with a sudden, wolfish smile. "We snatched a diamond and got away. Who does that? Nobody. Who beats the bosses? Nobody. Who out-runs the troopers?"

"Nobody?" Bea said.

"Nobody," Hazel agreed.

Hearing the strength in Hazel's voice, I felt something expanding in my chest, something fierce and happy. Something like hope.

"Who snuck onto the Rooftop?" Hazel asked.

"We did," Bea said.

"Who escaped Kodoc? Who haggled with mutineers?"

"We did! We did!"

"Yeah," Hazel said. "And next, we're going to cure Mrs. E."

"How?" Bea chewed her lower lip. "There's no way we'll reach the Port now."

Hazel turned to look at the growing speck of Port Oro. "I don't know how."

"Neither do I," Swedish said. "But only an idiot would

bet against *legends*."

In the silence that followed, I gaped at him, shocked by this sudden burst of optimism.

"Are there fishing ships?" Bea asked, a minute later. "Can you see them?"

"The lake's on the other side of the mountain," Hazel told her.

We'd heard that a fleet of airships lowered nets into a massive Fog-shrouded lake every day, trawling for fish hundreds of yards below. We'd heard that farms and mines dotted outlying mountaintop "islands," and even that a few bits of Port Oro were built on the tops of ancient skyscrapers that rose from the white. Which was completely loco. How could super-tall buildings still rise above the white?

"What about skyscratchers?" Loretta asked.

"Scrapers," Hazel corrected. "I don't see them. Not yet."

"You don't actually believe in those," Swedish said. "Do you?"

"In the old days," Hazel told him, "there were hundreds of them."

"There were big bens, too," I said. At least, according to my dad's scrapbook. "And wall streets."

Loretta squinted at me. "What's a big ben?"

"A huge clock," I said. "Named after Big Ben Franklin."

"The guy whose face is on fancy toilet paper?" she asked.

"That's the one."

"There!" Hazel pointed. "Warships. Nine mutie warships, coming toward us."

"How far away are they?" I asked, my grip tightening on the rail.

"Too far," she said. "Unless Vidious slows Kodoc down."

As if in answer, a sudden *BOOM* echoed across the sky.

Airsailors shouted, and I spun toward the noise. The gun deck blocked my view, so I climbed the mizzen rigging until I spotted the *Night Tide*.

High above and far behind us, Vidious's airship seemed tiny in the shadow of the *Predator*. Kodoc's steel-ribbed balloon cut through the air as his warship swooped in for the attack, her big guns thundering again.

The crackle of Vidious's cannons answered—too softly, like a cricket's chirp after a lion's roar.

Hazel climbed beside me, and we watched the one-sided air battle. Three times in ten minutes the *Predator* blasted the *Night Tide* with a terrible volley, then swiveled to chase the *Anvil Rose*. To chase *me*. But every time, Vidious managed to fire one more harpoon or war chain at Kodoc's ship. Just enough to make him turn back again.

Just enough to slow him down.

In the end, Vidious didn't have a chance. The *Predator*

was too fast, too armored, too powerful. Flames spat from Kodoc's guns, and cannonballs tore into the *Night Tide*. Even from miles away, I almost *felt* the damage, almost heard the hiss of foggium and smelled the bitter stench of smoke.

Vidious's cigar-shaped zeppelin buckled, then sagged in the middle. The *Night Tide* tilted, and for one heart-clenching moment, I thought the entire airship was going to flip over, hurling everyone into the Fog. Instead, the hull cracked. The elegant stretch of railings splintered and the rigging twisted into a gnarled knot. Broken rudders and charred fans tumbled into the white.

I held my breath, waiting for the ruined ship to plummet. It slumped under the limp zeppelin, drifted helplessly in the air . . . but stayed aloft. Hanging broken in the sky, under a cloud of smoke.

The *Predator* pivoted toward us. She hovered for two heartbeats, then rocketed forward, propellers blurring.

"How long before Kodoc reaches us?" I asked Hazel.

"Thirty minutes," she said. "Maybe forty."

"And the mutie ships from the Port?"

She looked through her spyglass. "An hour. At least."

"So he'll catch us."

"Yeah," she said. "He'll catch us."

46

I FLOPPED ONTO THE sweep deck and stared toward Port Oro. So close—yet we'd never reach it. The nine mutineer warships still looked like toys, while the *Predator* loomed ever larger.

Minutes slipped past, way too fast. I wasn't ready to lose, not yet. I wasn't ready to say good-bye to my dreams, I wasn't ready to say good-bye to my crew.

If only I'd done things differently. If only I'd been born normal. If only the *X-Wing Enterprise* would fall from the stars to save us all. I touched the scrapbook in my jacket and remembered Mrs. E's words. *What if the* X-Wing Enterprise *already landed? What if the rescue party is already here?*

"Oh," I said under my breath.

Maybe Mrs. E meant that nobody would save us . . . so we needed to save ourselves. But how? I didn't know. It wasn't possible. I closed my eyes and lay back in defeat. The deck shuddered beneath me. The shouts of the airsailors sounded far away. The glow of sunlight on my eyelids reminded me of the Fog, and I daydreamed about diving—about the freedom and the speed.

Then a terrifying thought rose in my mind, like a jaguar's growl rumbling through the Fog. *No.* No, it was a dumb idea. A deadly idea.

I swallowed a few times. "Uh, Hazel? We can't outrun Kodoc, right?"

"Right," she said.

"So either he pounds Nisha's ship and *then* grabs me . . . or he just grabs me. We have to sneak off the ship and hand me over."

Her eyes narrowed. "Give you to Kodoc?"

"Yeah. To keep the *Rose* out of it."

"No."

"Do you have a better idea?"

She didn't answer.

"It's our only choice," I told her. "Either I surrender, or I dive without a tether."

Hazel cocked her head and gazed past me, like she was reading our future in the fields of Fog.

"I'm no expert," Loretta said, "but isn't 'diving without a tether' the same as 'jumping overboard'?"

"That's what Chess is saying." Swedish glared at me. "Even though he knows I'll stuff him in a chest before I let that happen."

"Wait," Hazel murmured, her eyes dark with thought. "Maybe that's it."

"Maybe what's it?" Loretta asked.

"Diving without a tether."

Swedish squinted at Hazel. "What're you talking about?"

"I think," she said slowly, "I have a plan."

"Is it better than Chess jumping overboard?"

"No," Hazel said. "It's not."

"Captain Nisha is going to kill us," Swedish grunted twenty minutes later.

"She'll thank us," Loretta said. "Are you done with those bolts yet?"

Swedish raised his head from the harpoon. "She's going to thank us for stealing her lifeboat?"

"You're not a pokey little *lifeboat*, are you?" Bea crooned, fiddling with the cargo raft's engine. "No, you're my smuggle-buggy!"

I was too scared to smile at Bea, too numb and nervous. My mind kept snagging on Hazel's plan, especially the part where I surrendered to Kodoc. It had seemed like a better idea before we'd started trying to make it happen.

I spun on my tether to look at Hazel, but she didn't

309

notice. She was perched in the access hatch that opened beside the lifeboats, her eyes half closed. Plotting and planning as Swedish bolted a stolen harpoon—which I'd lowered alongside the *Anvil Rose*—onto the cargo raft deck.

"That's right," Bea murmured to the pistons. "You're fast as a greasy cheetah."

Swinging beside Hazel, I unlatched from the tether and closed my jacket around the harness we'd lifted, along with a pair of goggles. My hands shook too much to work the buttons—because pretty soon I'd be alone on the *Predator*, face-to-face with Kodoc.

"You can do this, Chess," Hazel said, fastening my buttons. "Swedish, are you done?"

He patted the harpoon. "The pig-sticker is in place."

"Bea?" Hazel hopped from the warship onto the still-deflated cargo raft. "How's the engine look?"

"One minute, Cap'n! The spark plugs are a weensy bit scared."

"Well, sweet-talk them—quickly."

I crouched at the base of the harpoon and pretended to check the long rope coiled there. Trying to look busy instead of petrified.

"How about you, Loretta?" Hazel asked.

"I am awesome." Loretta flashed a gap-toothed smile. "I get to shoot a harpoon directly up Kodoc's nose."

"Loretta!" Hazel snapped, grabbing a strap near the

mast. "Do not aim at Kodoc. You only get one shot."

"I know, I know," she grumbled. "I'm just kidding."

"The plugs are happy!" Bea chimed, lifting her head from the hatch.

"Swedish?" Hazel called.

Swede ran his fingers over the steam organ keyboard. "She's just like the salvage raft," he said with a satisfied grunt. "But slicker than a snail's sneeze."

"Then everyone fasten down—we're going for a ride!" Hazel reached for the emergency inflation handle . . . then paused. "Um, Chess? Would you please keep Loretta from plunging to her death?"

"I'm fastened!" Loretta insisted, gripping the railing tighter. "Stop picking on me!"

"Well, just in case," I said.

"Thanks," she muttered. "How come all this airship stuff always happens in the *air*?"

"In three," Hazel said. "Two, one . . ."

She turned the handle, and the tank of foggium coughed to life. The hose stiffened for a few seconds, then the cargo raft woke. The mast unfolded on pneumatic hinges, pulling the rigging taut. The propellers straightened, the deck snapped straight, and *whoosh*, the raft's balloon inflated like a frog's throat.

Loretta stumbled, and I steadied her as we drifted free from the *Anvil Rose*. A shiver of excitement ran across my skin, along with an edge of terror. I was on a raft again, flying over the Fog with my crew . . . and heading for Kodoc's ship.

I lowered Bea through a hatch, where she started scolding and tinkering as the cargo raft dropped through the air. Swedish was taking us beneath the *Anvil Rose*, because we needed to get to the other side, closer to the *Predator*.

"Okay," Hazel said, chewing her lip nervously. "So much for the easy part."

"Look on the bright side," I told her. "Now we're stealing from muties. We've come a long way."

She raised her spyglass to look behind us. "What's next, mugging the Five Families?"

"Either that," I said, "or winning a fight with a goose."

I followed her gaze and caught a glimpse of the nine warships approaching from the Port, closer than ever. "How long before they get here?"

"Fifteen minutes," she said.

"That's great! We can wait for them to catch up instead of—"

"No," she interrupted, pointing her spyglass in the other direction. "Look."

As we flew out from beneath the *Anvil Rose*, the *Predator* swooped into firing range.

47

THE PREDATOR'S BIG GUNS swiveled toward Nisha's airship, and a roar slammed across the sky. A volley of cannonballs barely missed the *Anvil Rose*'s zeppelin—a warning shot.

"Give me the boy!" Kodoc shouted into the sudden silence. "Or the next blast guts your ship!"

"Come get him, you slime-sniffing roof rat!" Nisha shouted back. "If you can."

"Sweet," Loretta murmured beside her harpoon. "The captain knows how to sling an insult."

The *Predator* fired again. The sound of the blast almost split my head—and the impact almost split the *Anvil Rose*'s propellers. Smoke billowed and bits of wood and copper rained around us.

"Watch out!" I shouted to Swedish. "It's going to squash us!"

"Not today," he said between gritted teeth. "That's what *they* want."

His fingers danced across the keyboard organ, and we zoomed from the shadow of the *Anvil Rose* as flaming debris plunged around us.

"Whoa," Swedish said. "This thing really moves."

He spun the wheel and clattered on the organ. With a hiss of foggium, the propellers sliced through the air as explosions and screams sounded high above. A quick glance at the *Anvil Rose* made me wince: jagged holes pocked the hull, smoke poured from two gun emplacements, and the rigging crew frantically patched the balloon.

"Lord Kodoc!" a roof-trooper cried from the *Predator*. "Down there! There are three boys in that raft! Is that him?"

"Heh-heh," Loretta snickered to Hazel. "They think you're a boy."

In middle of the fear and the danger, Hazel and I looked at each other and almost smiled. Did Loretta really think that the trooper had mistaken *Hazel* for the third boy?

Then the cannons roared again. "Catch him!" Kodoc roared. "I need him alive!"

Swedish swooped low, speeding away from the Port,

away from the *Rose*—away from the safety of the nine incoming mutineer warships—and dove under the *Predator*. The cargo raft zigzagged, swerving in sharp angles to avoid harpoons and nets, and I closed my mind against the racket, trying to tame my fear.

Then I heard Kodoc's voice directly above me, cutting through the air. "You will never escape me, Chess. Not ever."

My heart beat so hard in my chest that my ribs ached. I raised my head and saw Kodoc standing on the bridge of the *Predator* forty feet away, pinning me with his stare. I couldn't do this. Hazel's plan was loco. How could I walk onto Kodoc's ship . . . and then defy him?

What if I couldn't stand up to Kodoc? He'd created me. He'd transformed me from a normal baby into a cowardly freak, just like he'd transformed the *Teardrop* into the *Predator*, and I couldn't do this.

The wind of his propellers blew the hair from my face, but I was too scared to even raise my hand to cover my eye. I wanted to scream at Hazel—*Run! Hide! Get me away from him!*—but fear paralyzed me.

Swedish slammed the organ and we veered forward, past the *Predator*, heading away from the *Anvil Rose*. We needed to draw Kodoc as far as possible from Nisha. The cargo raft spun and swooped, swerving so hard that the rudders squealed, staying fifty yards over the highest crests of Fog. Loretta gripped the harpoon, Bea peeked from a hatch, and Hazel scanned the sky, her jaw clenched.

"It's time," she said.

I swung from the rigging to the deck as the *Predator* dove from the sky in front of us. Swedish spun the wheel and hammered the organ, and we slewed to a halt.

We were ten feet from Kodoc, with nowhere to run.

48

A HEAVY BOARDING PLANK shot from the *Predator* and slammed onto the deck of the cargo raft. The *crack* sounded like a bone snapping.

Kodoc stood at the far end of the plank, watching me with hungry eyes. "Get over here, boy. You've caused enough trouble."

"Y-yes, sir," I said.

My stomach ached as I edged onto the plank with quivering legs. A sour taste rose in my throat, and I forced myself to step forward.

From the crow's nest, Hazel said, too softly for Kodoc to hear, "Goggles down, Chess. Tether free."

The wind stilled. I paused, wanting to look at her but afraid I'd start crying.

"Dive at will," she whispered. "And come back safe."

I ducked my head and crossed the rest of the boarding plank.

The instant I stepped onto the *Predator's* deck, the plank retracted with an ominous scrape. I almost whimpered: utterly alone, cut off from my crew, stranded on a warship with Lord Kodoc, as his troopers hunched over their wicked-looking harpoons and cannons.

The big warship wheeled in the air, turning away from the crew, away from the Port . . . away from the nine mutineer ships that slipped into view behind the *Anvil Rose*.

"The Port Oro navy is ten minutes from firing range, m'lord," an airtrooper said, watching the warships through a spyglass.

"They're too slow," Kodoc said. "They can't catch us now."

My teeth chattered from fear, and darkness dimmed my vision. What if I fainted? If I fainted, I was finished. So I took slow, shaky breaths as the *Predator* picked up speed, starting the long journey back to the Rooftop.

Kodoc looked down at me. "You will find the Compass. My other divers failed, but not you, you were born for this. Now show me your eye."

"Y-y-yes, s-sir—"

"Stop stammering and show me!"

My mind writhed with terror. Kodoc was the monster who'd chased me every night while I slept, the beast who'd killed me a thousand times. Now he was standing two feet away. He was *real*. I saw the faint lines on his forehead and the cruelty in his eyes. I smelled the sickly sweetness of his breath.

"Now!" he screamed.

I flinched, then pushed my hair aside.

He grabbed my head and stared at my eye. "So you lived in the junkyard?"

"Y-yes."

"Hidden by that coward Katherine," he sneered. "What does she call herself now? I'll find her next."

Despite my fear, a spark caught fire in my heart. "N-no. You won't."

"Never say no to me!" Kodoc cuffed me, and my goggles clattered across the deck. "You're not a tetherboy anymore, you're not a slumkid or a bottom-feeder. You're not even human, not anymore. You're just a tool. And I'm going to beat you into shape."

At first, I almost wet myself with fear. But as he kept ranting, a strange thing happened: my terror started to fade.

Seeing him this close, I realized that Kodoc *wasn't* a monster, he wasn't a nightmare beast who'd created me by snapping his fingers. Spittle flew from his mouth when he shouted, and one nostril hair dangled from his nose like a curly wire. He wasn't a monster—he was just a cruel Rooftop lord with too much power.

319

For my whole life, I'd been afraid to call attention to myself. My whole life I'd worried that being a freak also made me a coward. But Kodoc was just an evil man, not my creator. Which meant I was not his creature. Just a kid with a freak-eye.

And I was no coward.

"You will obey me," he snarled. "You *will* dive. You *will* find the Compass. And once the Fog is mine—"

A shrill whistle interrupted him, a sharp note from across the Fog.

Kodoc turned at the sound, and I peered past him. The cargo raft hovered a hundred yards away. Hazel watched from the crow's nest, while Swedish stood at the wheel, and Loretta slouched beside the harpoon, two fingers in her mouth.

She stopped whistling, and Hazel gestured with her spyglass, like she was showing us the entire sky. High above her, the smoldering *Night Tide* limped toward the Port. And far behind her, the nine mutineer warships guarded the *Anvil Rose*.

Whatever happened now, Mrs. E was safe. *Suck pigeon eggs, Kodoc.*

Kodoc narrowed his eyes. "Nine warships could beat me, boy—but they can't catch me."

"They don't have to," I said, and kicked him in the shin.

He gave a shout of pain, then lunged at me, but I ducked and raced across the deck.

"Grab him!" he bellowed.

I dodged an airsailor and scrambled onto the railing, balancing at the edge of the airship as Hazel shouted, "*NOW!*" and Loretta fired her harpoon, attached to a long, coiled rope—a tether.

The world moved in slow motion. My heart thudded to a stop and my breath faded to nothing as a silver spear arced through the air toward me, trailed by the tether. A good shot, straight and true.

I tracked the motion with my gaze, my knees bent, my focus absolute. The harpoon flashed under the *Predator*, the rope streaming behind . . . and I jumped.

"Turn the ship!" Kodoc screamed behind me. "Battle stations! Catch him! He's *mine*, he—"

The rush of air in my ears silenced him. The wind whipped my face and ruffled my jacket, and my heart pounded with sudden, thrilling hope. I'd done it. I'd walked onto Kodoc's airship of my own free will, I'd kicked him in the shin, and I'd walked back off again.

Well, I'd *jumped* off. Without a tether. Maybe it wasn't time to celebrate yet.

But everything was going according to Hazel's plan . . . so far. "You're going to dive without a tether," she'd told me. "You'll jump from an airship a half mile above the ground and catch a rope in midair."

"What—what airship?" I'd stammered.

"The *Predator*," she'd explained. "We'll fly you to

Kodoc and hand you over. That'll buy time for the mutie warships to reach us. Then you'll jump overboard and catch the rope."

"What rope?" Bea asked.

"The one Loretta's going to shoot, attached to a harpoon. Like a tether."

"No way." Bea chewed her lower lip. "Shoot from where?"

"From the cargo raft we're about to steal."

I'd gaped at Hazel. "Are you trying to kill me? You want me to jump from a ship and catch a rope in midair? There's no way I can do that."

"You listen to me, Chess," Hazel had said. "I know *exactly* what you can do."

And I'd seen the truth in her face: she trusted me the way I trusted her, she saw me the way I saw her, as someone special, someone extraordinary. She believed in me, which made me believe in myself.

Except now, falling through the air, I couldn't see the rope. Without my goggles, the wind brought tears to my eyes, and the endless white crests of Fog, five hundred feet beneath me, reflected the sunlight too brightly.

Where was that tether? C'mon, c'mon. . . .

"Yes!" I breathed, spotting the rope below me.

Ha! Can't stop the tetherboy. I spread my arms to catch the tether, and a blow slammed into my shoulder from behind, spinning me off course.

Then a grappling hook sheared past.

Kodoc was trying to fish me from the air.

I lashed out with my left leg and barely caught the tether on the tip of my boot. But when I curled in midair to bring it to my hands, a harpoon shot from the sky and grazed my leg.

I flinched at the pain, the tether slipped from my boot—and another harpoon flashed past. Kodoc was trying to *spear*fish me from the air.

Which was definitely *not* part of the plan.

Twisting wildly, free-falling hundreds of feet above the Fog, I lunged for the tether. A dozen more spears fired at me from the *Predator* as Kodoc attempted to spike me and drag me back on deck. The harpoons burned through the sky. Too many too fast. Too *accurate*. One drilled directly toward my stomach. With a panicked yelp, I arched in the air, and the razor-edged blade only sliced my hip.

I'd lost the cargo raft tether completely, and the next three harpoons were dead on target: two shooting at my chest and one about to sink into my leg. Moving too fast to miss. I couldn't dodge them.

They were three seconds from skewering me. Two seconds, one second—

49

I HIT THE FOG, and the world disappeared into a silent blur of mist. Time stopped. Coolness touched my face and quicksilver filled my veins.

The closest harpoon sliced toward my chest—and I snatched it from the air.

Whirling as fast as a hummingbird, I swung the harpoon like a sword and deflected the second two. The clash of metal sounded soft inside the Fog, and the harpoons tumbled away into the thick mist . . . but more scythed at me from above.

I dodged and twirled, yanking hard on the harpoon in my hands.

The line immediately tightened. The harpooner must've thought she'd caught me, so she stopped the rope from unspooling from the *Predator*. It hung firmly in the air. Which meant that the roof-troopers weren't just shooting harpoons at me: they were shooting *tethers*.

Despite everything, I laughed. Maybe I wasn't good at fighting or fixing or flying—but nobody beat me in the Fog.

Nobody.

Within seconds, dozens of harpoon ropes—all fired from the *Predator*—dangled around me, like a forest of tethers in the mist. A Fog diver's dream. Grinning wildly, I yanked on a nearby rope, then another. Anchored on Kodoc's warship, I swung between them like a monkey on a vine, cartwheeling to dodge the harpoons still slicing downward as I scanned the billows of Fog.

There! The tether from Loretta's harpoon was a sideways slash across all the vertical lines, falling slowly through the white vapor below me.

I swung hard, released my grip on a harpoon line, and somersaulted into the blankness. Fog surrounded me. White on white. Free-falling. No sounds except my ragged breathing.

So peaceful that I almost wanted to stay forever.

Then the cargo raft tether rose through the whiteness and curled gently into my fist.

50

WITH MY HEART PUMPING and my fingers clumsy, I hitched the tether to the harness under my jacket. Safe. Connected. I slumped in relief, inhaled the cool whiteness . . . and was jerked sideways through the Fog.

"Ow!" I shouted toward the sky. "Swedish!"

The tether jolted me again—to the left, then the right—then it whipped me in a wide circle. Which meant that high above, Swedish was speeding away from the *Predator*, racing toward the mutineer ships.

Towing me to safety.

Pain flared in my slashed leg as the tether whiplashed, and I slumped in my harness, dazed and drained and exhilarated. The ripples and billows of Fog swam in my vision. My breath sounded loud, the world faded into a blur. . . .

When the tether started winching me upward, my head jerked and my pulse pounded. I must've fainted for a minute or two. Or five. I shook my head as I rose higher and higher, until in an instant, the Fog fell away.

My body felt leaden and my leg throbbed with a steady ache, but my vision suddenly extended for miles. I swiveled in my harness and saw the mutineer warships standing guard nearby. Dozens of big guns were aimed at the *Predator*, which hovered in the distance—too far to pose a threat.

Mrs. E was safe, and Kodoc would never catch me now. He didn't control me anymore—maybe he never had. Because Hazel and Swedish were right. I didn't belong to Kodoc, not even close.

The sun warmed my face as I spun to look at the cargo raft flying above me. Bea beamed from the engine, waving her cap wildly and hopping around like a flea. I lifted a hand to her as the tether dragged me upward. A minute later, Swedish dragged me on deck and into a back-thumping bear hug.

Yeah, I knew *exactly* where I belonged.

"For a second there," he muttered in a choked voice, "I thought *they* got you."

"*They* wouldn't dare," Loretta said. "You've got a

fighter in the crew now."

"Ow!" I said as Swedish thumped me again. "Ouch!"

"He's bleeding, Swede!" Hazel snapped. "Let him go."

"Oops!" he said, releasing me. "Sorry."

When I swayed, Hazel grabbed me—and hugged me even tighter.

She didn't say anything. Neither did I. We just held each other as the deck shifted beneath us and the propellers spun. Maybe she cried a little—maybe we both did—but for once I didn't care if anyone was watching. For once, I wasn't afraid of being seen.

"You did it," she finally said.

"*We* did it," I told her. "How long before we reach the Port?"

Her smile was the brightest thing in the world. "Look behind you."

I turned and there it was: the jagged green gleaming peaks of Port Oro, framed by the sun. We'd fought the bosses and the troopers and Lord Kodoc himself, and we'd won.

"We made it," Hazel said. "We're home."

Acknowledgments

Many thanks to Caitlin Blasdell, Alyson Day, Renée Cafiero, Toni Markiet, Joel Tippie, Jenna Lisanti, Gina Rizzo, and Tina Wexler.

Turn the page for a look at
the exciting sequel to *The Fog Diver*!

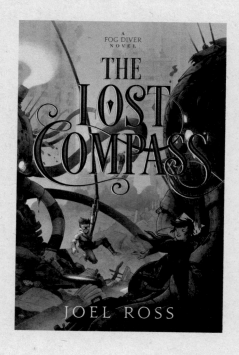

MY NAME IS Chess, and I was raised in a junkyard.

Imagine a slum floating on rickety platforms above the deadly Fog that covers the Earth. Now picture a kid shivering in an alley, terrified of the same Fog swirling inside his right eye.

That was me, before Mrs. E gave me a home.

Then Lord Kodoc found us. He ruled the Rooftop, the mountaintop empire that loomed over the junkyard, and he was obsessed with an ancient machine lost in the ruins. Kodoc needed a tetherkid with a misty eye to get this "Compass," so he hunted my crew across the sky until he captured me.

There's only one way off a warship in flight—I leaped overboard in midair.

My crew caught me before I splattered on the ground, and we headed toward the safety of a distant mountaintop called Port Oro. All we want is to heal Mrs. E's fogsickness and start a new life, but Kodoc isn't finished with us yet. And neither is the Fog.

1

Lord Kodoc's warship swooped through the sky like a falcon. Her propellers spun, and her long-range guns swiveled to target us . . . but she didn't fire.

"We're out of range," Hazel said from beside me on the cargo raft. "And Kodoc is out of luck."

As she spoke, the warship veered away, and I gripped the rigging harder, dizzy with relief and aching from harpoon wounds.

A few minutes earlier, I'd kicked Kodoc in the shin and jumped off the *Predator*'s main deck. I'd plummeted toward the ground, toward certain death. But a few seconds before impact, I'd caught a tether fired from our cargo raft. Safe at last—except that two of Kodoc's harpoons had slashed me before the crew towed me away.

"After all that," I said, "we're still standing."

Then my injured leg buckled, and I sprawled across the deck.

"Spoke too soon." Hazel knelt beside me and frowned at my wound. "Look at that cut."

I looked at her face instead, watching her braids sway like a beaded curtain. She was a couple of years older than me, and pretty enough that people noticed. But more important, she was the captain: she thought faster, and farther, than anyone I'd ever met.

She pressed a cloth to the harpoon slash on my leg, and a sharp edge of pain clawed at me.

I hissed. "You're making it worse!"

"It's not that bad," she said, wincing.

"It's a wound," I told her. "I'm wounded. Like a warrior."

"That's you," she said, tying the bandage tight. "A strong, silent warrior."

"Ow!" I yelped. "Hazel, ow-ow-ow!"

The clatter of clockwork engines grew louder as two mutineer warships roared closer to our little cargo raft. I almost smiled at the sight of them. The mutineers flew airships from the mountaintop settlement called Port Oro: our goal, our hope, our haven. And their convoy—led by the kind Captain Nisha and her brother, the kind-of-scary Captain Vidious—was the only reason that Kodoc wasn't chasing us down.

Our raft swayed in the warships' wake as they sped

4

past. "Why aren't they stopping for us?" I asked.

"Captain Nisha must've told them to chase off Kodoc first." Hazel's voice grew softer. "We—we did it, Chess. We reached Port Oro."

"Of course we did," I said, like we hadn't almost died a hundred times. "You're too stubborn to give up. Now we just need to get Mrs. E healed."

"That's first," she said, her eyes dancing.

"What's second?"

"Brand-new lives! Not in a slum, working for the junkyard bosses. Not rummaging for trash in the Fog. Real lives. Good lives. Working for ourselves." She raised her voice. "Swedish! Head for the *Anvil Rose*!"

"Why?" At the wheel, our pilot, Swedish, jerked his thumb in the other direction. "Port Oro is that way."

"We need to return the cargo raft to Captain Nisha," Hazel told him.

"We *stole* the cargo raft from Nisha." Swedish gave a lopsided grin. "We should definitely head in the other direction."

He had a point. Captain Nisha had flown us most of the way to Port Oro, pursued by a murderous Lord Kodoc—until we'd realized that we couldn't outrun him. That's when we'd stolen the cargo raft, to buy the *Anvil Rose* enough time to arrive.

Which had been a terrible idea, except for one thing: it worked.

"We don't have any time to waste." Hazel peered at Nisha's ship, the *Anvil Rose*. "We need to get Mrs. E and bring her to the Subassembly. They're the only ones able to heal her."

Swedish grunted and pulled a lever with one big hand. He was burly and shaggy and, at about sixteen, the oldest member of the crew. "You really think the fogheads will heal her?"

"Not if you keep calling them 'fogheads,'" Hazel told him as the cargo raft spun in the air. "From now on, they're 'Assemblers.'"

"I still say we ought to stay away from them," Swedish muttered.

I knew what he meant. I'd never trusted the Subassembly either. No slumkid trusted the so-called fogheads. They were *different*, and when you spent every moment scrambling for survival, *different* meant "dangerous." But then we'd met a Subassembly leader and realized that sometimes *different* just meant "not the same."

"They got us here in one piece, didn't they?" Hazel asked.

"Not really," Loretta said, squatting beside me. "Chess is in three pieces."

"I'm okay," I told her.

She squinted at Hazel. "You call that a bandage?"

"What?" Hazel asked her. "The bleeding stopped."

"Barely. I'll sew him up proper."

Hazel eyed her. "*You* know how to sew?"

"Not dresses and shirts," Loretta said, wrinkling her nose in disgust. "Only knife wounds and ax slashes—you know, the good stuff."

"The good stuff," I repeated faintly.

"Hey, I ran with a junkyard gang till last week, remember? Plenty of practice sewing up wounds."

"More practice making them," Swedish said.

Loretta's eyes gleamed. "More fun, too."

"Let's wait until we get to the Assemblers—" Hazel started.

"Nah," Loretta said, and ripped the bandage off my leg.

I howled, swiping at her. "Loretta!"

"You missed the cut on his hip," she told Hazel, batting away my hand. "You know what we need?"

"Painkillers," I moaned.

"A parade." Loretta gave a gap-toothed smile. "We got from the Rooftop to Port Oro with evil Kodoc nipping at our butts. We deserve a parade."

"I'd settle for a nap," I muttered.

"You sleep and I'll sew." She started patting her pockets. "I've got a needle and thread somewhere."

I closed my eyes. I couldn't stand to watch Loretta stitching me up. To distract myself, I started thinking about my father's scrapbook, pages of historical facts from the time before the Fog rose.

"In the old days," I said into the darkness, "they threw

a parade every year for a festival called Thanksgiving, where they stuffed turkeys and ate cramberry sauce."

From beside me, Loretta's voice said, "What'd they stuff turkeys with?"

"Stuffing."

"If you don't know, that's okay," she said, sounding cross. "You don't have to make something up."

"I *do* know!" I said. "They stuffed them with stuffing."

"Sure, and instead of knives, they stabbed people with stabbing."

"Was cramberry sauce made from actual cramberries?" Swedish asked. "Or was it a bunch of different berries all crammed together?"

"It was a kind of berry, but . . ." I paused, knowing that they weren't going to believe me. "Uh, they were too sour to eat."

"That's the opposite of 'berry,'" Swedish said.

"You can open your eyes now, you liar," Loretta told me, tapping my shoulder. "I don't have a needle. Also, the *Anvil Rose* is about to run us over."

My eyes sprang open, and I saw the *Rose* swooping toward us, propellers whirling and rigging snapping beneath the sleek balloon. Captain Nisha stood at the prow, her yellow hair flying all over the place. Not running us over exactly, but speeding in our general direction.

"Where's she going?" Loretta asked.

"To help her brother." Hazel looked across the sky

toward the half-broken *Night Tide*, still smoking from Lord Kodoc's attack. "So he doesn't crash before he reaches the Port."

A hatch clanged open in the center of the cargo raft, and Bea's head popped through, her leather helmet askew. "The *Tide* won't crash!"

"Are you sure?" Hazel asked.

Bea squinted at the *Night Tide*. She was the youngest member of the crew, and a brilliant gearslinger who spent half her time chatting to machinery. She wrinkled her nose, listening to the distant grind of the *Tide*'s engines.

"Oh, look at your poor hull," she muttered to the far-off ship. "And your mizzenmast is all cattywampus."

"Is that bad?" Loretta asked me. "Cattybombom?"

"Cattywampus," I corrected her. "It's only a *little* bad."

Bea chewed on her lower lip. "She says her gearwork is strong, though. She'll be okay for a few hours."

Bea didn't only talk *to* engines; she insisted that they answer.

The *Anvil Rose* swerved to a halt nearby, her fans blowing hard enough to tilt the cargo raft's deck. Loretta swore, Swedish goosed the engine to keep us in place, and Captain Nisha swung from the *Rose*'s crow's nest to the deck nearest us.

"I need your geargirl!" she yelled to Hazel.

"She says the *Night Tide* is okay," Hazel called back. "For a few hours."

Nisha eyed Bea. "Are you sure?"

"Yes, ma'am, Cap'n!" Bea sang out. "As long as she doesn't get hit again."

Captain Nisha slumped in relief. She knew Bea was never wrong about mechanical things.

"Come on board, then," Nisha said, tugging at her beaded necklace. "And give me back my cargo raft!"

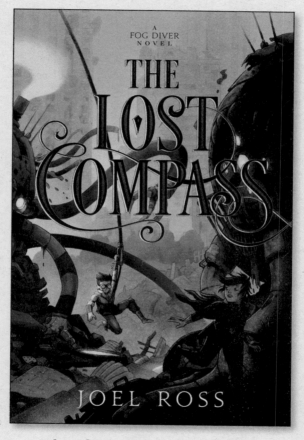